IN HIS OWN IMAGE

JEREMIAH COBRA

IN HIS OWN IMAGE

ISBN: 978-0-9999043-2-9 (hardcover)
ISBN: 978-0-9999043-3-6 (ebook)

To my mother

PART ONE
AUTUMN OF 1858

Chapter 1: Crossing the Mississippi

October 12th, 1858

*Y*et am *I a slave.*

Blood is supposed to be thicker than water. But he made my blood spill like water. So I crossed waters to leave blood behind, hoping that I don't leave a trail that will lead him back to me. I sit on earth that does not cool my feet but leaves my soles calloused and cracked. The crisp air does not soothe my aches but steals the moisture from my skin. Gentle breezes are menacing hisses, and the sun does not shine for me but looms beyond the thick canopy of branches. I sit hidden by the foliage, coiled among the protruding roots of an old oak, my head tucked into a nook at the base of its trunk, my knees drawn tightly to my chest. I imagine what it may some day feel like to lie in the open fields and admire these last moments of autumn.

The moss might feel cool upon my back where I now feel the cold sting of dried leaves against tender scars. I might seek the sun's warmth or run about the fields of golden grass and fallen leaves. But, I dare not do any of these things. The reach of my master's hand is long. His bounty hunters might be close, and a sudden move or unfortunate cough will reveal my hiding place. Then I will be returned, a slave. He doesn't like the word. Slave. Said it would make us feel like there was something to get away from. He preferred 'servant.' At one time, I wondered how he would have felt about the word 'son.'

The circumstances of my birth were not unusual. As is evident by the many shades of brown that pepper the population of Howard County, slave owners are quite taken with the idea of wantonly increasing their property. If, by chance, a Missouri slave should look into a mirror, he might be haunted by the image. And, while many slaves may only hear rumors and speculations about their parentage, I am peculiar in that I know mine for sure. I am Percival Bishop, the bastard son of my master, Joachim Bishop.

Though he is no more in the dark on this matter than I, our shared blood afforded me none of the comforts befitting an heir to a rather profitable tobacco plantation. He gave my body strength so that he might command it to rise and toil for his purposes. He let me learn my letters but only so that I might know by my own eyes God's will for me. He did not mean for me to aspire to freedom. Nevertheless, here I am. Coiled beneath an old oak. Waiting for the cloak of nightfall so that I can cross the Great River to freedom. I have stolen my body from him.

Yet, am I a slave?

October 13th, 1858

There is an unsettling stench in the air. Last night, I built a fire to keep from freezing to death after the icy Mississippi had leaked onto my crudely-made raft and soaked my ragged clothing. But it is not the smell of dying fires that unsettles me; the sweet smell of embers might have been comforting were it not accompanied by a the foulest odor, the kind that sets into a working man's skin when he does not wash himself of weeks-old sweat, stale tobacco smoke, and whiskey vapors. I open my once slumbering eyes, and my heart seizes up in my chest when I see him. A man sits on his haunches with a rifle balanced upon his knee. He seems relaxed. Comfortable. Perhaps he has been watching me sleep for hours. I scurry backwards on my hands and knees until a large tree keeps me from retreating farther.

"Well, good morning," the words seep past his rust-colored teeth and a grin that had no bit of kindness in it. The brim of his hat hides his eyes, but the glint of the morning sun reflects off his tobacco tin to highlight his filthy, wind-scorched face. He spits a filthy brown stream onto the frostbitten ground beside me and replaces a old clump of tobacco between his cracked lower lip and blackened gums. He wrinkles his nose and furrows his brow. Then, he offers me the tin.

"You hungry?" he asks.

I work my mouth to speak, but no words come out.

"Of course you are," he says. "Out here all alone. I bet you're just glad to see a familiar face. But you did alright for yourself, didn't you? I mean, you're not dead. Not yet."

He looks away, losing himself in some thoughts for a moment as he uses his tongue to adjust the brown clump between his teeth and gums. Then he spits again. "You read anything in them books about the kinds of creatures that can get ya?" He looks at me again, his eyes gleaming with a sinister thought. "Read anything in them books about creatures like me?"

Fact is, I didn't have to read any books to know about creatures like Chester Albert McAllister. I know all I need to know. He was my father's first overseer, but his cruelty made him unfit even for that job. He would have beaten the slaves into submission, but Mister Joachim did not like that method, didn't think it was necessary when he first became master. The one time Chester went to cracking his whip to hit anything besides air was to teach my mother to lower her stare. When Mister Joachim found out, he knocked Chester down a peg to foreman until the dirty Irishman finished his own indentured servitude. Then Mister Joachim let him go. A newly-freed man, Chester turned his appetites to the role of slave-catcher. He never worked alone, though; he never could. I know that much about him, too. He was never fast nor clever enough to do the job alone. Still, it was his name that became known throughout the town of Fayette and especially among restless slaves.

I also know that Chester Albert McAllister likes to be addressed by his full name, but when he wasn't around, we called him 'Skunk.' Even now, he stinks of whiskey and for want of soap. There is also the smell of tobacco on him, but all of the slaves have that. There is no washing it from our palms or fingernails. Even a week-long passage in the woods had hardly cleansed it from my nose and mouth.

"Come on, have a taste," he says, smirking and shaking the tin before me. I long to cut that smirk from his face. I have a small penknife tucked into the waistband of my breeches, but when I go to retrieve it, it slips from my fingers and lands close to Chester's badly-worn boot. I look up to see a sneer in his slack jaw and muddy-green eyes.

"What were you gonna do with that thing?" he asks. "You gonna fight us, boy?"

With the barrel of his rifle, he points to my gaunt figure. I press myself against tree, my scars keeping me from truly feeling the bark there.

"I don't think you have the strength," he says. "Hell, I almost didn't recognize you. I says to Goliath, I says, 'Goliath, you sure that's Bishop's boy? Why, he look scrawnier than a crippled dog trapped in a cemetery, I swear.' But Goliath was sure, and after I got closer, I says to Goliath, I says, 'Well, I'll be goddamned, that *is* the little niglet.' And wouldn't you know it but I was right the second time.

"You've been away from home a mighty long while, haven't you? Your mama misses you, though she don't say nothin'. But I can tell. I can always tell the silent ones what want to pretend they ain't scared. She think you dead. I took you for dead, too. But ol' Goliath, if he ain't the most talented, nigger-finding redskin, I don't know who is."

Chester again works the chaw from one side of his jaw to the other, never taking his eyes off of me. He spits another shit stain onto the ground and winces from some pain that has settled into one of his remaining teeth.

"Good ol' Goliath. He knew you was alive. Ain't that right?" Chester says looking to his left where I finally see the tall, mountain of a man who lurks there, somehow hidden by the overgrown foliage.

"You didn't really think you'd stay escaped, did you? They don't call him Shadow Wolf for nothing. Word got out that Bishop was missing his boy soon as you stepped one foot off his land, and you know, this old wolf here just got to sniffin'. I about laughed my ass off when he said how we ain't need no dogs to catch you. But I'll be doggone," he paused to chuckle at his own joke, "He caught your scent all by hisself, and then we just come a runnin'. Family helpin' family. That's our way, ain't it?"

A fool's blush warms my cheeks and ears. For the audacity to step foot from the plantation and carve a path to freedom, for the pride I felt at having evaded my pursuers and made it across the river, I nevertheless stand before the whim and judgment of this scoundrel. With a few words and a sneer, he turns my courage and cunning to pitiful fantasy, and I must look down, away from his bloodshot eyes.

"Why don't you let us feed you something," he says, waving the tobacco tin again. "See? We're in this together. Any of them other hunters catch you, maybe you don't make it back home whole. But we family. Your master is like a brother to me. Hell, Goliath and him been hunting together since they was little papooses. Ain't that right?" Chester chuckles to Goliath, who snorts in derisive reply. "We don't wanna harm a hair on your head. Besides, you're worth more whole than cut up. Let us help you find your way back home. To your mama."

"I don't have a home." My voice is hoarse, and I hardly recognize it. I look from Chester to Goliath, who has crept closer. His dark skin masks his expressions, and his straight black hair whips about in the cold, autumn wind. He uncoils the rope in his hands and walks slowly toward me.

"Oh, everybody gots a home," Chester says. "It may not be the one you wants, but it's the one God gives you. Ain't your place to question it." He spits once more on the ground before my feet as he stands and looks away to the dirt road. He leaves me to Goliath.

"Ha!" Chester guffaws, "This feels just like when we chased that Diggs nigger all them years back. Remember him, Wolf?" But Goliath is not listening. I can see in his eyes that he is aware only of the muscles in my body. He is waiting for one defiant twitch.

"You think if we get this one back to Bishop, he'll stop worrying 'bout that other one he lost?" Chester asks. Then addressing me, he says, "Of course, Bishop was only a boy then. He ain't know no better. And neither do you. You about nearly starved to death already. Come on back where you belong."

Goliath takes one step forward, and my body jolts into action. I dash away as Chester's laughter rings out behind me. Branches snag at my ragged garments and rake at my dry skin. I hear Goliath huffing behind me, and I become aware of the emptiness in my body. I haven't the strength to run or fight him off. However, I have the will, and that is enough for now. I sail forward as though a gale carries me.

Blow, oh mighty wind.

The trees rush by. My feet splash through shallow, frigid puddles that have thawed in the rising sun. For a brief moment, I am energized by the crispness of the morning air. I hope that I may be carried away by some divine breeze. Except that there are stones and branches on the ground below that catch my toes. Then, I can no longer move forward. I move down. All the way down. Down to the ground. When I land there, hellfire shoots through my entire body.

Get up! I think just before the weight of Goliath's massive hands stamps my chest into the ground. I tighten my grip on my knife as he grabs my arms.

"Whoa, Percy!" Chester hollers in the distance, "Look at the scraggly mutt trying to outrun a wolf. You knew how fast he was!"

Goliath tries to clasp my arms behind my back to work the rope around them, and in this moment, I think to press the blade of my penknife into his hands.

How much freedom will this gain me? How much pain will it cost?

I wriggle my hands loose from his rope, and in frustration he picks me up and slams my back against the ground. The fresh wounds there reopen and I cry out. Wild-eyed from the pain, I look to my hand which holds the knife. I look back to see that Goliath sees the knife, too. Before I can swing it, his forearm smashes into my jaw. There is a sudden flash of light. Then, the world goes black.

When I open my eyes, I am being carried by Goliath. My wrists are bound before me. The blade of my knife glints in the grass behind us. Soon, I find myself before Chester's fiendish grin again.

"Tie him to the wagon," Chester says, but though he stands right before me, his voice sounds a great distance away. Louder is the ringing in my ears. When Goliath releases me, I swoon and stumble to the ground again. He steadies me before Chester who looks into my eyes and cackles.

How I loathe this man! I think.

I do not avert my eyes from his gaze, and his smile and laughter fades. He turns away to retrieve a whip from the wagon and returns to rub the braid of its thong down my cheek.

My God! I pray, not with grace but with fire, the fire that must have set me upon this journey. *Is this Your lesson for me? Have I taken this path only to discover the persistence of Your will? Then kill me now! Let this man beat me into the cold earth below, that I may pass through it into your hottest hell, for it must be better than this life here. Strike me down. I promise that I do not have the strength to take the blow.*

I clench my eyes closed, but this does not keep a tear from escaping down my cheek. Chester sneers. Perhaps he thinks he knows the well from which this water is drawn.

"Hmph," he utters. "Maybe he has the fear of God in him, after all. Come on, let's go." But, before he turns again to the wagon, a roar of thunder stops him cold. It seemed the sound of the whole world rushes back to my ears as I watch Chester's eyes roll back in his head. He collapses with a thud at my feet, and a large, crimson circle spreads through the fibers of his coat, slowly saturating them, slowly seeping onto the frostbitten earth.

Goliath looks with bewilderment at the suddenly lifeless body before him. Then, with skittish eyes, he looks around the woods in search of the gunman. We notice him at the same time— a slender but rugged man with dusky skin, a stalker hat, and a long, wool-lined coat. He emerges from the tall grass, his revolver aimed at us. Goliath uses me as a shield while he edges toward the wagon. He looks for Chester's rifle and finds it at the dead man's feet. He reaches for it, but the gunman fires another shot and dislodges some frozen dirt. The woods echo with the sounds of gunshots, and the harnessed horses neigh and stomp the ground in their panic. Goliath releases me to duck behind the wagon, and the gunman fires once more, missing the Indian but splintering one of the wheel spokes. It crackles as the horses pull the carriage forward. Goliath scrambles behind the immense tree, and I hear another shot. It seems that the air it stirs brushes my cheek. I flinch as a branch splinters behind me. I fall to my hands and knees as the sound of Goliath's retreating steps rustle away into the woods. Several paces away from me, the sunlight glints on my penknife, and I crawl toward it.

Will the gunman seize me next? Or will he kill me?

A voice calms the neighing of horses. The echoes of gunshots settle. Then there is silence.

For a long while, I can hear only the thump of my heart and the heave of my exhausted breaths. When I reach the knife, I cup my bound hands over it and struggle to stand, turning to face the ruthless gunman who approaches. His face is stern. The gaze of his gray eyes is unwavering, like calm waters.

Must I wade in those waters? I wonder. *And if God were to trouble them?*

My legs tremble to hold up my emaciated body. When the man holsters his gun and attempts to take hold of me, I avoid his grasp by falling to one knee. My heart aches in my throbbing jaw. The taste of my own blood reminds me of the smell of iron after it rains. The gunman lowers himself to grab my shoulders, and I elude him once more, collapsing in the dirt. I can go no farther.

"I don't need help," I utter.

"No," he says. "No, you don't." He pauses for a long moment, studying me. He reveals a canteen of water and holds it to my lips. I do not drink. He pours the water into my mouth, and I spit it out, hoping to remove the taste of shackles as well.

"Drink," he commands. I ignore him. He grips my jaw and forces the water past my lips. I choke in protest. He pulls the canteen away and looks at me with sympathetic eyes.

"He ain't calling you home yet," the gunman says. "In fact you've come a long way from home. Haven't you, Percy?"

I feel the hairs on my neck stand at the sound of my name. I strain to look upon the man's face, and perhaps there is something there that I recognize. However, a greater power stills me against my will. The pain in my back and jaw fade though my heart throbs in my ears. My vision blurs and my eyes close.

"I won't be a slave again," I utter.

"We'll see," I hear.

Then, the world fades away.

Chapter 2: Reflecting on My Departure

The Reflection

My father meant to beat me for the first time, but he hesitated. Twelve days before my escape across the Mississippi River where I am now a fugitive, I was discovered away from Elysium Plantation past the time of the slaves' curfew, long past the night and on into the dawn. Joachim had thought that I meant to escape, and so he ordered Wolf to fetch me from the woods. In truth, I had only meant to indulge a dream: to venture into the woods at night, to smell the aroma of a passing storm, and to be lulled to sleep by the sounds of the creek. But alas, the dreams of a slave must dissipate with the morning fog, into the murky revelations of every dawn. By the time I awakened and realized the nature of my folly, I was too far from home to be in the fields by sunrise. The bounty hunters returned me to the plantation, and my own mother had to watch as I was bound by my wrists to the large pecan tree that had long ago become the landmark of Elysium. I stood there through the morning and afternoon, and by evening my father stood before me with the coiled whip in his hand. The Lord's command was that he beat me. But he hesitated.

Slave. Obey, in everything, your earthly master and do so for fear of the Lord.

My father glared at me through whiskey-glazed eyes, his jaw trembling from the force with which he kept his mouth shut.

I shall bid my slave to be submissive to his master. And if he is not, he shall bear

14

the punishment that must fall upon the disobedient.

Not a sound came from his mouth, yet the words seemed to linger in the air as the ghost of his past sermons. I only imagined that they might be words he would call upon, for I could see that he was a man in need of scripture. He clutched the whip and looked upon his slave as a son he ought to have loved. But, he had both a lawful and moral duty to uphold, and he meant to carry it out.

My wrists were raw from the rope that bound me to the pecan tree, my bare flesh exposed to the autumn air. My heart ached from my mother's distant cries, and my body trembled from having been bound and dragged through the woods by Goliath and Chester Albert McAllister. Nevertheless, I looked at my father, and I knew that his was the greater hell. I had spent hours contemplating that trauma of the flesh that the slave should suffer for the sin of stealing himself from his master. However, on this day of reckoning, my mind was occupied by the sight of a most pitiable creature, this man who himself seemed perturbed by his own reflection. In me, Joachim saw his broad shoulders that slumped against the tree, his long legs that trembled from the trauma of having been dragged through the woods, his jawline that was etched out in sweat and blood, and his fiery black eyes that glittered in the last sunlight of dusk. Naught but a few shades and a few decades stood between us. The rope that bound my hands was the cowhide that bound his. And when that cowhide tore through my flesh, he knew that his blood would be spilled.

He took one inebriated step forward, but he stopped himself again. As I looked at him, I was reminded of words my mother had told me when I was eight years old.

"Hell," Miriam had said then, "is earth. And men make it that way. They nurture it in their souls and carry it with them. And they give birth to it in their words and grow it up in their acts." She had said this on a morning when the sun was shining, a cool breeze was finally stirring in the scorched atmosphere, and the other slaves were dancing jubilantly on the plantation. The harvest had come in bountifully as usual, and Joachim, ever the generous master, rewarded us with a holiday.

On that day, he gifted us new clothes and tools, and he provided a barrel of bourbon. He invited the slaves to celebrate this harvest, and celebrate they did. Old Cyrus fiddled a lively tune while the others looped arms and swung each other in circles. A few of them stumbled about in a drunken stupor. Solomon the Preacher told lively stories to the young children. An older girl named Serafina played a kissing game with some of the older boys though even some of the men chased her around with groveling hands. Everyone was taken with the spirit of our generous master. Everyone except my mother. She sat brooding from the porch of our shanty.

"That's what this is," she said. "Hell. A bunch of demons whooping and hollering around like the devil himself done gave us our freedom." She grumbled while her nimble fingers turned reams of straw into baskets for next year's harvest. On the ground beside her, I used my own similarly nimble fingers to whittle away at a tree branch I had found near the edge of the plantation. So engrossed was I in my task that I paid little attention to my mother's grumblings.

"Ain't nothing worse than foolish happiness. Fancy clothes, drinking, and carrying on. Ain't nothing but the devil. I ever find that kind of foolishness in you, I'll whip it out of you myself. You hear me?"

I did not respond, but it was not that I did not hear her; a mother's words have a way of writing themselves onto the souls of their children, even inattentive ones. It was simply that in that same moment, a most unholy ghost had taken hold of my fingers as I whittled away at the branch. A pleasant sensation welled up from the pit of my stomach as I looked upon the face that was forming in my eight year old hands.

Wait until you see what I can do, mama. I thought.

However, my mother was not pleased. When she looked down to discover why I had not replied to her, she gasped in horror.

"Boy, stop!" she shouted. Again, I did not hear her. In my

imaginings, I was neither a slave nor a child but a master of the Renaissance, raising nose and cheekbone from stone. It took a tremendous blow from her coarse hand to return me to the plantation.

"Boy, look!" my mother shouted at me. I looked from my work to her terror-filled eyes and back to my work before I discovered what had frightened her so.

"Boy, you're bleeding. Put that knife down and come here!"

Indeed, the blood trickled from a small cut I had nicked into my pointer finger. Enough had trickled out that it stained the carving in my hand. I had not noticed any blood or pain until now, and when I dropped my work and held my hands up to my mother, she burst into tears. I felt that my mother's reaction was much greater than the amount of blood or pain deserved, and yet I cried too, for a child can hardly resist the tears of his mother. She rushed me away to the well, and I watched as the crimson swirled and mingled with the water. She wrap my hands so tightly in cloth afterward that I could hardly move my fingers. When she was done and her own tears no longer flowed, she ordered me to our cabin. I went away then, but I paused before our porch to search for my carving on the ground. I found it sullied and stained. I retrieved it along with my penknife, and I carried the items inside. I held them as best as I could, close to my chest as I dozed off. However, when I awoke, the sun was gone, and so were these pieces of my heart.

"What you want with something so dangerous as that knife, anyway?" my mother asked me on the following morning.

"I can make things with it," I replied. "Beautiful things, maybe. One day…"

"Put that idea out of your mind," my mother said.

"Yes'm."

We sat quietly for a while, but the I felt an urge to continue on.

"I didn't cut myself so bad," I said.

"Cut yourself bad enough," she replied. "Maybe next time you cut yourself to death."

"But I won't," I promised. "I'll stay alive. Maybe more alive than before."

"What you think you know about being alive? Or about dying?"

I worked my mouth as if I would answer, but no words came out.

"You don't know," she answered for me. "But I do. I learned about it when they took me from my mama. Then I learned some more when I gave birth to you. I fear every nigger mother knows death. She knows it when she births you, and she feel it over and over again every time you weep or get sick or feel hungry. You know what feeling that is? Deep and dark. Like a hunger you can't never fill. Lord knows I tried not to feel it, but I did anyway. And ain't nothing made me feel closer to death than seeing all that blood pour out of your hands yesterday."

"It was only a little bit," I replied quietly.

"Put it out of your mind."

"Yes'm."

We sat quietly again, but still I felt compelled to say something more. I do not know what made me. A sense of injustice, perhaps. A feeling that my position was right, and I ought to say so.

"I won't be happy, then," I murmured.

"Good!" my mother snapped, "Ain't no happy for a slave. Not here."

"Then maybe I'll go somewhere else to find it."

At first, my mother's expression was blank though she trembled like a tea kettle on a hot stove. Then, she shook until I thought she would break. At last she did break, rising up like a shot and striking me across the face with all of her strength. The pain had hardly begun to settle into my cheek before she pulled me close to her. Silently. Tearfully. Remorsefully.

It is jarring, the first time one is struck by his mother. Fathers, perhaps not so much, for they are hard. But, mothers ought to be soft. My mother was not soft, nor had she any reason to be. However, in that moment, perhaps she wished she were, for all she could do was cry all the tears of being a slave first and a mother second.

"Ain't no running no where," she whispered in my ear. "Elsewheres is all the same, and ain't none of it for slaves. You stay put. You stay here. Safe. That's all the happy I want."

As a child, I nodded against her bosom. I wanted to understand and to obey. Nevertheless, curiosity overtook me.

Is it all truly the same elsewhere? Were there slaves elsewhere? Would they even know I was a slave if I went there?

I was hardly a troublesome child before this age of curiosity took hold of me. From that moment, however, I did not cease to find myself in some mischief or other. I stole my knife back from my mother who had it sewn inside a patch in her mattress. I suppose she could not bring herself to truly get rid of it. Or perhaps she feared that I would find it somewhere else. When she discovered that I had torn the patch off her mattress, she beat me with a switch she had cut from the pecan tree behind the cabin. It was my mother who gave me my first beating. She commanded me to hand over the knife, but I would not. So, she beat me until we were both sore and exhausted. Yet, she never found where I hid the knife. And, I never showed her anything I made with it.

When I was thirteen years old, I stowed away on a wagon to see what *elsewhere* looked like. For this misdeed, my mother beat me with a switch again. She beat me harder than she ever had, for she hoped that her beating me would keep my father from doing it himself. After this second beating, it would be five years before I again mustered the courage to venture away from the plantation. On the day that my courage returned, I found myself alone at the edge of the property.

There was a most violent storm in my eighteenth year. That storm terrified everyone on the plantation, slave and master alike. Its thunders still roared in the distance when I found myself alone outside, contemplating *elsewhere*. The other slaves huddled in their quarters and imagined the divine, I supposed.

"Storms are just God doing his work," they often assured each other when thunder cracked like a whip. They dared not venture outside until the skies were completely silent. I, on the other hand, sat drenched before the crooked row of ash trees, which stretched menacingly toward the stormy skies. Those trees became a gateway to an unknown world, and I marveled at their appearance against the darkened sky. With each sudden flash of lightning, they became like menacing specters. Then, just as suddenly, they were trees again.

Harmless, I thought as I stared past them into the deep darkness of the woods. The earth had been softened to clay, and I curled my toes in it. In the midst of the summer scorched air, a cool and subtle breeze wafted by. One deep breath of it enticed me to take a few tentative steps toward those trees. The moon peeked through the slowly dispersing clouds, but the storm still raged in the distance. The black of the woods cloaked me, and so I took a few steps more. The trees loomed before me, and a bolt of lightning scorched the sky for several moments. Branches became long tendrils that threatened to strangle me lest I retreat. But, they remained still when the darkness returned, so I stepped beyond them.

Thunder sounded once more, but no ill would come of it. I was sure, for the bullfrogs began to croak. The field mice began to squeak. The hush of the breeze, like mesmerizing whispers, beckoned me to the creek. There was life beyond those scattered trees, and I started to run as fast as my legs could carry me toward it. I ran, and my heart pounded, and the thick, warm air brushed my face and stuck in my lungs. As my heels splashed water from the puddles, my wiry arms swiped away the low hanging branches, and drops of freshly fallen rain cooled my face. The woods opened onto the high grass of the rolling hills, and there was nothing to hold me back. The air became a little cooler and my legs carried me downhill so that I felt that I was flying. For a brief moment, I pretended that I was.

I closed my eyes and imagined the swooping of the night owls from treetop to treetop. Then I ran uphill, mimicking the boundless gallop of the wild horses and the graceful prancing of the deer. As the whispers of the creek grew louder, I longed to feel their currents wash over me. However, I stopped before I arrived there. My chest heaved. The clouds had thinned, and the plantation was far behind me. I looked back, but I could not see it. Nor were there any trees or stones nearby. The moon shone brightly, the breeze blanketed me, and the music of nature played all around me. Nevertheless, in the midst of this splendor, a terror seized my body. There were no hiding places in this field, nothing to keep the moonlight off me. I turned to go back. I hurried over the hill and across the plains. I rushed toward the entrance of the woods. I froze before I could reach it, for a voice cut through the darkness.

"Percy!" it cried out. "Get over here!"

The pale moon revealed a figure coming toward me. I stood transfixed by the revelation of that light. When she was close enough, I felt the sting of her calloused palm across my sweat-dampened cheek. I made no sound. She struck me again before pulling me close to her bosom and holding me there tightly. I did not make a sound. I did not hold her in return.

It is only the first time that a child is struck by his mother that the sharp pain impresses greatly upon him. Every strike thereafter is a dull and duller sensation. Then, there comes a time when he outgrows the pain altogether. When that time comes, and a mother strikes her son, he feels nothing. He is numb to the pain, and thus it does not stir his soul. On this night, such a time had come.

We stood silently, my mother and I, amidst the whispers of the creek, the croak of the bullfrog, and the squeak of the field mice. I towered over my mother then, and I had to kneel to feel the heaves in her chest. I felt that we might have made a tranquil scene but for the tremors of her sobbing and the pulse of fear in each of our chests. After a long while, she whispered again.

"You're a fool! You think you're all grown up, but you're just a big fool. You could've gotten lost. You could've gotten caught. You could've gotten..." She sputtered broken thoughts into the thick air as we hurried back to the plantation.

That night, my mother tried to cradle me before the fire that burned in our slave cabin hearth. I thought that she wished to turn my tall frame into the babe it once was. She cried and pleaded. She rocked back and forth. She sang every hymn in her memory. When she was weak from crying, and her voice was raspy from singing, she whispered to me:

"Don't make them take you away from me. You're all I have— all I could never want."

My heart pounded in my chest because I wanted to say "Yes'm," and nod obediently the way that a child ought to. But I was no longer a child, and I knew that I would venture away again. I began to long for dark clouds and thunderstorms. I came to revel in the low rumbling bass of the thunder and the staccato melody of the raindrops. I became a masterful thief, stealing myself away to discover new paths into the woods and returning before anyone could discover that I was missing. Perhaps I grew too confident in my skills or too comfortable on these journeys. Or perhaps I was simply fulfilling my mother's prophesy, nurturing hell in my soul and inviting its fire in my actions. And so, eight days before today, I found myself being hunted for the first time.

I was too frantic and the woods were too dark for me to know if it was Chester or Goliath who slipped the rope around my neck. Only the stench I endured during the struggle provided a clue. I had just enough time to stick my fingers into the loop of the rope before it tightened as I was being dragged the entire way back to the plantation. The ground, which had once cooled my feet, scoured my body. Twigs and fallen branches left splinters in my arms, and mud caked my eyes and nostrils. I blacked out before long, and when I awoke, dawn had broken into morning. I was bound to the pecan tree. The sun moved across the sky, illuminating my shame for the whole day and for everyone to see. Then evening came and my father slumped before me with a drunken crook in his spine and a defeated scowl on his face. He meant to whip me for the first time. But he hesitated.

"But he's your own flesh and blood!" my mother cried out, and though this was perhaps meant as a deterrent to my father's actions, it instead served as a provocation. His back straightened and his chest swelled. A fire flashed in his eyes and his nostrils flared. He raised the whip.

I closed my eyes, and a blood-curdling shriek ripped through the night air and clawed into my back. Every muscle in my body convulsed and my jaw clenched. I swallowed a cry, and just as that cry settled at the bottom of my stomach, another of her shrieks came and tore down my spine. Lightning and thunder had converged upon me, and a crimson rain fell from my flesh in torrents. I tried not to hold my breaths, but each time I exhaled, it seemed the air rushed to fill my lungs. I heaved several invasive breaths before the scream and the whip struck again. This time my head snapped back and my spine arched. I gasped, but I did not cry. The earnest fire within me refused to give utterance to my pain.

My mother's shrieks turned to helpless sobs, but the strikes continued. Lightning without thunder. My torso fought against the rigidity of the pecan tree and my fingers dug into its bark. After the tenth lash, my legs trembled beneath me, but when I fell, there was no pain. It was as if the earth had fallen away and the tree had vanished. My last thought was that I had become a ghost, that my body had been taken from me.

The Departure

I awoke several hours later, and a reminder of my punishment flooded to me in one immediate sensation: searing pain that sent tremors through my body and tears to my eyes. I let out an agonized groan. Then I heard the song of a familiar voice.

"I got wings. You got wings."

As my mother applied a salve to my wounds, I bristled at her words, for they belied the lacerations that twined like roots and branches upon my back.

"All of God's chillun got wings," she drew out each note with a vibrato that turned the oft-jubilant song into one of requiem. I grumbled and spat dirt as I struggled to turn my face from the floor of our cabin. When at last I could look upon my mother's face, I found an unfamiliar expression there.

My mother often assumed a most somber temperament when awful things happened, especially when those things happened to me. However, she did not seem somber. In fact, she did not seem herself at all.

"You almost bled to death," she said.

"But I ain't dead. I'm still alive, mama."

"You are, aren't you?" she remarked.

I wasn't even close to death, I thought. However, I did not say these words aloud. I knew that my mother would not want to hear them.

"When I go to heaven, gonna put on my wings, gonna fly all over God's heaven," she sang.

As I listened to this song, I decided that I hated it. I hated its lyrics and melody. I hated that it was familiar to me and that it sometimes rang in my head when I toiled away in the fields. I hated that she sang them while I lay in agony. I hated that her singing was louder than my thinking. So, I cursed my mother who sang. Then, I cursed my father who had beaten me. Then, I cursed God— He who is merciful but would make a man long for heaven at the price of living through hell. The notes of my mother's song sank into the pit of my stomach and churned with the words of Solomon's sermons.

Slave, be submissive for this is a virtue and the righteous path into the kingdom of heaven. Slave, obey your earthly master. Slave, fear him as you fear the Lord.

My body ached then, not from my wounds but from an enlightened anger that shook tears from my eyes and stirred the soul in my tortured body.

Yes! I am even more alive than before!

My soul longed to stretch my body rigid against that pecan tree, strain my wrists against the ropes, direct my gaze into my father's eyes, and declare, "I do not fear the Lord!"

For six days, I learned to walk upright again. On the seventh day, I was sent back to work. But on the eighth day, I gathered my few belongings: the clothes on my back, my small knife and my carving, and a cut of bread smaller than my fist. When I heard the thunder rumble in the Indian summer sky, I headed toward it.

Chapter 3: A Curious Stranger

October 14th, 1858

The gunman observes me curiously as I eat. Having seen the frailness of my body, he conceded to me all of the meal except the whiskey. He gladly drinks the whiskey. Grateful though I am for this kindness of his, I cannot help looking askance at him. Hungry though I am, I cannot help eating slowly as we speak.

"Where are we?" I mumble through a mouthful of bread. I notice that I can hardly hear the river.

"We have traveled a few miles north and east from where I found you," he replied. "We needed to move. We still do. There may be other bounty hunters by the river."

"You aren't one of them?"

"My name is Winthrop Goodfellow. I am no bounty hunter."

"Mister Goodfellow…"

"You may call me Winthrop."

"Mister Winthrop… You know my name."

"I do."

"Why?"

"It is my business to know."

"Like a bounty hunter."

"I am not a bounty hunter."

"Then what is your business?"

"I help runaways get to freedom. You are a runaway in obvious need of my help."

"What kind of stranger helps runaways?"

"Well, most fortunately for you, the kind with a gun."

"Like a bounty hunter."

"I am not," he sighs. "Well, I suppose I am kind of like a bounty hunter. You may call me just Winthrop. And I shall call you... ?"

"But you seem to know already," I say.

"But do you like to be called 'Percy' or 'Percival'?"

Winthrop notices that I have stopped chewing. He sighs again.

"I am a keen eavesdropper," he explains. "I heard the bounty hunter say your name in the woods. This, of course confirmed to me what I had already suspected."

"Suspected?" I say once I manage to swallow the lump of food in my mouth.

Winthrop reveals a thick fold of paper and hands it to me, but he does not wait for me to read it.

"You are Percival Bishop, aren't you?" he asks.

"I do not know that name," I say, trying to seem confident.

"You do," Winthrop says.

"And you know this because you *are* a bounty hunter!"

"In a way, I suppose I am. A good kind, though. I find bounties before bad men do. To foil their plans, you see. I have no intention of turning you in. You may remember that I rescued you."

"I should thank you, then?"

"No need to thank me. But, rest assured, I mean you no harm."

"Why must I be assured of that?"

"Because you would be dead, otherwise."

"Not if you meant to claim my bounty."

"I am not... " he groans and sits upright. "Look, how may I prove that I am a friend?"

"Let me go."

"You are free to go, then. Is that what you'd prefer? To finish devouring my food and water, and then be free to starve until you make it to— Springfield? Or Chicago, perhaps?"

"My destination is my concern."

"It is. However, whether or not you make it there should also be. I can help. I have some land a bit farther north from here. You need to rest. Eat. Heal. Wherever your destination lies, it is yet many miles away, upon a path ridden with hunters. I can provide shelter while you recover your strength and a safer passage once you're ready to move on."

"You are so eager to help a stranger," I remark. "It is dangerous to help someone like me."

"There would be no reason to help you, otherwise."

"It is also dangerous for a runaway to trust strange men."

"The irony of a white man seeking the confidence of a runaway slave is not lost on me. After all, trust is your most valuable and scarce resource these days, isn't it? One ought to be careful where he spends it. So, I will simply suggest that you invest in yourself. Decide on whichever way seems best. You've made it this far. Perhaps you can make it a bit farther, alone."

He rises and walks over to the horses. I stare at the two horses, a mustang and a fox trotter. I know them. They are called Soba and Nuki. Soba has a buckskin coat like the color of rich farm soil, but Nuki is dapple gray and shines like the moon even in the day time. I once cared for them at my father's plantation. Solomon even taught me to ride them and harness them to the buggy and wagon, anticipating that I might some day run errands for my father. I ran away before I ever had the chance to. In that escape, I had hoped never to see anything from that plantation again, including these horses. Winthrop must have taken them from the bounty hunters' wagon in order to carry me this far. I ought to be grateful for their presence. Nevertheless, I shudder to think that such a reminder of my enslavement has followed me here.

"If you wish to accompany me, my home is another fifteen miles north," Winthrop says as he tethers the mustang to his thoroughbred horse. "If not, Springfield is about one-hundred miles due east. Chicago is another three-hundred miles from there. Of course, you may wish to stay away from the main roads. Ride at night and hide the horse as best as you can during the day. Given a deliberate pace, and good food and water for you and your horse, you may arrive at Springfield in a week's time. Chicago, a bit longer than that."

He mounts the thoroughbred and begins to ride away. I look down at the poster in my hand once more. Then I look at Nuki. She cannot hear my racing heart nor my hurried breaths. She does not know what it is to look around at the strange and expansive land and worry about who might discover her. She is calm, and I envy her.

I tuck the poster into the waistband of my breeches and walk over to mount the horse. In that moment, I am grateful for our familiarity with each other. I look to the northward path to find that Winthrop is nearly out of eyesight. Nuki seems anxious as I ponder a bit longer, and she becomes grateful when I finally turn her in Winthrop's direction. It is not long before we catch up to him.

"Men are curious beings, aren't they?" he speaks as if I have been beside him all along. "It is quite difficult for them to believe in one another. They believe in God easily enough. That only requires imagination. But it is much more difficult for men to believe in other men."

"And what about the devil?" I remark. "I reckon the devil has done me far less harm than the other two put together."

"Ha!" Winthrop scoffs. "You know the devil well, don't you? Tell people there is a God or devil, and they will help you make up the details. Yet, they see men before them every day and must be convinced of his nature. You have had the chance to see me before you with your very own eyes, and still you are not sure if I will betray you or not."

I give him a puzzled glance, and we ride in silence for a moment before he continues.

"No, we do not believe in men. When he does good, God gets the glory. When he errs, it is his own weakness. When a bird sings a beautiful song, we hear the glory of God. And too, when a ferocious beast commits an evil, we know that it is only in its nature to do so. It cannot help itself. But—"

"Some men *are* no better than animals," I interrupt.

"*Some* animals are useful as beasts of burden," Winthrop says. "Which ones ought we keep in chains?"

"I—"

"You," Winthrop interrupts me, "were a beast of burden."

"I am not an animal."

"You are not," he says. "But you must some day tell me how a beast of burden comes to realize that he ought to be free."

"I simply wanted to live," I respond.

"So do animals!" Winthrop retorts. "Even a plant wants to live. I imagine they'd say as much if they could speak."

"The tobacco does not protest when I cut it down."

"Ha! Neither do men!"

"They can," I say quietly.

"They don't. Not the majority of them. Or even enough of them."

"I did."

"Ah, so you did. But what did it take?"

As if my body should answer his question in spite of me, a sharp spasm shoots down my back, and I straighten my posture to alleviate it.

"Hmm," Winthrop says as he notices my discomfort. "It seems we are using 'live' in two different ways. Certainly, one does not have to kill a man to keep him from living."

He appears satisfied with the point he has made, and to signal an end to the conversation, he hastens his horse to a canter. The woods around us are immense and full with shadows, and I try to keep pace as we ride toward a clearing. Nuki seems reluctant to move at more than a trot, but soon she relents, and we approach the sprawling hills ahead. Long, golden blades of autumn grass move in waves against the wind, and rays of sunlight break through the clouds to melt the glittery frost upon those golden blades.

Winthrop slows once to cut the tether between his horse and the mustang. Then he gallops away. The mustang soon diverges from his path, and I look at the two paths being cut before me. To the north, a horse gallops at the direction of a self-assured rider. To the east, a horse is unfettered, returning to an untamed nature it once knew so very long ago. It must find its own way in the world. It must survive. I shudder to think of the ways in which it may find its end. Shifting in my saddle, I command Nuki to a gallop and we head northward.

The cold air streams through the holes of my tattered garments and against my face, prying tears from my eyes. Yet, I feel exhilarated. Never before have I experienced this role of master. As I command the horse about the hills and around the bends of the winding paths, as I feel it yield to my unspoken will, I become aware for the first time that I no longer toil with it as a beast of burden. I look about me at a world that moves at my own beckoning, and I feel that I can hold it in the palm of my hand, that the winds are my own breaths, that the rivers are my blood, that the rains are my tears of release. I feel that the sunlight is my gaze, its infinite capacity to know and rule the world, that the clouds are my uncertainty but that they shall soon disperse.

Before long, Winthrop and I come upon a rushing stream, and we stop for a rest. A large tree rises up with arching branches that seem to cradle the low-hanging sun and keep it from setting.

"How long must I stay with you?" I ask once we dismount.

"That is entirely up to you," he replies as he gathers water from the stream and washes his face with it. I notice that his hands and forearms are scarred and that his face is deeply tanned. His scars suggest that he is no stranger to hard work or the outdoors. So, too, do the muscles drawn taut in his neck and shoulders. Strands of silver pepper his copper beard, and when he removes his hat, I see that he has rather springy hair for a white man. Finally, there are the slight creases about his brow and deep creases around his mouth that indicate many angst-filled years of living.

"You're a good rider," he says. "You learn anything else on the plantation?"

"I suppose."

"Well, you'd probably like to forget them all, but there are some things worth remembering. How to work with your hands. How to feed yourself. There are quite a few things that a free man ought to know."

As I watch him crouch by the stream to wash his hands, I wonder what he could possibly know about the life of a slave.

"I learned to read and write," I admit. He does not look up from his task, nor does he seem surprised.

"I don't suppose you learned to fire a gun," he replies.

"No."

"Ain't no use in having the one without the other," he says as he dries his hands on a kerchief. He works the fabric over each crease and finger. Then, he unholsters his weapon and holds it out to me. I look at him with bewilderment and he steps toward me to place it in my hand and direct me to the tree nearby.

The revolver is heavier than I imagined any gun would be. I wait for further instruction, but Winthrop is silent. He simply stands behind me and waits. My hands tremble to raise the gun and steady it, but I soon hold it before my target. I pull the trigger. A tremendous force propels my arms upward, and a thunder cracks and quickly fades to a ringing in my ears. When the ringing stops, I hear the lingering sound of flapping wings in the trees and scattering paws in the brush. Winthrop gazes at the unscathed tree, as do I. A feverish determination washes over me, so I aim and pull the trigger again. And again. And again. However, there are only empty clicks. Winthrop takes the revolver from my hand and holsters it. Then he places my penknife in my hands.

"That's all for your first lesson," he says and heads back toward the horses.

"What lesson was that?"

"Sometimes you miss the only shot you get."

I look down at my trembling hands and Winthrop places my

penknife in them.

"You dropped this," he said. "I saw you retrieve it even when you were too weak to run away. Figured it must be important."

I look at the knife, suddenly so small in my hands that it seems to drown in the echoes of the deadlier weapon I held moments before. I shudder to remember my encounter with the bounty hunters that morning. I think that my old home lurks too closely behind me.

"You missed, too," I blurt out.

"I beg your pardon?" Winthrop says.

"The Indian. You should have killed him, but you missed."

Winthrop lies down against the trunk of the tree, crosses his legs, and begins to tilt his hat over his placid-water eyes. But, before he covers them completely, he glances up at me.

"Good thing I get more than one shot, huh?"

He pats the second gun holstered by his off hand. He closes his eyes and uses his hat to shield his face from the sun. He becomes still and quiet. As he sleeps, I cut a branch from his resting tree and begin whittling away as I ponder how much farther we have to go.

Chapter 4: I Learned of My Father

A Presence in the Dark

I found out who my father was on the first day of my sixteenth year. Solomon told me. The week before that, my body was stricken with fever, my sleep was restless and fitful, and my dreams were of an incomprehensible angst. For many days and nights, my body fought this affliction, this unseeable ghost that possessed my body and sought to consume it. Sometimes, my mother soothed my suffering with her song. Other times, Solomon watched over me and told me stories. Then there was one time when I awoke to a silhouette seated in my mother's chair. It stared over me like a specter in the dark.

The creak of the old, wooden rocking chair rang against the weathered walls of the cabin. The leather soles of his boots thumped against the earthen floor, muted and rhythmically. A fire warmed the room. It crackled softly and in contrast to the heavy raindrops that pattered heavily against the shoddy shingles and dirt-frosted windowpane. The fire shone subtly on his cream-colored breeches and veined hands. The light of the fire could not reach his face to illuminate it, raising a void that spread from his chest, to the ceiling, and along the walls that the light of the fire also could not reach. Only his hands were lit, dusky hands whose knuckles only grew pale as they stuck out from the shadows and clutched the arms of the rocking chair. Were it not for those hands, I would have thought him another slave.

At first, I was suspicious of his presence, for our master did not often visit the slaves' quarters unless he was retrieving something. I wondered if he could see that I was looking at him. I wondered if he was seeing me at all. He rocked slowly. The tips of his fingers glowed red in the dim light. His foot thumped rhythmically. He said nothing. Then once, when my fever grew hottest, I awoke to him leaning over me. I thought for a moment that I saw a sadness in his eyes. My head ached unbearably, and I closed my eyes. When I awoke the next morning, my fever was gone. And so was he. I rose from my bed and sought Solomon in his cabin.

"Why should Mister Bishop bother with me or my illness?" I asked while Solomon shuffled back and forth along the dusty floors of his plant-filled cabin.

"Because you're a bother to him," Solomon replied, "perhaps more than anyone else on the plantation." He plucked black berries from one of the many plants and fed them to a pet rabbit he called Macbeth. I held that rabbit in my lap.

"Why me?" I asked.

"Your mother hasn't told you?" Solomon looked about the cabin as if he were ensuring that only he and I were present. "Well, I suppose it is time to put away childish things, isn't it?" He took the rabbit from me and returned it to its cage. Then, he began his tale.

"You see, once upon a time, the sun rose and a willow grew with the soul of an ebony tree. And the sunlight gleamed from afar to admire what it saw. And it traveled from the horizon to its summit in the sky, its gaze all the while fixed upon the willow and her beauty. He delighted, did the sun, in his power to feed the willow. He longed to touch her leaves, her branches, her flowers.

"Now, the willow does weep, for it needs lots of water, and it ought to have been planted by the life-giving currents of the river. It grew, and it stretched its roots towards that river. But the sun, in his longing to touch the willow, reached down and slowly dried the river. And the willow did droop and wither; her branches did bend hither and thither beneath the sun's lustful gaze. Then the sun retreated behind the horizon, where it would shine its dreams on the moon for the willow to see at night. And he courted her in the day and lusted after her in the night for the entirety of her spring.

"Then one summer, when the river was low and the willow was weeping, the sun ventured to touch her leaves, her branches, and her flowers. He kissed and groped her with fervor, fire kisses and brimstone caresses. And the willow wept, for the sun's desire for her was insatiable and unbearable. Though some fires are tranquil, and others do flare, though the caress of a fire is as light as the air, its fierceness is there; they all devour without care. By the autumn, the willow was all used up. Her flowers were gone. Her leaves had fallen. Her branches, once aflame, lay ashen.

"By the winter, the willow wept often and bitterly. It never again blossomed in spring. However in her weeping, the willow's seeds did fall from her fruit." Solomon looked at me gravely. He held his arm up to mine to contrast his coal-black skin to my pecan-brown before continuing, "And the sun does shine brightly upon the seedling."

"Surely drying up the river would kill the tree," I remark.

"It ought to have. Yet, the willow stands, deeply rooted to the land, starved and hollowed," Solomon said.

"And the sun?"

"The sun is powerful. It does what powerful things do."

"And the river?"

"The river?" Solomon chuckled softly. "It just goes on about its business. Even when it seems to run dry, it is simply rising into the sky to one day blot out the sun. When the rain falls, the river has its day."

"Perhaps it is best to be the river."

"Perhaps it is," he replied.

"Solomon?"

"Yes?"

"Must you always speak in riddles?"

"Yes! Riddles sharpen the mind."

"But they're mighty hard to understand."

"That's how they work. Understand that story, and you'll understand how things work in this great, awful land. Did you understand any part of it?"

"I understand that the sun is Mister Joachim. And the willow is my mother. I am the seedling, aren't I?"

"You are," he replied.

"And who is the river?"

"That's a story for another time."

Chapter 5: A Labor of Love

October 16th, 1858

I have been in larger rooms than this, but none more splendid. As I awaken, I stare in awe of the lustrous wooden surfaces that capture the sunlight such that they, themselves, seem to illuminate the room. A chair with oaken legs that curve and wind up from the ground to its seat overlooks the landscape outside the large window. A wardrobe stands like a magnificent tower against the far wall. Beside me is a stout and handsome nightstand upon which sits my penknife and the whittled branch of an old oak tree. I cannot help but think how crude they are in comparison to this nightstand or anything else in the room. Even the beams that hold the bed together at its four corners ascend toward the ceiling as if they might break through and reach the heavens. I think to raise my hand to them, but I know that I shall never reach the top as I lie upon my back. Slowly, I rise to my knees to reach further and caress the carvings. I rise to my feet to reach the topmost bead. But then there is a knock at the door, and I sink down and beneath the covers to shroud my skin and bones. A long moment passes before I hear a voice.

"May I come in?" Winthrop asks from behind the door.

I look down to see my exposed and ashy ankles jutting out from the blankets. I quickly cover them just as Winthrop enters with clean clothes and a small, wooden box. He places the shirt and trousers at the foot of the bed. Then, he looks at me and chuckles.

"There are usually one of two answers when one hears a knock at the door," he explains, "unless, of course, you think that death stands on the other side of it."

"What should I do then?" I ask.

"That depends on whether or not you are waiting for it."

"Who waits for death?"

"More people than you'd think."

"Well, I'm not waiting."

"No," he says, "You're hiding from it. That's almost the same thing." He strides across the room and settles into the chair by the window. He reveals a pipe and a pouch from the wooden box he holds and packs the pipe as he continues. "In my experience, one does not accomplish very much by hiding. It is in the seeking that things are done."

"I have to hide," I reply, "from a world that doesn't want me to live."

"Well, hiding is certainly no way to live. Sitting around hoping to remain free? That is not how freedom works. Freedom is a *doing* thing. You awake every day and *do* it. No matter what obstacles come your way, what conditions you are born under; in spite of any man who wishes for your enslavement or even your death; if one who wishes to live he must ensure that his every waking hour is an act of liberation."

"And what would you know about this *doing thing*?" I ask.

"What wouldn't I know?" he replies.

"It's we slaves who must wake up every day and worry about freedom."

"No," he says. "The white man must worry, too. Those who are apathetic toward the plight around him stand by as their apathy ossifies into oblivion. Then he cannot tell slavery from freedom, neither his own nor anyone else's. Look at your master. Tell me you haven't seen how much this dreaded institution has eaten away at his soul."

"You speak as if you know my master," I remark.

"I know all masters in a way. Slavery is a cancer. No man, white or black, master or slave can survive it."

"Is that why you do what you do?" I ask.

Winthrop lights a match and holds it over the pipe bowl, taking several puffs and then one deep draw before exhaling a fragrant plume of smoke. He looks out the window, his mind seemingly elsewhere.

"I never knew tobacco could smell like that," I remark.

"That is a shame," Winthrop replies, "considering how well you have come to know tobacco."

I grow tense beneath the covers.

"Why do you think that I know tobacco?" I ask.

"Well, you just implied it," he chuckles. "But that is not your concern today, is it? Your hardest acts may be behind you."

"Then what should my acts be today?" I ask.

"That's a good question," Winthrop says. "Might I suggest eating?" He smiles. I do not.

"Is this to be my new condition?" I ask. "Shall I spend the rest of my days worrying that slave-catchers will find me in my sleep?"

"So long as you feel the need to hide from them, you will worry about them catching you," Winthrop says.

"You got that the wrong way around," I say. "They are hunting me. It is obvious that I must hide from them."

"Perhaps," Winthrop says, drawing pensively from his pipe. He exhales another fragrant plume and continues, "When a man does wrong, he must run because he should be pursued. When he does right, he can only be pursued if he runs. Criminals must run, but I never saw a free and righteous man who should not boldly stand up to wrong and declare his freedom and righteousness to the world."

"I am a criminal," I say. "I have broken a law."

"In a just world, there ought to be no such law as the one you have purportedly broken."

"Then maybe this world was not made for someone like me," I say.

Winthrop frowns. "Only if you believe yourself a criminal," he says. "But, I cannot help but think that those are not your words. I do not know who gave them to you, but they do not match your actions, and I will hear no more of them. Rise from that bed and put on those clothes there. We can eat, and then we'll see if we can find you a task or two."

"Hmph," I mutter, "I run away from slavery only to find that I still must have a task."

"Or *two!*" Winthrop declares. "A task or two. Like I said, freedom must always lie in the doing of things, so we must find you something to do."

He rises from the chair to head out of the room, and I wait until he is gone before I remove the covers and dress slowly.

The hall outside of my room is shallow and dark, but it opens directly into an almost cavernous chamber with high, vaulted ceilings, and large picture windows. On the west side of the chamber is a simple yet quaint dining table and chairs while on the east side is an upholstered sofa and chairs along with a more elegant table. Against the near wall behind the sofa is a piano and a shelf full with leather-bound books, and on the opposite wall is a stone fireplace that stretches to the highest point of the vaulted ceiling.

The east-facing windows catch the morning sunshine and turn the long, wooden planks of the floor into a path of light that bisects the living and dining rooms as it leads into a second hallway. As I head toward that hallway, I am struck by the austerity of the home. No paintings or wallpaper adorn the wooden walls, yet the polish of those bare walls belies their simplicity. The moldings along the ceiling and floors are carved with a subtle elegance, and were it not for a tall grandfather clock that stood on the far wall of the dining room, I would have suspected Winthrop of living a meager life.

As I reach the end of the hall, I see a closed door to the east, and an adjacent open doorway, through which is a most handsome kitchen with waxed tile floors and a broad, wood-burning stove. Winthrop sat at the table with a steaming cup of black coffee. Across the table from him is a bowl of porridge, a plate of sliced fruit, and an empty seat.

"So," he begins, "you were on your way to Springfield?"

"I do not know Springfield," I reply.

"What do you know, then?"

"I knew to find the river and cross it," I say. "Then I knew to follow it north."

"Quincy, then?"

"Who is that?"

"It's a city, the city you would have found if you would have continued north from where we met. It would have taken a few days, but if you did not starve, the people there could have helped you—that is if you knew which ones to look for. Doesn't sound like you do."

"Do you?" I ask.

"I do. I can take you to Quincy and introduce you to my friends there. The city is right on the river and receives boats from Hannibal. In fact, it was at the port that I learned of your bounty."

"I thought this was a free state," I remark.

"The general sentiment here tilts away from slavery. There are good people, people who can help. But there are also those on the other side of the aisle. And there are certain laws. Quincy is a bit close to home, I think."

"Whose home?" I ask.

"Not yours," Winthrop says pensively as he clenches his pipe between his teeth. "Not any longer."

"It never was," I say.

I look away from him and down at my coarse and dry hands. There are blisters there from climbing into the trees that hid me from bounty hunters. There are scars, too, from cutting and braiding willow bark and branches for my raft. Making those cords in the shadows away from daylight reminded me of the baskets my mother made. Finding the three felled logs that would further my journey in the dark reminded me of the slave cabins I helped to build. My raft hardly survived the trip across the river, but I did. Perhaps I learned more at Elysium than I had wished to admit when Winthrop asked me that question.

I close one hand to hide the cuts there, and I use the other to lift the spoon from the bowl of porridge.

"The human spirit is resilient," Winthrop muses. "It can withstand a great deal, even while it is being broken."

I swallow a spoonful of porridge and spoon some more. There is a sweetness in it that I have never tasted before, a sweetness far more splendid than molasses. Perhaps it is the cane sugar I had only heard about as a young child. I nearly swoon from the taste of it, and it is not long before the bowl is empty. Winthrop turns to the window and takes more pensive puffs from his pipe. He gazes at a large tree in the yard.

"So you know a few things about wood," he says. "What else do you know?"

"It burns," I reply.

"It does. Anything else?"

"It breaks," I say.

"Clearly, you've made a few things with it."

"Yes."

"What kind of things?"

"All kinds. Doors. Tables. I've mended fences. I made a chair once."

"Do you think you could make a chair for me?"

"What use would that be to you?"

"It doesn't have to be of any use to me. It has to be of some use to you. However as it so happens, I need one for a customer. In Quincy, in fact."

"What if I cannot make one worth selling?" I ask.

"You probably can't," Winthrop says with a self-assured smile. "But if you were to learn, you might be more useful to yourself."

"You can teach me?" I ask.

"I know a thing or two. You might even say that carpentry is my occupation. When I am not hunting bounties."

He winks and reaches for a scarf that hangs by the door leading to the backyard.

"Eat up," he says. "Then join me outside. You can use this coat and these boots."

Winthrop wraps the scarf around his neck and heads outside.

When I follow him, I discover that the cabin is much smaller than it seemed from the inside. Having stumbled outside in Winthrop's boots, which are a bit tight, I discover that the house of wood and stone is only slightly bigger than Solomon's slave cabin.

The shed, however, is much bigger. Smoke rises from one of its four chimneys, which are set at each of the edifice's four corners. Large piles of logs sit beneath an awning before the entrance, and as I approach the large door, I can smell the freshly chopped wood and their shavings. Inside, Winthrop slides an extravagant metal tool along the smooth grains of a trunk that has been cut flat. The tool is a familiar one, a hand plane. However, I am sure that I have never seen one like it. Its bronze handle glints in the sun, and its body is adorned with ornate carvings. Thin layers of wood fly from it with each of Winthrop's forward strokes. He ceases his work and wipes his brow when he sees me.

"Here," he says, rising to lead me back outside to where the logs are. "Not with these. With that." He points to a tall and slender birch tree, whose trunk is not more than two feet in diameter. "You have the day. Get to it."

"A day?"

"That is all the time we have. I am due in Quincy on Thursday."

"It is not possible to make a chair in a day. Even four slaves are given two."

"It is not possible for a slave to make a raft from nothing and sail across the Mississippi, but here you are."

"What if I cannot do it?"

"Is that a question you asked yourself when you fled through the woods and across the river?"

"Yes. Many times."

"Then you have had quite the battle between words and actions," Winthrop says. "I am glad the actions won. It proves that there is something in you that is bigger, louder than the words you have been taught."

I look away from him to the ax, the hammer, and the wedges he has placed here for the purpose. Then I look up to the top of the birch tree.

"The sun never stops its journey," Winthrop says as he returns to the shed. "Neither should you."

I take the ax and begin cutting the tree. Soon, my muscles ache with the familiarity of work. It is a full hour before the trunk is severed from its roots, and it falls with a bristling surrender. A compulsive mechanism guides my hand as I swing the ax to divide the tree into manageable logs. Each swing binds my muscles into knots. Each knot bids my body to rest. However, I have long ago become impervious to this bidding. I swing with the axe. It strikes the wood. The wood splinters. The logs break. The sweat stings my eyes and turns to tears. Before long, there are eight logs— one to be split into the legs of the chair, two for its splats, one for its seat, one for the stiles and three in case I fail in the crafting of the others.

I use the wedges and hammer to split some logs into their necessary parts. I use the axe again to cut other logs into slats. There is a workhorse to render the slats smooth and even. A chisel and lathe allow me to round out the logs for the chair legs. New blisters begin to form in the crooks between my thumbs and fingers, and old blisters become raw once again. Old cuts in my palm redden and a new cut opens when the chisel slips from my sweaty fingers. However, I find solace and purpose in the pain, and I hold in my mind a vision of the finished chair. Winthrop goes and returns and goes again. At some point, I realize that he must have placed food and water on the workbench, for the smell of fried pork and biscuits distract me from my work. I stop to eat, noticing a similar sweetness in the biscuits as there was in the porridge earlier in the morning. I finish quickly and return to work.

The sun moves across the sky and a solitary lantern illuminates the moments when I must fit the pieces together in the dark. It is deep into the night when I finally sit upon the fully-formed chair. I do not sit for long before Winthrop joins me in the shed. I feel flush about my ears and collar as he looks over my work. I immediately want to dash the chair to bits with the ax.

"It is done, then," he remarks.

"How is it?" I ask, but I immediately regret the question.

"It is certainly a chair," he says. He retrieves the ax I used earlier and hands it to me. "Now, destroy it."

"What?"

"Go on," he says. "I do not sell to slave owners, so I fear that I shall never find a buyer for it. Break it up. We'll use it for fire wood."

I feel now that a fever overtakes me as I hold the ax tightly, its smooth handle chaffing my raw palms. I look back to Winthrop.

"Go on," he says.

I scowl and raise the ax. He snorts.

"I would have expected some resistance from a runaway," he remarks.

I want to destroy the chair, but I hesitate.

"You have worked all day on it," Winthrop says. "It took your energy and effort. And now you'll just destroy it?"

"It is no good."

"Is that what you think?"

"That's what you said."

"I said no such thing. I merely said that it was a slave's chair. Of course, I hoped I was mistaken. Clearly I am not."

"What do you want me to do with it, then?" I ask.

"Why is that any of your concern? What do you want to do with it?"

"I don't know," I say.

"Do you love it?"

"Love what?"

"The chair."

I look at it, and I feel a sudden urge to cover it with the blanket I awoke under this morning.

"Who loves a chair?" I ask.

"So you don't?"

"People do not love chairs."

"Don't they?" Winthrop retorts. "Sounds like an awful way of life for the chair maker."

Winthrop walks over to the chair. He picks it up and thumps twice upon the floor with it.

"You have never made a chair for a man, have you? These slats would be unforgiving on any man's back, but they are perfect for the yielding slave. You toiled away on these legs, but they may just as well have remained branches because they are not much more than well-crafted stumps. I think a man could sit on this chair or a felled log and not know the difference. The joints are quite strong, but that only ensures that this will survive for decades, maybe centuries to come. It is a perfectly good chair for a slave. And that is why I would destroy it. But you must do so for a different reason."

"And what is that?" I ask.

"Because you are ashamed of this chair. I can see it in the way you look at it. But you are not ashamed because it is bad. You are ashamed because you loved it until I saw it for what it was. Every man puts a little of himself in the things he makes. You think that when I look at this chair, I see the slave who made it."

"I am not a slave," I utter.

"I know," Winthrop replies. "That is not what I see."

"Then what do you see?"

"I see a young man who could have learned to do anything with his hands but was instead forced to make chairs for slaves."

I look down at my hands. The blisters are there. So are the scars from forging a path to freedom. And when I look more closely, I see the faint crease in the top of my pointer finger.

"You should not be making chairs for slaves," he says. "You shouldn't even be making them for me."

"What should I be making?" I ask.

"I don't know. Something to love. Something with soul."

"How do I make something with a soul?"

"I'll show you tomorrow."

He turns to leave the shed.

"After you do away with that thing."

I retrieve the ax and lift it to destroy the chair. However, I hesitate, and instead of bringing the ax down, I rest it upon my shoulder. Then I head outside into the dark woods, in search of a thing to love.

Chapter 6: A Labor of Loathing

A Memory of Solomon's Lessons, 1850

"Again!" Solomon commanded with a strike from a willow branch across my dried knuckles. I scratched three lines over and over on the gray slate in front of me. Each time, I made a small mistake. With each mistake, the willow hissed a stinging reprimand across my hands.

Once, the lines did not touch at the top.

Hiss.

Then they crossed.

Hiss.

I was rushing.

Hiss, hiss!

I slowed down, and the lines touched perfectly. But the rung in the middle went past one leg. On my next try, it did not go far enough. Then it touched neither leg. An ache settled into the center of my palm. Thin, red welts rose on the brown skin of my hand and crisscrossed like spiderwebs to hide the veins. At first, the pain and scars unsettled me. Then I grew used to them. I almost came to expect them.

Hiss!

Hiss!

Hiss!

Then nothing. I made the three lines come together perfectly, and I felt... nothing.

"At last, your *A* is an *A*," Solomon said, and I dropped the chalk to touch a single finger to one of the welts on my hand. Except for the discernible burn that one hand felt from the touch of the other, it seemed that I touched the hand of a stranger. I winced.

"Sometimes it hurts to do things right," Solomon said. He grabbed the board and wiped it clean. "Again." he commanded.

"Why?" I asked. Solomon looked at me with a raised eyebrow.

"Because you do as you are told," he snapped.

"Do the other slaves read?"

"No. Just you. And me."

"Then why should I learn to read at all?"

At this, Solomon struck the board with the willow branch, which sounded like the crack of a whip.

"You don't ask why!" he declared. "You do as you are told, and you count your blessings."

With fear that his next strike would rake at my already chafed hands, I drew the next row of A's too hastily and he nevertheless struck me with the willow. The sting of the blow brought tears to my eyes. Seeing these tears, Solomon's expression softened, but only a bit, and he remarked,

"Mister Bishop sees something special in you. He doesn't let just any slave learn his letters."

"What's so special about me?" I asked.

"Maybe some day you can ask him yourself," Solomon replied. "But today, you need to do as you're told.

More carefully this time, I wrote one row of perfect A's like pitched roofs on slave cabins, and Solomon finally dropped the willow branch.

"Your mother would be proud," he said, "but don't you go telling her a thing about these lessons, you hear?"

"Even though she would be proud?" I asked.

"*Would be*," he replied, "In any other life, maybe she'd allow herself to be."

"How can she not allow things of herself?" I asked.

"All of us slaves know what is allowed and what isn't," he said. "Some things the master doesn't allow, but even those things they might encourage, we know better than to allow ourselves. Pride is one of those things. Fortunately for you mother, her melancholy keeps pride at bay." I did not know this word.

Melancholy

"Is she sick?" I asked.

"In a way, yes," Solomon replied. "She has a spiritual sickness. The kind that doesn't let her see the goodness in things.

"She was quite hard-headed when she first came to Elysium. She didn't like nothing or nobody. But then you came along, and she liked you. A whole lot. Maybe too much to where it eats her up sometimes. That's why you can't tell her about these lessons. She'll think you're getting away from her."

"I wouldn't want to get away from her," I remark.

"You don't know what you'd want," Solomon snapped. "You ain't hardly even lived yet. What would you know about wanting?"

"I know I don't want to get away from mama," I replied.

"Good," Solomon said with smirk. "I'm sure she'd be glad to hear that. You keep thinking like that. Maybe you'll learn something from me after all."

"Yes," I agreed. "I'll learn my letters."

"You'll learn more than that, child," Solomon remarked. "Still waters run deep. I stay still and move the world in my currents. Mister Bishop is our master, but who do you think is his?"

"I didn't know masters had masters," I said. Solomon tapped the Bible in his hand.

"Everyone has a master. Mister Joachim's wrote all the laws in this here book. Learn these, and you learn laws that rule men."

"Why would I want to do that?" I asked.

"To rule men," Solomon said with a smirk. Then, with a certain softness in his voice, he continued, "At some point, you will get tired of men ruling you." He sighed. "You'll understand when you're older. I suppose for now, you'd rather make them than rule them, huh?"

"Make them?" I asked.

"Your mother told me about that cut on your hand." He chuckled. "Boy did that stir her melancholy! Show a nigger a statue and he wants to be Michelangelo! Listen: learn your letters; learn the Word. Then you can make all the men you want."

He left, and I busied myself with my letters. C's like scythes. H's to separate the corn from the potatoes. A's for gable roofs. I's in neat rows of tobacco. N's for the slats of wood that kept the cabin doors from coming loose in their frame. At the edges of the pages I made sketches of men I had read about. Not the slaves nor their chains from the stories Solomon told me about in the Bible. I was never very interested in those stories. When my chores and Bible lessons were done, I retreated to stories more suited for my disposition.

Out, past the crooked ash trees at the end of the plantation was a large tree that bore no leaves. Upon climbing it one day, I discovered high up in its trunk, a nook. Inside it was a book bound in black, ornate leather whose beauty paled in comparison to the wonders inside. When I reflect on the happenstance that brought this book into my possession, I understand fully why the slave is not taught to read or write. There is such power in the word. To learn just one begets the learning of others. Words widen the lens of the mind.

On the first page of my book was written the title *The Slave-King*. These few words alone filled me with wonder! That a slave could be a king was awe-inspiring. That this slave, whom his captors named Peirrot, could be so filled with love, honor, and friendship in spite of his condition confused me at first. But, by the end, when I learned that he would die for these things, I was so struck with inspiration that I longed desperately for a friendship such as his, for the capacity to keep my word such as he did, and to love someone so deeply.

I do not know who put the book in that tree, but I sometimes dreamt that he had placed it there for me. In that dream, I meet him when we are both very old, and I thank him. In my waking hours, I found myself at this nook as often as I could steal away. Countless times I have read this tale about this African who was born a king, lived as a slave, but died as king again. The words in those pages wrote themselves indelibly on my soul. I recreated the one illustration I found inside. Once, I even attempted to carve it. And, I kept all, the book, the drawings, and the carving inside of the nook where I hoped no one would ever find them. It was a most unfortunate day when Solomon caught me asleep beneath that nook, pages fluttering in my right hand, a pine box of drawings in my left.

"What are you doing out here?" Solomon asked, startling me awake.

"Didn't you hear me calling you?" he asked. "Mister Bishop sent me looking everywhere for you. He wants to show you off to his guests. Bring yourself! We'll get your Bible along the way."

He grabbed the book and shuffled through the pages.

"What's this?" he asked.

"I don't know."

"Where'd you get it?"

"I found it."

Solomon looked over the book again. He frowned.

"Put it back, wherever you found it and leave it there." He shoved it in my hands, causing me to drop the box. He watched anxiously as I climbed the tree and put the book away. When I returned to him, he grabbed me by the cuff.

"Come on," he said, pushing me ahead of him just after I reached down and grabbed the box.

The sun yet gleamed above the horizon, casting its light upon the path between the slave quarters and the mansion so that our shadows stretched out far ahead of us. The light of the setting sun lay upon the golden leaves of tobacco so that they, themselves, seemed like lanterns lighting our way to the master's house. The air was heavy with their sweet aroma and the stickiness of a summer day settling down. The cicadas had been singing all day, and the June bugs buzzed softly in their midst. Solomon rushed us toward the looming mansion ahead, our footsteps kicking the dust up from the path. As we grew closer to the house, the cicadas and June bugs gave way to the laughter of guests and the music of Cyrus, the best fiddler on the plantation, even better than Solomon, though Solomon was older and had taught him. Solomon used to play for Mister Joachim's guests, but once Cyrus began to pass him in skill, he was the one called upon to play in the mansion.

Entering through the side entrance of the mansion, Solomon and I passed through Esther's Kitchen, as we called the main kitchen in the mansion. This was because Esther was the head cook, and she had christened it that long ago. We all knew it by that name, and even Mister Joachim called it that from time to time. My mouth watered at the remnant scents of collards and pork and the lingering aroma of cinnamon and vanilla from the cobbler Esther had made, a piece of which remained in a pan atop the center table. Esther was there with my mother and another slave named Opal, Cyrus's wife. Together, the three had cooked dinner for Mister Joachim's guests and were now cleaning the many dishes used for serving. My mother gave me a solemn gaze as Solomon and I passed through, and I could hear Esther scold her as we entered the hallway.

The walls on either side of the hall were adorned with candles and two paintings, the one on the left depicting Mister Joachim's father Aaron Bishop, and the one on the right depicting Aaron's wife, who passed before Mister Joachim was born. Solomon and I also passed the dining room entrance on the left, across from the kitchen, but not before I could get a glimpse of its oblong, dining table, its ornate chandeliers, and the majestic drapes that hung from the tall windows.

Entering the foyer, I marveled at the balusters of the staircase that seemed to wind upward to heaven. Then we passed into the parlor in which so many lights shimmered from the chandeliers and danced upon the faces of Joachim's many guests. I had never before seen the chandelier lit, and it must be what the sun would look like if I could ever get a good look at it. I had also never before seen so many people in the mansion. There were several men in the parlor, including Mister Joachim, all dressed on various shades of gray, blue, or brown. In the next room, I could hear the musical voices of the women who had accompanied these men, but were no doubt being spared the smoking, drinking, and cursing that was taking place here.

Wispy layers of cigar smoke wafted about the room, and there mingled with this haze the sweet aromas of brandy and bourbon as well as laughter and the music of Cyrus's lively fiddle. The room was very much alive, then, with the murmur of various conversations accenting all that overwhelmed me about the large square room with its tall windows and long, crimson drapes framing the darkness outside. When Joachim saw me, he shouted with drunken cheer.

"Ah, my boy!" he shouted. "Now y'all will see what I have been saying: that you will never again see a more talented nigger in all of Missouri!"

The men stopped their conversation to gaze down upon me, their cheeks flush with the most fervent shades of red, no doubt the effects of the brandy and bourbon which glittered gold in their crystal glasses. I found the sudden silence to be daunting, and I struggled to look into their expectant faces. I most certainly would not have approached them had Solomon not pushed me into the crowd and Mister Joachim not pulled me forward by my shoulder. He picked up a Bible from from the mantel and shoved it into my hands.

"Read Ephesians, chapter six," he said, the cigar and whiskey aromas pouring from his mouth.

"Read?" a gentleman with a slight Irish accent scoffed.

"Recite," Mister Joachim corrected himself.

"Then why does he need the Bible?" another man's high and raspy voice cut through the rising hum of disbelief.

"For effect," Mister Joachim stated.

"You taught this nigger to read?" asked a third man whose voice had a peculiarly gruff quality.

"Of course not!" Mister Joachim said. "That would be illegal, wouldn't it?" He sipped bourbon from his glass and narrowed his eyes menacingly at the crowd. "Would anyone here accuse me of breaking the law?"

"Did you?" asked the Irishman. Mister Joachim turned quickly and staggered toward the man until their noses nearly touched.

"Where is your brother?" Mister Joachim grumbled.

"I ain't his keeper," replied the Irishman.

"And yet, shouldn't you be? Doesn't the Bible…"

"Don't you preach to me!" the Irishman cried. "I read the Bible, too. I am his brother, but…"

"Oh, you read do you!?" Mister Joachim cried in disbelief, and the Irishman pursed his lips and clenched his jaw.

"That's right," Mister Joachim interrupted. "Because if you read, you'd know that you ought to be your brother's keeper. And yet, it is I who know all about his dealings. And I know who he deals with. So let me warn you that unlike some in our present company, I'm not in the habit of breaking the law. But I could pick up that habit real quick." He pushed his nose against the Irishman's and clenched his fist. "Just let me know when."

The Irishman took a step back.

"Let's not ruin a good time," he said sheepishly. Mister Joachim grinned, closed his eyes, and stumbled back a few steps.

"Yesh!" he slurred with a sly grin. "Let ush enjoy thish evening. Percival! Read the Word to us! Teach the heathens in our midst!"

I searched for the page as murmurs continued around me. When I found it, I looked with sheepish eyes toward Solomon who urged me on with a wave of his hand. I looked at the glossy eyes upon me. Then, I looked down and read with a steady pace.

"Servants, be obedient to them that are your masters according to the flesh, with fear and trembling, in singleness of your heart, as unto Christ; Not with eye service, as men pleasers; but as the servants of Christ, doing the will of God from the heart; With good will doing service, as to the Lord, and not to men: Knowing that whatsoever good thing any man doth, the same shall he receive of the Lord, whether he be bond or free. And, ye masters, do the same things unto them, forbearing threatening; knowing that your Master also is in heaven; neither is there respect of persons…"

I hesitated to continue as the murmurs around me grew to a deafening drone. It was as though I stood in the midst of a swarm of cicadas.

"He does read!" shouted a man with a gruff voice.

"Fools!" Mister Joachim shouted, swinging his hand to point at the man and with it, his glass of bourbon that landed with a splash upon the man's boots. "It is but a parlor trick, as it were," Mister Joachim explained. "I will bet that half of you do not know the Bible so well as he, for he is a slave of scripture, a humble servant who knows the word of God and thereby knows his place in the world."

"It sure looked like he was reading," spoke the high and raspy voice.

"It sure did!" the Irishman chimed in. To these words, Mister Joachim approached me and snatched the Bible. He then stormed toward the Irishman and thrust the book toward his hands.

"There!" Mister Joachim growled. "Since you know so well what reading looks like, why don't you find the passage and read it for us."

The Irishman's ears grew red to match his cheeks, and he looked nervously at the other guests. Mister Joachim smirked.

"Go ahead," Mister Bishop nudged the Bible toward him. The Irishman was reluctant but defiant, and he took it. As he thumbed through the pages, his eyes glossed over the words. Before long, he settled on a page and began to stammer through the words there. The guests were quiet, but when he slammed the book closed, the man with the gruff voice rumbled with laughter. This broke the Irishman.

"You know I ain't an educated man, Joachim!" he shouted angrily.

"Ah, so you would admit to a nigger being able to learn what you yourself cannot?" Mister Joachim jeered.

"It is not that I cannot, it is just that… that…" he sought desperately for some sort of reason that would silence the sniggering about him, but unable to find one, he changed course.

"Oh ho, Joachim!" he said with a feigned grin. "I see what you've done here. Clearly you have taught this nigger of yours some trick to make a fool out of me! It was a good trick. A good trick indeed."

"Oh ho, Mister McAllister!" Mister Joachim guffawed. "If my niggers could read, what would I need you for?" The other guests joined him in his laughter.

"Next, he'll be telling us that niggers can be slaveowners," said one man with a snobbish drawl. He wore a paisley shirt beneath a red vest. Both articles of clothing stood out among the mostly brown and blue attire of the other guests.

"As a matter of fact," the Irishman began.

"A matter of fact!" the snobbish man cried.

"Why yes!" the Irishman continued. "There is a nigger slave owner in the next county over."

"You don't say!" Mister Joachim teased.

"He bought his own freedom and then bought himself six others to work for him," the Irishman explained. "My brother caught one of his runaways just last month."

"My God, the niggers are evolving!" Mister Joachim guffawed to the delight of his guests, though a few seemed a bit uneasy. "I say you and your brother ought to drop the bottle and pick up a book while you still can." He tilted his head back and finished the bourbon in his glass.

"To hell with you!" the Irishman cried.

"My name is already on the list," Mister Joachim mumbled. "Anyone else here gullible enough to be out-witted by a little slave boy?" He waved the Bible.

"I was made to memorize the Lord's prayer in primary school," offered the raspy-voiced man as the jovial mood spread among the guests.

"Step on up and recite it," Mister Joachim said. "But not too quickly. We can't have the merchant embarrassed by a nigger *and* a bookkeeper in one night!" The man scoffed, but the guests roared with laughter, and Mister Joachim turned to pat me on the head. For the briefest of moments, there was a light in his gaze as he looked upon me. However, this waned quickly, and he turned to Solomon and returned the Bible. As Solomon took it, he shifted the pine box under his arm and it caught Joachim's eye.

"What is that?"

"Some sort of box," Solomon replied. "The boy made it, himself."

"Ah!" Joachim shouted to his guests, whose attention had shifted to some point that the bookkeeper was making. He did not seem pleased that the guests once again focused on their host. "He is a builder as well! I could put him to work on the fences. Better yet, maybe he will rebuild this old mansion!"

"That is some talented nigger you got there!" declared the snobbish man. "What would you say your price is for him? Or are you truly so fond of him?"

"He is priceless!" Mister Joachim said as he held up the box, rattling its yet undiscovered contents.

My heart swelled with pride at Mister Joachim's proclamation, but that pride quickly became dread as he passed the box to the crowd. He passed it around, and it went from hand to thoughtless hand. They all seemed to admire it, but it was the bookkeeper who had the idea of opening it.

"What is this?" He asked as he picked out the carving of my likeness and turned it over in his hand. Then he took another carving, a bird, and held the two wooden sculptures as if he might crush them in his palm. "Looks like nigger witchcraft to me!" He laughed, and a few men joined him.

Mister Joachim staggered over to the bookkeeper for what seemed to be a closer look. He took the carving and held it, first too close and then too far from his eyes.

"Did you make this?" he asked, looking to me with a discerning frown.

I did not answer. He walked over to me. He laid his large, heavy hand on the crown of my head, and he let out a thunderous belly laugh.

"What an artist!" he chuckled, and his guests laughed, too. "Who is this? Solomon?"

"Why, it looks like you!" said the bookkeeper as the laughter grew louder.

"But it's so dirty and ugly!" cried the snobbish man. "Surely that's a nigger of some sort!"

"Or maybe he sees you as a nigger just like him," the bookkeeper chortled. "Be careful, lest he cast some nigger hoodoo on you!"

The room erupted in laughter, but Mister Joachim's scowl silenced it quickly. With tilted gait, he approached the bookkeeper, but when he arrived, he stood as straight as an arrow. For a second time that night, Mister Joachim touched noses with a guest. The bookkeeper stopped laughing then and seemed to have trouble swallowing.

"I know your father, don't I?" Mister Joachim asked him in the same menacing grumble that he used earlier.

"You do," the man replied. "He runs one of your stores across the river. I-I-I'm a bookkeeper there."

"Hmph," Mister Joachim snorted. Then he stumbled backward and declared, "The day a nigger gets the best of me will be the day niggers become the masters of men!" Then he tossed the carving toward me onto the floor while the guests murmured uneasily. Mister Joachim spun around, took a bow, and collapsed into a chair, his head cocked back, his mouth open, and his eyes closed. He snored immediately, and Cyrus took this as his cue to begin fiddling again. The guests refilled their emptied glasses with their liquor of choice, and I hustled about the room to retrieve my box and my carving. I clutched these things to my chest. Then, I ran down the hallway and into the kitchen where I looked with teary eyes, first at Esther and then at my mother. Perhaps there was sympathy on their faces, but neither ceased her task. I stifled a sob in my throat and ran all the way to the cabin. When my mother joined me there, she did not greet me but instead busied herself with needle and thread. She also did not stop when Solomon entered our chamber.

He smiled sympathetically when he saw us, and he went about adding wood to the fire in our hearth.

"God was watching over us tonight," Solomon said, fanning the flames. "Luckily Mister Joachim is as cunning as he is proud. And the guests were too drunk to declare you be hanged. Hopefully they're all too drunk to remember anything in the morning. Do you see that right there?" He pointed to the pine box in my hands. "Get rid of it. We can find enough trouble without the townsfolk accusing us of nigger witchcraft on top of it all."

I looked away to the fire, but I did not move. I clutched the box tighter to my chest.

"You truly are your mother's son, aren't you?" he said. "Born with all of her hard-headedness." He looked to my mother and smirked, but she kept her attention on her embroidery. "I remember when she was pregnant with you, right before she gave birth…" He began telling the story as if she were not sitting there. Perhaps it was he who cast spells, for we moved at the pace of his words. She kept with her sewing, I slowly walked toward the fire, and he told us our story as if he had been speaking us into existence the entire time. I picked up the bird and turned it over in my hand before tossing it toward the hearth. It did not land in the fire, but the flames reached out and touched it anyway. With tears and anger, I removed another carving, a horse, and hurled it into the merciless light. When at last I got to the carved face, I paused to look at its bloodstained brow, broad nostrils, and high cheekbones. I looked back to Solomon who was now by mother's side. She was indifferent to his touch as he stroked the plaits in her hair, his eyes closed, his mouth spilling all of her secrets. He spoke of her pregnancy with me. Then he spoke of the days when she was new to the plantation. Neither of them paid any attention to me. So, I broke the spell. I looked back to the fire and tossed the pine box in it. Then, I tucked the carving away and turned my attention to Solomon's story.

Chapter 7: A Sculpture of Exodus

October 22nd, 1858

Winthrop turns the vises of a wood-bending mold like a captain steadying a ship through a storm. However, it is not the rugged waves of the ocean but the rigid fibers of the tree that he must bend to his will. They bristle and shriek in the vise as he works them into an unnatural curve. He holds his breath while the boiler expels plumes of sweet and musky steam that cause sweat to pour down his face. The shriek of the bending wood grows louder, and Winthrop pauses with caution. For a moment, there is silence but for the exhales of the boiler. Then, there is a great and sudden crackling as the lumber splinters and shatters against the mold.

"Well," Winthrop lets out an exasperated sigh, "that was to be expected, I suppose. What is wrought by nature is also made stubborn by her."

I retrieve more wood from the boiler and pass it to him. Winthrop clears the large splinters from the mold. He lifts a large hammer and pummels the beam into the iron fasteners. Then he begins anew the arduous task of turning the vises. This beam, too, whines and bristles, and he pauses often when the lumber threatens to splinter. This beam, however, does not break, and at last it is forged into a large arch.

"There," he says with a weary but satisfied smile. "It was once just a boring tree, but soon it will have purpose."

"Didn't it already have that?" I ask.

"No, it had utility," Winthrop answers, "shade for some woodland creatures or food for some insects. That is what nature does, it gives things utility. Men must give them souls."

"Now it will be a dead thing in a parlor."

"No! It will be a beloved thing in a home. It will be a resting place for men to laugh and forge friendships."

"Or perhaps men will argue and fight upon it," I say.

"Men do not sit when they fight."

"You have a peculiar way of looking at things."

"I am a romantic! No man can create a thing without a bit of the romantic in him."

He lifts the curved wood in its vise and holds it up as a pious man might hold up an offering. Then, he hangs it from the ceiling with the other molds. As I look at the rows of suspended, wooden arches, I consider telling Winthrop about a felled tree I found in the woods a few days ago. Then I would have to confess that I did not destroy my chair. I think better of these confessions, and instead I simply nod before we retire to the house. There, I wait until long after we have extinguished our candles to steal away alone with my hammer and chisel.

October 24th, 1858

Every night since I began the sculpture, I have ventured into the woods to work on it by the light of the moon. Tonight, it is exactly I have left it on previous nights: hopelessly unfinished. I sit in the chair that I did not destroy, and I gaze upon my artwork. I have stripped away bark on one side of the felled pine log and etched in its place the intricate details of a horse. It is a familiar horse, the one that I rode to this place. I wish that my carving were more than a tactile drawing on the side of this tree trunk, but I have never sculpted anything so big. I place my chisel against the grain and I raise my hammer. However, I freeze when I hear a man clear his throat behind me.

"What nature has wrought, indeed," Winthrop remarks." Sorry to startle you, but I was curious. I have been hearing my front door open and close in the middle of three consecutive nights. Yet, you are always in your bed the next morning. I was beginning to wonder why you kept returning. Now I understand. You were not plotting some kind of excursion."

"And if I were?" I ask.

He looks over my shoulder.

"You wouldn't get far on that," he replies. "It is quite good, however. I've known slaves to have hobbies— anything to pass the time. But this is quite good indeed. Very detailed."

"It is nothing— not even finished."

"I can see that it is not finished. However, this is not nothing."

"I wish to finish it," I say. "Alone."

"Don't carve there," Winthrop warns. "You will destroy it if you place your chisel there. The wood will split straight through the torso."

"How do you know?"

"I have little patience for sculpting. But, I do know wood, and you are cutting against the grain. In a carving, that might not do much damage, but in a sculpture, nature will take its course and split through the entire thing."

"How do you know it is a sculpture?"

"Because you are digging at the top here. You would have stopped long ago if you only wanted a carving. Instead, you are digging a grave with a spoon, so to speak. I can see that you want this to be more."

"What should I do, then?"

"Well, for starters, you should have brought this wood into the shed so that we could dry it properly. You should not sculpt on green wood. But, let's consider this a practice piece. If you wish to add detail, you ought to put it here." He takes the tool from me and places its blade along the grain of the wood. He makes a tiny cut, and I wince.

"Or you might place it here," he says as he positions the blade across the grain and gestures a second cut.

"Whatever you do," he continues, "don't rush. With details, it is better to make small, confident cuts than large, clumsy ones."

He hands the chisel back to me, and I make a few inconsequential cuts.

"Of course, since you intend to create a whole horse," he remarks, "a few large cuts will be necessary."

Winthrop dashes away to the shed, leaving me alone for several moments. He returns with an ax and a larger chisel.

"You ought to have made an outline before you added the details," he says as he begins to hack away at the trunk until the bark has been stripped away. "Even God did not create life with a blade of grass. He started big— light and dark. Heavens and Earth. Then he added the grass." He hacks some more until the trunk is a block of jagged edges with my carving on one side.

With the chisel, Winthrop teaches me to round the sharp edges and cut triangles where curves must follow. With the plane, I learn to render the rough surface smooth. With the hammer, I apply force where the strength of my hands is not enough. With these three tools, I cut away the tree trunk until the form in my mind begins to take shape there. Then it seems that I am not sculpting but exhuming and resurrecting some part of myself. There is a certain rhythm to sculpting; a music in the sound of the chisel and hammer against the wood; a poetry that I write in the grain.

Elegant wisps of shaved wood are like delicate flower petals as they form on my chisel and fall away. Some are whisked away by the breeze. Others form whispers beneath my feet as I shuffle around the sculpture. So fully immersed do I become in this work that there is no ache in my forearms or shoulders. Nor do the blisters sting as they form in my palms. There is only the horse that manifests from the wood grains, a monument to my passage into freedom. I work until I drift into slumber. Then, I awake and work some more.

October 25th, 1858

I dreamt about the curves and lines that give rise to movement frozen in time. I remember what it felt like to touch a real horse for the first time. Goliath named her Nuki, for her nostrils , but I shall give her another name: Moses, after she who led the enslaved to freedom. Nuki was big and powerful, and I was but a small child. But, Moses belongs to me, and I am large enough in spirit to fit her. I once feared that she would raise her strong hooves when I was behind her, strike me once in the head or chest, and end my story. Instead, she inhabits it.

There is nostalgia in the smoothness of the sculpture's crest and withers; courage in her nostrils that flare; ambition in her mane and tail that wave in the still wind; and victory in her legs and hooves that gallop forevermore. When I fall back to behold the completed sculpture, I know that I have given her a part of me, and it is only now that I grasp how fully self-possessed I am and must be.

"Perhaps there is a bit of the romantic in you, after all," Winthrop says, startling me with his presence.

"Perhaps," I respond.

"Trees don't grow with souls, but you have given this tree yours. Come inside. We have a trip to plan."

Following him back to the house, I consider both, the excitement and terror of journeying to a new place.

"What will happen to me there?" I ask.

"Nothing that you are currently prepared for," Winthrop replies, "but nothing prepares like experience, and we will take necessary precautions."

"Precautions?"

Inside the house, he leads me beneath the stairwell where he unlocks and reveals a doorway that leads down into darkness. The cellar into which we descend is cold and damp, and I struggle to see anything at all until I heard a curious hissing sound and a flame ignited at Winthrop's fingertips. He uses this to light a lamp, which illuminates the rows of brick that make up the walls of the cellar. Stacked along the walls in wooden racks and shelves was a small arsenal of rifles and handguns. My eyes grow wide with the discovery. Winthrop, unaware of, or unperturbed by my surprise, walks over to a shelf and removes a small revolver.

"Ever seen a pepperbox, before?" he asks, presenting the weapon to me with both hands. I marvel at its shiny, wooden handle and intricate metal engravings. I take it in my hands and find its weight impressive, unexpectedly so. It is, to me, a most peculiar weapon, having one large cylinder that contains six chambers and barrels. I imagine it firing six shots at once.

"This way," Winthrop says, grabbing a small leather pouch and guiding me from the cellar. Outside, we head toward the immense yard behind the house and between the work shed and horse barn. He shows me how to load each of the six chambers. Then, we approach a young oak tree. He stops within four yards of it, extends his arm to aim the pepperbox, and fires one shot into the tree. An ungodly thunder seems to shake the entire earth, and a cloud rises from the barrel as shattered splinters of wood scatter from the trunk of the tree. Winthrop then turns to hand me the weapon.

I look at the tree, raise my arm and pull the trigger. Again, the gun thunders and a cloud rises from the barrel. However, the splinters do not scatter.

"Fortunately for you, you get more than one shot this time," Winthrop says.

I fire again. Thunder. Cloud. Nothing.

"You should use your eyes when you shoot," Winthrop says.

I open my eyes, unaware that I had clinched them closed each time before firing.

"This is no different than woodworking," he says, taking the gun from me. "You would not look in one place on a block of wood and chisel in another, nor would you sculpt with your eyes closed. Your eyes tell your hand where to put the tool. You carve by looking. You shoot by looking."

I watch how he stands with his side to the tree. He looks a straight line from his shoulder down his arm and down the barrel. He fires. Thunder. Cloud. Splinters.

"This," he returns the gun, "is the tool."

He walks away, and I raise the gun. Then, in the last moment before I pull the trigger, I try to mimic his stance. I turn my head and my side to the tree. I look a straight line from my shoulder to the barrel. I fire twice. The first shot misses, but the second nicks the side of the trunk, dislodging the bark and turning it to splinters in the air. So elated am I with this success that I fire again and again. However, there is no noise and no rising clouds.

"Six shots," Winthrop says. "You get six shots to live. Then, you better run like hell."

He takes the gun from me and begins dismantling it.

"How many lessons do I get?"

"Every man gets as many lessons as it takes to kill him. You survive, you get another lesson."

I watch him clean the weapon meticulously, removing remnants of the caps and wiping away the powder before reassembling and reloading the revolver.

"Keep it clean. Keep it loaded." He hands the gun and the pouch to me. Then he returns to the house. I follow.

I spend the next day and the following eve of our departure constructing a new chair. I do not love it, but Winthrop assures me that we can sell it in Quincy. On the morning of our departure, Winthrop and I load six chairs— including my own, a dining table, and two nightstands onto the wagon. We also load the sculpture.

"Maybe we'll find a buyer," Winthrop says.

"What if I don't want to sell it?"

Winthrop shrugs, "Then maybe you know even less about where you're going than I thought."

Before we board, he hands me a folded document.

"You will need this," he says. I unfold the document to find freedom papers for a man I do not know.

"Who is Abraham Bailey?" I ask.

"He is you. For now."

I follow him back into the workshop where he takes an old chisel and places it on the iron, wood-burning stove.

"This says I'm free?" I ask, referring to the papers in my hand.

"Those words say that *Abraham Bailey* is free, and it is our first line of defense. When that fails," he says and points to the holstered gun inside my coat, "that is our second. This next part will hurt a bit," he warns.

"What?"

"Abraham Bailey has a birthmark on his cheek. You do not."

He comes to me and carefully brands a crescent into my cheek. I want to cry out from the pain, but I do not. Nor do I make a sound when he tilts my head and pours whiskey into the fresh wound. I am reminded of that day by the pecan tree. I hear my mother's cry in my own. I remember her face as she applied the salve.

The next morning, we climb aboard the wagon that is hitched to two horses: Tennyson, one of Winthrop's thoroughbreds, and Moses.

When we are ready to depart I ask, "Where are your folks?"

"A long way from here, I think," he replies.

"How far?"

He is silent for a long moment, contemplative as though he wrestles with a choice.

"Well, my mother and father were taken from me some time ago. As were my siblings."

"Did you marry?"

His jaw stiffens.

"I wanted to," he answers, but he does not elaborate. I want to question him further, but there are storm clouds in those gray eyes. I offer him silence instead as we embark on our journey. He graciously accepts.

On the road, I dare not relax. I search every space among the bushes, every corner to every bend, and every shadow that might hide the opportunist in search of his fortune. Every rustle in the grass is a threat upon which I must be ready to pounce; every swaying branch is a neck I must throttle lest it turn an eye upon me and see beyond the fresh wound on my face. How long must I fear the sun, that telltale to miscreants, those beams of betrayal? I clutch my breast pocket where the papers are folded. I feel the wood and engraved steel holstered and pressed against my heart. I wonder if they will be enough to keep my freedom.

Chapter 8: Journey to Quincy

October 26th, 1858

Blazoning the sprawling town ahead of us, the sun lingers just a moment longer, painting streaks of gold upon the billows and wisps of clouds above. When it sinks below the horizon ahead, the city of Quincy becomes a silhouette of jagged shadows against the dimming sky and shimmering river. Soon, however, those shadows grow into rows of brick houses and buildings dotted by swaying lanterns and flickering kerosine lamps. It seems to me that regal equestrians guide stallions, and stallions move chariots upon cobblestone roads. Meanwhile Winthrop and I amble in our humble wagon toward that road from our dusty path. When we arrive, I wonder at the neatly painted signs that adorn the businesses of grocers and butchers, cobblers, tailors, and gunsmiths.

The road beneath us shimmers with the glossy reflections of the lanterns and light from shop windows, and it is musical with the footsteps that trot, plod, or pitter-patter across it. I cannot resist staring at the high-heeled shoes of a pair of women who stroll by with their arms clasped tightly in each other's. Their faces and eyes are radiant with the delight of each other's company, and their laughter is a melodious song. They stroll past a negro with broad shoulders. He lifts a large barrel from a wagon and whistles as he hauls that barrel through a doorway marked "Saloon." Two young boys chase each other playfully while their mother follows hastily and worriedly after them. Two more negros walk toward the saloon with their fiddle cases. One chides the other who simply smiles amusedly. They walk toward the church at the end of the street. Before long, we come to a stop in front of a quaint brick building. Upon its door hangs a simple sign with white letters that read, "Markel Maertz's Market." Through its large front window is a marvelous display of goods and wares.

"Take these in there. I will be right behind," Winthrop instructs me as he positions two chairs for me to carry inside. I climb down from the carriage and onto the firm ground of stone. The door to the shop opens inward with a sturdy nudge of my shoulder. A young mulatto girl not much older than I but with a rather mature and discerning expression greets me.

"Good evening, sir," she says, approaching me with her hands folded purposefully across her skirts and a sternness in her expression that all but demands an explanation for my having crossed her doorway. She looks upon me with luminous, umber eyes. There is such a light there as could never have shone from the eyes of a slave. In her gaze, I wonder if the beholder cannot be made beautiful by the things he beholds.

"May I help you?" she asks.

I ought to respond. I cannot.

"Cassy!" Winthrop rescues me with a shout from the door. "You are looking quite well."

"Mister Goodfellow," the girl responds with an air of sophistication. "Cassy is a child's name. I like to be called Cassandra, now."

"But of course," Winthrop says as he removes his cap and bows deeply at the waist. I remember my own cap and remove it promptly, fumbling with it in my hands as I try to imitate Winthrop.

"Miss Cassandra," Winthrop emphasizes each syllable, and Cassandra blushes but smiles proudly as she turns to carry the chairs to an empty display table near fruit and candies.

"Ms. Maertz will be down soon," she continues. "I should warn you that she is already quite firm in her desire to have you stay for a few

80

days."

"Now, we must really be on our way," Winthrop replies. Cassandra turns to face us with a displeased yet determined look.

"Mr. Goodfellow, you of all people must know that by 'request' I mean 'insist.' Why, I have already prepared your rooms myself."

Winthrop flashes a discerning smile at Cassandra.

"Well, I suppose I am helpless and must oblige," Winthrop says with facetious resignation.

"Yes." Cassandra points her nose upward though a smile threatens to crack her stern expression.

"Ok then, we'll stay."

"Wonderful!" Cassandra nearly sings. Winthrop offers her an indulgent grin in return. Then he suddenly seems to remember that I am there.

"Ah! Forgive my manners," he says to Cassandra. "This is, uh, Abraham. Abraham Bailey, my new apprentice."

Cassandra looks at me with such an assured expression and gaze that I must look down. She curtsies and offers her hand.

"It is a pleasure to make your acquaintance, Mr. Bailey."

I hold out my coarse palm, only to be startled by the soft and slender hand that she places in it.

"He is very quiet," she says to Winthrop.

"This is all rather new to him," Winthrop replies. "He's still adjusting."

"To Quincy?" she asks.

"Sure," Winthrop replies.

"Well, we will have plenty of time to talk about your travels over dinner," she says. "Oh, how delighted I— I mean Ms. Maertz will be quite pleased to see you again, Mr. Goodfellow." However, she cannot maintain her airs and throws her arms around Winthrop's neck. Then she turns and saunters from the room, her skirts stirring the dust from the ground.

"I'm sure she will." Winthrop winks at me and with a quick nod gestures for me to follow him.

"We should bring in your sculpture," he says. "Ms. Maertz shall be quite impressed."

As I follow him outside, I find my voice.

"You know her. Cassandra, I mean." I remark.

"All of her life," Winthrop replies.

"She is negro."

"Enough to matter, yes. But she was born free here in Illinois. She was orphaned when she was born. I made sure she found her way to Ms. Maertz when she was a child. I suspect she will go away to a women's college in the east soon."

"She is important to you."

"Like my own daughter."

"But she is not."

"No. But sometimes we pretend that she is."

He positions himself beside the sculpture and together we carry it into the store before returning for the dining table, a dresser, and two stools. Inside we are greeted by a stern little woman with pursed lips, a tight French braid in her hair, and a frock whose collar goes all the way up to her jaw.

"I do not prefer evening deliveries!" Isabelle Maertz, with her subtle German accent, says as she enters. Her lips are pursed, and her brow is furrowed above her dark, spectacle-framed eyes.

"My dearest Isabelle!" Winthrop says. "Always a pleasure."

"My dear Mr. Goodfellow," Ms. Maertz responds wryly. "You are late!"

"You must excuse the passing of a few hours," Winthrop explains. "I had to find and train another apprentice. This young man has been a tremendous help already. You must know that it is nearly impossible to fill your orders alone."

Ms. Maertz raises a brow when she sees me. She adjusts her spectacles upon her nose and peers up at me.

"Another apprentice?" she asks turning to Winthrop. "What

happened to the old one?"

"He moved west. Probably made it to California by now."

"Mmhmm. Well, then." She turns back to me. "What is your name?"

"Abraha—" Winthrop begins.

"I asked him," Ms. Maertz interrupts, flitting her eyelids in a spell of irritation. "He does talk, doesn't he?"

"Not much," Cassandra quips.

"Abraham," I say. "Abraham Bailey."

"Very good." Ms. Maertz replies. "And where do you come from?"

"Missouri," I reveal.

"Missouri! You must be one of the very few free negros from down there?"

"There are some, if not many, mostly in the northern part," Winthrop explains.

"Well, aren't you lucky?" Ms. Maertz says to Winthrop. "One of them made it to you. I hope he won't be any trouble here in Quincy."

"Of course he will be the opposite of trouble," Winthrop chuckles. "You have never met a less troublesome negro."

"I'm very serious, Mr. Goodfellow," Ms. Maertz says. "Ever since that new law, they have been suspicious of us harboring fugitives. They even gave me trouble over Cassandra, who the townspeople have known all her life. The sheriff charged in here just a week ago, throwing accusations around, and I had to strip Cassandra near to nakedness in front of him just so he could look at her back and know she wasn't a former slave nor did she know the one they were looking—
"

"As if they haven't known me my whole life!" Cassandra interjects.

"It's bad for business!" Ms. Maertz continues. "You can imagine the talk in town after that ordeal."

"I understand," Winthrop says.

"Do you?" Ms. Maertz asks, looking at him sternly. "I find this slavery thing as abhorrent as anyone, but I cannot afford to have that kind of attention on my store."

"If it would make you feel better, Abe here could strip down to his bare back," Winthrop jests.

"That won't be necessary," she says, peering up at me again. "Abraham, then?"

"Yes'm," I reply.

"Mr. Goodfellow rarely brings me wares by anyone's hand beside his own. I suppose I should take a look, then."

As she heads toward the wagon outside, I feel as though a noose might slip around my neck. I bring a hand to my collar bone to remember bruises that were once there.

"It is quite dark and vulgar, isn't it?" I hear Ms. Maertz say as she, Winthrop, and Cassandra gather around the wagon. I am not keen to follow, but I do nevertheless.

"Such violence in its sinews," Ms. Maertz continues.

"But it is also rather majestic, isn't it?" Cassandra chimes in.

"Hexenmeister," Ms. Maertz mutters. "It looks like it may trample me dead where I stand."

"It is really not so good—" I begin.

"No," Ms. Maertz interrupts. "Its proportions are off in some places, and the whole subject lacks subtlety."

"Freedom is not subtle," I say before I can think better of doing so. She turns to glare at me. She seems startled and appalled.

"An artist ought to be!" she declares. "And more refined. Or do you already know better than I?"

"Ms. Isabelle Martz was an art—" Winthrop begins explaining to me.

"Was!?" Ms. Maertz scoffs. Winthrop smiles politely.

"In her old country," Winthrop continues, "she was a purveyor art."

"You are as successful as you are because I *am still* a good judge of art," Ms. Maertz retorts, "and of course I am never mistaken." She turns her attention back to me, her eyes as wide as saucers. "You are wasting your talents as an apprentice to a carpenter. Raw talent is nothing if it is not nurtured, it is like the clay itself. And a good master is like the sculptor. If you expect to be good, you shall get no such molding from the likes of a carpenter. No, that shall never do. You mustn't toil away in a workers shed making chairs and the like."

"I happen to like toiling away, thank you," Winthrop says.

"His work does have a certain charm, though, doesn't it?" Cassandra says, though Ms. Maertz merely waves her hand and flits her eyelids in response.

"You should leave this piece with me," she says firmly. "I have some connections. I may be able to find you a proper apprenticeship in town here."

"There is a matter of money," Winthrop remarks.

"For a novice?" Ms. Maertz replies.

"For a young man who is still finding his way in the world," Winthrop says.

"And what should a work of mere potential fetch?" Ms. Maertz asks. "Twenty dollars? Two-hundred? Two-thousand?"

"It is not worth anything," I say.

"Of course it is!" Winthrop declares. "It is worth whatever his effort is worth."

"Effort is worth nothing if it cannot yield a good result," Ms. Maertz counters.

"And it has," a soft voice rises above the debate. We look to see Cassandra turning back toward the sculpture.

"By whose standard?" Ms. Maertz asks.

"By mine," Cassandra responds.

"Then you will purchase it?" Ms. Maertz scoffs. "With what money?"

"I have saved some."

"Enough for fine art?"

"Then it is fine?" Winthrop asks with a smirk.

"For a beginner," Ms. Maertz replies, sensing that she is losing the debate. "With the proper guidance and effort, he might be able to make himself worth something."

"Well, I shall guide him as best as I can until such time as you can contact a proper teacher," Winthrop says.

"And I shall be his first buyer," Cassandra says before sheepishly adding, "with a little help perhaps." Ms. Maertz discerns the hint.

"I will purchase it," she concludes, "for ten dollars. And you, Miss Cassandra, shall earn every penny of it back. You can start with the chandelier in the store room; they need a good dusting."

"Thank you!" Cassandra beams before heading back into the store.

"We were hoping for a bit more," Winthrop begins once Cassandra is out of earshot, "but we are nevertheless tremendously grateful for your kindness."

"The boy might say so," Ms. Maertz remarks.

"Thank you," I say quietly as I look at Moses standing in flesh and blood before the wagon but also frozen in pinewood atop it. Perhaps the proportions are off a bit. The intensity of her stare, however, is unmistakable. Those arrowhead-nostrils point resolutely toward a promised land, and in my sculpture, she does gallop most violently toward it. I have renamed her appropriately.

"Now that we have settled that," Winthrop says, "I hope you might afford us a bit of rest and hospitality. Cassandra mentioned that you have had rooms prepared for us."

"Of course!" Ms. Maertz responds. "Where are my manners? It seems I have been all business and no pleasure today. You must both pardon me. Come this way, Mr. Goodfellow. You must tell me all about your travels…"

The three of us return to the store, and their words fade away from me as I watch Cassandra saunter about the storeroom, preparing to close it for the evening. She climbs down from the ladder beneath the chandelier, which she has dusted. She locks the doors and draws the curtain on the large display window. She takes one last look around the store, in the middle of which sit four large wooden tables. One is topped with an assortment of candies while others hold assorted grains

— flour, barley, oats, and coffee beans. The shelves nearest the door hold bottles of bourbon, canisters of tobacco, boxes of ammunition, and various cans of fruits and vegetables. The furniture is displayed throughout the store and along the side wall furthest from the door. The counter and register are at the back, and to the right of that counter is a door that serves as the rear exit. We leave through this door once Cassandra is satisfied that everything is in order. Her last chore is to extinguish the light of the gasolier.

Outside, we climb aboard our wagon while Cassandra and Ms. Maertz enter a much more elegant brougham, upon which a young, broad-shouldered negro driver sits.

"You have a new horse," she remarks, referring to Moses.

"She certainly makes the load easier on Azalea," Winthrop replies.

"Ah! A new apprentice and a new horse. You ought to be bringing me double the inventory, then," Ms. Maertz smirks before she closes the door. She raps on the door with her knuckle, and the driver rides them away as Winthrop and I follow.

It is a short ride to Ms. Maertz's home, a charming, moderately-sized white house with a flat roof, cornices, and pedimented windows and doors. When we arrive, a negro servant named Louise greets us at the door. Her husband, Henry, is the stable hand, and he appears from there to lead our horses away.

"Cassandra will show you to your rooms," Ms. Maertz says. "Be quick to wash the road off you. Dinner will be served shortly."

The house is decorated in a baroque style, with scrolling foliage and garlands of flowers printed along the walls and carved into nearly every wooden surface. I am impressed by the beauty and pristine look of everything. Upstairs, I discover that I am to sleep in the cleanest, most beautiful bed I have ever seen, and I almost forget not to say so.

"The servants have drawn you a bath," Cassandra says to us. "I regret that it will not be so warm for one of you, but it will get the dirt off of you."

She embraces Winthrop about the waist as a child might.

"Do be quick!" she says, "I want to hear everything about your travels, and I have so much to tell you, too. So much has happened since we last met, and I am very pleased that you'll be staying with us."

Winthrop kisses her forehead.

"Me, too," he replies.

Beaming with delight, Cassandra curtsies to me and heads off downstairs.

"You first," Winthrop says to me.

I enter the bathing room, but I hesitate. I ensure that the door is closed firmly behind me. I take the wooden chair from its corner and lodge it in front of the door, beneath the doorknob. I disrobe slowly and deliberately. Then I enter the bath. It is quite hot, but it feels hottest upon my back.

October 27th, 1858 - Morning

I dream of meadowlarks in spring, the subtle flutter of their wings and blissful melody they sing. The scrolling foliage upon the chamber walls becomes a sprawling field of blossoms, and I become enthralled with this enchanting and tranquil forest that has joined me in my chamber.

Might I stay here forever?

I wish that I might, but there is a knock at my chamber door. I try to ignore this emphatic and persistent tapping there. I strain my ears for the song which grows farther away, but alas, the knocking is deafening, unbearable. I rise to answer, but when I open the door, no one is there. Just an empty corridor at the end of which are the mere echoes of the euphoric sounds I had heard only moments ago.

I enter the hall and peer through its depths and darkness to see a door at its distant end. I walk toward it, but the corridor becomes endless. I walk faster. I trot. I run. I sprint. Then, when it seems that I will never reach the end of the hall, the door looms suddenly before me, tall and ominous. I hesitate. I peek through the keyhole to find no danger there. Only the legs of a familiar rocking chair. I open the door to discover myself as a slumbering boy in my mother's cabin. She cradles me and rocks in the chair. She hums the melody to the song I had heard before. Only, there is no bliss in her rendition. The notes neither flutter nor scroll but twitch and crawl forth from her vocal cords and murmur against her pursed lips.

I jolt forward with my arms extended toward the little boy. I lean down to awaken him, but before I touch his shoulder, my mother looks at me with a wide-eyed scowl and opens her mouth to scream. But, her voice does not come out. Instead, the cacophonous plucking of piano keys sounds and a flock of crows pour forth from her mouth, their wings flailing about. They make the world as black as night, and I close my eyes to shield them from the violent beating of wings. In that darkness, I hear the last lingering note of a piano. When I open my eyes, I am awake, in the real world. And the song begins again beyond my chamber door.

I rise from my bed to feel cold sweat matting my shirt to my back. I open the door and pass through it, grateful that the hall neither looms nor stretches, and the music that so stirred me in my sleep does not fade as I walk toward the door ahead. When I peek through keyhole of this second door, I see not a reminder of my nightmare, but quite the opposite, indeed.

Cassandra sits at her piano by the morning light of the window, yet the sunshine cannot silhouette her. She welcomes the sunrise with a sonata and turns the dawn behind her to dusk. Here, by her hand, plays the music that stirs my heart so that if the whole of my life has been moving toward this moment to end here and now, I would die content, grateful for every lash upon my back and every callous on my palm. I listen to this second rendition with pure delight, and when at last she plays the final note, I feel that it lingers in the air, and holds my breath with it.

"You are a perfect audience," Cassandra says with much delight. My only utterance is to clear the night from my throat.

"But won't you please say something? Surely you won't be so silent as you were yesterday. Or is my playing so dreadful?"

"No," the word falls with a grumble from my still slumbering vocal cords.

"It was good, then?"

"Good," I clear from my throat.

"Delightful? Magnificent? Soul-stirring? Does it justify the hundreds of hours I have spent before this dreadful instrument?"

A soul was stirred in earnest, but in earnest, he is speechless.

"Oh! What's the use? Of course, I am not ready yet. I shall play before an audience, and they shall laugh at the little mulatto girl who wished she could!"

I must rescue her from this sense of hopelessness.

"What shame I should have for placing such a burden on your judgment."

"It was good," I utter. "I have never heard anything like it."

She smiles at me.

"You are a gentleman, after all, then."

I raise a puzzled eyebrow.

"You would come to a damsel in distress. But oh, what is worse! To remain in distress or to be rescued by such an unsophisticated man?"

I frown. She blushes.

"My apologies," she says. "I didn't mean to… Well, that is to say that it is your ear that is unsophisticated. Oh, bother! I sometimes wonder why we shouldn't say exactly what we think. It would make things much easier, don't you think?"

I do not offer an answer, for I do not have one. Hers is a question I have never considered.

"Well," she says rising from her bench and approaching me, "wouldn't we make a fine pair. Me the mutterer and you the mute."

She stops mere inches before me in the doorway, and she looks up into my eyes.

"But, we are artists, aren't we?" she says. "What use have we for words?"

I close my eyes a bit longer than it takes to blink, and when I open them, she has passed from the doorway and down the hall toward the stairs. Her skirts stir the dirt from the ground such that she leaves a path behind in which I follow.

"Not so many are quite so taken with Bach as you or I," she says as she reaches the end of the hall and descends the stairs. "It disturbs the mornings, as the servants around here have taken to telling me on more than one occasion. But, I have no other time to practice. I must be off to the store by seven, and I am much too tired to practice in the evening. I should be so lucky to have an audience, even yours, when I fear that I am merely waking people at the crack of dawn."

I am pleased to be your audience.

When we reach the kitchen, the servant is already preparing breakfast.

"Good morning, Louise," sings Cassandra.

"Good morning, my dear," Louise says with a southern-heavy accent. "Now don't you let Miss Cassandra talk you're ear off, young man. She ain't used to having somebody her age to talk to. These northern folk ain't nuthin' like we Virginia folk. As you can see she has forgotten all of her manners."

Cassandra's face becomes flushed, and she smiles that inward smile of hers. She takes the cup of coffee that Louise holds out for her.

"There," says Louise turning to address me more directly. "Now, that mouth of hers is busy. Perhaps you can get a word in. I hear you have traveled a long way to find Mr. Goodfellow."

"All the way from Missouri!" Cassandra declares after an abrupt swallow.

"Well, I'm sure you're glad to be away from there," Louise addresses me but gives Cassandra a stern look. "I'll bet you can't get far enough across that river to suit you."

I nod.

"You don't hear about too many free negros that come here from there," Louise continues. I do not notice her curious glance. "You must be one of the railroad workers. That about the only work for men across the river that ain't cotton or tobacco."

I nod, again.

"Well?" Louise inquires, dissatisfied with my nodding.

"Oh my!" Cassandra chimes in. "The railroad? It must be mighty exciting to work on them. They are dreadfully big and loud, but still I think it would be delightful to ride one away from here."

"You have the 'dreadful' part right," Louise chuckles. "Big and loud and filthy. I never seen a man work on them who isn't blacker at the end of the day, no matter how black he is at the beginning." She and Cassandra laugh, and I hope that we are moving on from the railroad talk. It is Winthrop who rescues me when he enters.

"What are we all laughing about?" he asks, adjusting his suspenders with one hand and carrying a pipe in the other. He discards the old ashes from the pipe into a bucket of old coffee grounds, vegetable shavings, and animal trimmings.

"Did you know that Mr. Bailey used to work on the railroads in Missouri?" Cassandra asks.

"Ah," Winthrop says with his pipe balanced in his teeth. He searches his pocket for a match to light. "I guess Mr. Bailey here is full with surprises. He neglected to mention that. But I guess that's why he's so good with a hammer." He winks at me and strikes the discovered match.

"Isn't that exciting?" says Cassandra.

"Loud and filthy!" Louise grumbles. "Speaking of filthy, don't you light that thing in my kitchen!" Winthrop pauses with the match and looks at Cassandra, who shrugs. He extinguishes the match and tosses it into the bucket of food scraps.

"How about breakfast? That sounds the most exciting to me," he says. Louise, suddenly remembering the importance of her task, springs to action.

"Lord, y'all gonna get me in trouble if I don't stop messing with y'all," Louise says. "Go on in that dining room. I don't need y'all crowding my kitchen, no how. Shoo!"

"Very well," says Winthrop. He winks at me and I sigh with relief.

"I think Mr. Bailey is quite taken with the music of Johann Sebastian Bach," Cassandra says to Winthrop as we pass into the next room. I become tense again.

"Is that so?" Winthrop replies.

"He came to listen this morning. He seemed quite pleased with my playing." She smiles at me. My face grows warm.

"Oh, we all listened this morning," Louise shouts from the kitchen.

"Yes, but he was much less disagreeable about it," says Cassandra. "Speaking of disagreeable, when will you bring me a new bench?"

"The one you have isn't good enough?"

"It is a dreadful thing— quite the pain in the—"

"Miss Cassandra!" Louise scolds her as she arrives from the kitchen. We settle in the chairs around the table, and Louise places before us a tray with a bowl of oat porridge, a platter of fried pork, and an assortment of sliced pears and apples.

"We'll see about a new bench," Winthrop says to Cassandra. "And what about Ms. Maertz? How does she feel about your playing?" In that moment Isabelle Maertz enters the dining room through the door connecting to the anteroom.

"Why, aren't we all full of the bird's twitters and bee's buzzes this morning," she says in a more cheerful tone than I expect.

"We were just talking about you," Winthrop replies. "Cassandra says her playing is coming along. What do you think?"

"It is," Ms. Maertz replies. "It won't be long before she will be far from here."

"Oh Ms. Maertz," says Cassandra, "you will miss me terribly, won't you?"

Ms. Maertz smiles. "As a worker, dear. As a pupil, you are quite hard-headed."

"But capable?" Cassandra retorts.

"But hard-headed," Ms. Maertz reiterates.

"But capable," Cassandra says to Winthrop.

"This is very good to hear," Winthrop says. "New England will be very good for a young lady of your talents and temperament. But I am in no rush to see you off."

"Why, Mr. Bailey could fill the artistic void, couldn't he?" Cassandra jests.

"I do not think the young man plays the piano," he replies.

"Yes, but sculptures last longer. He doesn't even have to be in the room for you to enjoy them," Cassandra says.

"That is only if he should ever part with his creations," Ms. Maertz interjects.

"Must we return to this conversation so early in the morning?" Winthrop asks.

"No, of course not," Ms. Maertz says. "I am only surprised that someone of such little means should balk at my payment. Or my judgment."

"He does not question your judgment," Winthrop explains. "But it is his first work. He is understandably attached, you see."

"I do," Ms. Maertz says. "But, I also think he means to better his station. And his appearance. Pardon me for saying so, but he looks as though he has not eaten in weeks."

"Ms. Maertz!" Cassandra cries.

"I pardoned myself for saying so!" Ms. Maertz replies.

"Very well," Winthrop says. "Let us discuss it on our ride into town. I wish to show Mr. Bailey the public square and a few of Quincy's other splendors."

"I'm sure you will treat him to quite the adventure," Cassandra says.

"We are all wary of Mr. Goodfellow's adventures," Ms. Maertz warns. "Bar fights. Duels in the streets. No one would imagine the artisan is a hooligan.

"Hooligan?" Winthrop protests. "I only defend what is right. If a man wishes to challenge me over my opinion—"

"Drunken opinion," Ms. Maertz interjects.

"Then it is his loss. Besides, I have only ever dueled once."

"So did the other fellow," Ms. Maertz quips. "Now, don't you go starting fights in town. Between the new laws and that debate between those lawyers down there, sentiments between the townsfolk are about ready to boil over. I hate slavery as much as anyone. But I'd hate even more to lose my best *artisan*."

"Why, Ms. Maertz, do I seem like the fighting kind?"

"No, you do not. But you are all the same!"

"Oh, I think I like the sound of 'artisan.' It sounds a bit like 'artist,'" Winthrop says.

"Chairs are not sculptures, Mr. Goodfellow," Ms. Maertz retorts.

"Indeed they aren't."

"No adventures!" Ms. Maertz demands. "Stay out of trouble and keep the law from my doorstep. My reputation will not always save you."

"But dear Isabelle, without adventure how will we ever hope to court Mr. Bailey?"

"With money," Ms. Maertz replies.

Chapter 9: A Lesson Before Living

October 27th, 1858 - Noon

I have my mother's hands. They are bigger, but they look the same. The fingers are slender and rounded at the ends. The palms are wide and the creases cut deep and dark. My hands are tough and my fingers are nimble. Like hers. I use them to whittle a block of pine into a perched bird whose song I imagine as we ride into town. The song fits nicely with the rhythm of horseshoes against the cobblestone. There is something tranquil in the calmness of the horses and the orderliness of the road. I am mesmerized by the circular array of the stones as they seem to radiate from the steps of the horses. Again, the road leads us to that paradise of opportunity as the river gleams behind it all.

With an expression of admiration, Winthrop looks down at the meadowlark in my hand. When I notice how intently he observes me, I stop and place the carving in my breast pocket.

"She would like it," he says, returning his gaze to the road.

"I am not making it for her."

"You should."

"Why should I?"

"Because you aren't exactly winning her with your words."

"Who says I am trying to win her at all?"

"No one. "

We ride on for a moment in silence. I think about Serafina and moments when she would flirt with the boys and men on the plantation. I remember that when she was charmed, her cheeks would glow a rosy color upon her pecan complexion. I am grateful, now, for being darker.

"Clearly, however, we are speaking of *someone*," Winthrop says, "and if you were trying to win her over, you ought to make something for her."

I tuck my hands under my arms and sit, hunched over. Seeing my discomfort, Winthrop changes the subject.

"Ms. Maertz's price is a bit low, but you are fortunate to sell it to her."

"Am I?"

"She presents an interesting opportunity, doesn't she? If you sell to her, you're an artist, a sculptor, aren't you? Of course, I am not opposed to keeping you on as an apprentice if you don't."

"Is it so easy? I sell one thing to a stranger, and I'm an artist?"

"That's usually the first step. And of course, Isabelle Maertz is no ordinary stranger. She knows art. And she has influence in Illinois. A sale to her today is almost certainly a sale later. Perhaps many more after that. You will have as many buyers as you want before long."

I hunch a bit lower on the wagon bench.

"Of course, you don't have to be seen," he adds, "only your work. Or you can go on working for me. It will take a bit longer to earn the money you ought to get from a proper art sale, but once you have it, you can go as far as you need to— wherever you think you'll be free."

"And where will that be?"

"Depends on how far you're willing to go. The further you're willing, the less likely it will be that you will go anywhere at all."

He slows our wagon to a halt at the top of a hill overlooking John's Square. He points to the splendor blow, but I look, instead, to the immense river behind the buildings and the grand steamboat that sits upon it. A rail engine roars along the river bank toward Quincy Station. Plumes of smoke rise from its chimney to greet the sky. It's whistle screams a powerful announcement of its arrival. The steamboat calls back in a low, rumbling hum to the men ashore. They hustle to receive her at the dock. Never before have I witnessed such grandiose movement. Never before have I been so aware of the world, the whole of it, and its movement beneath my feet. Looking upon this grand spectacle, I feel that Elysium Plantation is both a part of me and apart from me. Its life is so minuscule in comparison to what I witness here, and yet it is true that my life there has brought me here.

"She is lovely, isn't she?" Winthrop echoes my thoughts.

"How terrific and terrifying it must be to travel on either one," I say about the boat and train that slow to stops at their respective ports.

Winthrop nods and says, "Let us get a closer look."

We hitch our wagon at a post on the cobblestone near a very loud butcher. Then we walk toward the wooden planks of the pier.

"Fresh off the boat! Best catch of the day!" a fisherman shouts as we pass him. Merchants push and pull crates to and fro on carts and wagons. One man rides a donkey led carriage full with Indian corn. Another pulls a cart full with sacks of flour toward the docks. Winthrop and I come to a stop on a plank where the view of the steamboat is unobstructed.

"How could anyone ever want to leave this splendor?" Winthrop says, drawing in a deep, invigorating breath and clenching his pipe in his teeth. He packs it with tobacco and strikes a match to it.

I tilt my head back to feel the breeze from the river bank. There many sounds of busyness, and I revel in the image of the men making those sounds. A few negros whistle as they labor to load and unload the crates at nearby shops. Three white men speak harshly to each other in a language I cannot understand.

"Would either you or your boy mind helping me with this?" a frail man with an Irish accent and a heavy wagon beckons Winthrop and me to his aid.

"Of course, friend," says Winthrop through a cloud of smoke.

"Bless you, sir."

Winthrop and I rush over to him just as he is losing control of his wagon load. I keep two crates from toppling to the ground, and as I right them on the wagon, I notice the branded emblem of a pecan tree upon them. I look away to the frail man who is quite frantic with the unpacking of his wares.

"This way," he says, guiding Winthrop and me along the dirt road behind the shops. We pass the butcher, a cobbler, and a blacksmith before we happen upon a tiny tobacco shop.

"Just place them here," the man says. "They will be off to the mills tomorrow. Here, have this for your troubles." The man shuffles away into his shop, and we follow him. Inside, he hands Winthrop a tin of pipe tobacco.

"Best smoke in all of Illinois," the man says with pride. They're having a little trouble down there, what with all the slaves running this way nowadays. But still, it don't get no better than good ole Missouri tobacco."

I look at the merchant more closely this time, but he hardly glances in my direction.

"I'd beg to differ," Winthrop says to him, looking the tin over pensively.

"Oh, well that's just 'cause you ain't tried the good stuff yet. I can smell it in your pipe. You must get that New England stuff. That shit sits on them trains until all the flavor is gone from it. Here." He hands another tin to Winthrop who hands it to me while placing the other in his breast pocket.

"I appreciate your generosity," Winthrop remarks.

"Likewise. Much obliged for your help." The merchant says.

"Glad to offer it," Winthrop replies.

They shake hands and we take our leave. We visit the gun shop next, and I am a bit too eager to find myself inside. So eager am I, in fact, that I walk straight through the front door without a thought. The first thing I see is the barrel of a gun. Second is the man pointing it at me.

"Niggers don't come in through the front door of this

101

establishment," he says. He cocks the hammer of the rifle.

"He's with me," Winthrop says calmly when he enters behind me.

"Then he ought to know better," the man says.

"Well, he doesn't."

The man looks askance at me, but he lowers his rifle and offers Winthrop a wry smile.

"One of these days, you're gonna get 'em killed before you can rescue 'em," the man says.

"You wouldn't," Winthrop chuckles.

"I would," the man replies. "I spare no obstacle in the pursuit of freedom."

"I am aware," Winthrop replies.

"Good. So who have you brought to me today?"

"This is Abraham Bailey."

"Nice name. Who is he really?"

Winthrop looks to me and nods.

"Percival Bishop," I say.

"No shit?"

"No shit," Winthrop says.

"You found him before they did," the man says.

"I always do," Winthrop replies. I offer a confounded look to both men.

"I am Mr. Pullman," the man says, offering me his hand. "You can call me 'George.'"

"George," I say taking his hand. He shakes it vigorously.

"Mr. *Bailey*," he says. "There is quite a bounty on your head in Missouri."

"Would you like to claim it?" I ask.

"On the contrary," George replies. "My job is to make any such attempt as futile as I can. It is fortunate that you found me. Quincy is a safe enough place for now, but we must get you farther east as soon as we can." He looks to Winthrop. "Does he have any money?"

"We're working on that," Winthrop replies.

"Does he have a gun?"

"He does."

"Does he know how to use it?"

"That's why we're here."

"Come this way," George instructs us. He locks the front door to his shop and leads us through another doorway behind the counter and into a small pantry. In that pantry, he slides a shelf to the side and lifts a plank in the floor, revealing a stairwell to a basement. I count fifty steps until we enter a room with an arsenal of rifles.

"Let's see what you got," George says to me, prompting me to remove the pepper box from its holster. George positions a target in the room, and he steps behind me with Winthrop. I raise the gun and fire twice. The first shot misses, but the second lands in the middle of the target.

"Not so hard, was it?" Winthrop asks. He steps in front of me and opens my coat. He searches inside for the meadowlark I was carving earlier. He goes over to the target and places it atop the wooden post there. Then, he returns to his place behind me.

"Hit that," he commands.

I fire once and miss. Winthrop pushes me forward. I fire and miss again. He pushes me until I am a mere yard away from the meadowlark. I miss and fire again. He pushes me until I can touch the meadowlark with the barrel of my gun. I raise my gun, but I do not fire.

"I see you have learned my previous lessons well," Winthrop remarks. "But there is one that supersedes the others."

"What is that?" I ask.

"George said it when you barged through his door earlier," Winthrop says. "Spare no obstacle in the pursuit of freedom. That there bird is your obstacle."

After our practice, George shows me how to reload the pepperbox. Then he offers me the same advice that Winthrop did.

"Keep it clean and loaded."

As we head away from the pier toward Maertz's General Store, the morning sun has risen high to crown the afternoon sky, and I find that it shines a bit too brightly upon the town. I remember the tobacco tin that I received from the merchant, and place my hand in my pocket to retrieve it. I feel the engraved emblem, and decide against looking at it. I remove my hand from my pocket, leaving the tin there, pressed against my gun.

October 31st, 1858

"Don't you miss your family?"

"No."

My curt response seems to pain Cassandra such that I am glad she cannot see me, cannot see how little it pained me to have uttered such a cold response to such a warm invitation to converse. She looks away, out of the large storeroom window as I hide behind the curtain that shields her eyes from my work in progress until it is done. I busy myself with the sculpture, worried that she has already decided I am a loveless creature.

But how in love I truly am!

Like the gallant hero, Peirrot, hiding from her gaze but professing my love through art. Whereas he sang, I sculpt. I wonder if would die.

Die? For this love?

It occurs to me that this is the true tragedy of Peirrot's story, that he should have to die for love. Was such a reality the cause of my mother's melancholy? Didn't I even see a glimpse of it in my father's eyes? I look to the girl perched on the stool as she gazes at the passersby outside the large storefront window. I wonder that they go about their lives without the same worry as I, and this realization makes my own condition larger in my mind.

No, I resolve. I shall not die like Pierrot.

With my mother's hands and my father's eyes, I carve Cassandra's likeness in oak, all the while pondering her question.

No. I do not miss them. I slave is not permitted such sentiments. So, when my father whipped me until I could only be held up by that pecan tree and my bindings to it; when my mother could do naught but cry and look on; when I knew that I must forge and scrape my own path to salvation or die, I felt the lashes upon my back, the burn of the salve, the cold, the thirst, and the hunger in the woods. And, I could feel nothing in my soul, for I might have indeed perished the first time my father's whip drew his bastard's blood.

"But you must feel something," Cassandra insists.

"No," I maintain. "We were poor. My father was a drunk, and my mother was—" I pause, "Coldhearted. It was necessary to get away."

"Still, you must've felt something," she replies, "even if that something comes out of the feeling of nothing. I did not know my parents, but it fills me with sadness at times to think that I shall never know what it feels like to miss their presence. Or to lose them, to truly lose someone after you once had them."

"Your sadness cannot bring them back."

Cassandra gasps.

"What a *coldhearted* thing to say," she remarks.

"And yet it is true," I reply. "If I should miss my father, would that change who he is? Or my mother? Would it change the fact that I..." I trail off.

"That you 'what'?" she asks.

"That I was born to a life of misery."

"And yet you were able to get away from it. Surely they taught you something. Something that stayed with you."

From my mother and father, I learned that there are forces in the world that can keep you from loving a thing. No matter how strongly inclined you are toward it. No matter how much your soul longs to reach out for it. There are forces in the world strong enough to make you harm a thing you love and be harmed by it. And if you don't harm that loving thing yourself, there are forces strong enough to make you stand by and watch harm done to it.

"No," I say. "Nothing at all."

Cassandra turns away from the window and my eyes widen in horror. I drop the chisel and hammer immediately and cover the sculpture.

"Perhaps you took more of your parents with you than you think," she says to me.

"Please," I implore, "it is not done yet."

Satisfied that she has touched upon some truth, she turns back to the window. I can see the light of the morning in her eyes as they are reflected in the window. Reflections are funny things. They have all of the semblances of reality, all of the colors and shapes and textures. But you cannot touch them. You cannot feel with your hands their flesh, blood, and bones though it may seem that you can. There is a safety in reflections, and I must only touch upon them with my chisel and hammer.

I carve away until I can see her delicate chin and jawline. Her nose is rounded yet dainty, and her eyes though not yet finished, threaten to stare into my soul as if I were the sculptor and she, the creator. I feel that I am conjuring life from this dead tree, and she will rise from its emptiness and teach me how to live. I have been working on this sculpture four days, but I am terrified of completing it. I cover it with a muslin to finish another day. In the meantime, I hope that the real Cassandra never looks upon my reflections beneath this shroud.

November 1st, 1858

"Would you like one?" Cassandra asks me in her sweet, sing-song voice as my eyes wander over the candy shelves of the store. I try to seem surprised by her presence, though I was acutely aware of her from the moment I approached the store. She walks over to me and, with her finger tips, lightly touches a glass jar filled with rainbow-colored wafers.

"These are my favorite," she continues. "We get them from Boston. Have you ever had one?"

"Never," I respond.

"Then you simply must."

She removes the lid from the jar of pastel candies, each like powdery coins. She holds out the jar to me. I take one between my finger and thumb and place it carefully in my mouth. The sweetness dissolves quite unexpectedly on my tongue, and the sensation brings water to my eyes.

She laughs.

"Are they so bad?" she asks.

"No, but I did not expect that."

"The taste?

"The sweetness."

"My goodness! Have you never had candy before?"

Of course, I had been given a swallow of molasses on occasion for good behavior when I was a child. However, that did not prepare for this sweetness that seemed to melt and spread throughout my entire body even as I still tasted it upon my tongue.

"How dreadful it must have been for a child to not taste candy."

She still holds the open jar before me.

"Would you like another?" she asks.

Hesitantly, I take another. She smiles.

"What was it like?" she asks, "Growing up in Missouri, I mean?"

I look away from her eager eyes.

"Quiet," I reply.

"Not many people?"

"Plenty of people. But quiet all the same."

"Is your mother still there?"

"Perhaps."

"And your father?"

"I suspect so."

"You do not know for sure?"

"I have not been home. Not in a very long while."

"Have you even been alive a long while? You seem so young— at least as young as I."

"Are your parents where you left them?" I snap.

"I did not expect such a cruel tone," she says. "But in the spirit of conversation, I will say that I did not leave them. They died from a terrible illness when I was yet an infant. Mr. Goodfellow knew them a bit. He speaks of my mother when I ask, though not much. I would have been given to an orphanage were it not for him. He raised me until my fourteenth year. Then I came to live with the Maertz Family, before Mr. Maertz died— Markel Maertz, his name was. I helped to nurse him before he died, and I have been here ever since. Five years in autumn."

"I see," I reply.

"Will you go back there some day? To Missouri?" she asks.

"I do not know."

"I see," she closes the candy jar abruptly and places it firmly in its place on the shelf.

"I have spoken of my parents already," I say.

"Not much."

"Enough. They will always be what they are. And I have no desire to return to them."

"Will you always be what you are?" she asks. "Are you even what you were?"

"I am what I am."

"How biblical of you. Were your parents very religious?"

"Must you pry?" I ask, losing patience.

"I must," she responds. "How else am I to know you?"

"And why must you know me?"

"Because that is our lot in life. We must all go through the humdrum of life, but things become much more colorful with the meeting of others, those who have gone about things in different ways than ourselves. I am curious about the ways in which you have colored the humdrum."

"Curious?"

"Yes. Aren't you curious about me?"

She walks across the storeroom, past the furniture to be sold, and settles before the muslin-covered sculpture. She touches the muslin lightly with her slender, pointed fingers, and I hurry over to distract her.

"What can make you curious about me?" I ask.

"Well," she begins, "you aren't the first apprentice Mr. Goodfellow has had. I suppose I am curious to know if you will stay a while."

"Maybe not," I reply.

"Oh," she sighs. "That is disappointing."

"Is it?"

"It just seems that his apprentices are always leaving for one reason or another."

"I'm sure they have their reasons."

"Maybe," she says. "It does make it hard to become attached to any of them."

I clear my throat.

"Have you ever found yourself attached to any of them?"

"Not yet," she says, fingering the muslin again. "What will you do with this one?"

"It is not done," I say. "I suppose I will take it with me."

"Then how will you finish it?" she asks.

"Perhaps I won't."

Cassandra frowns.

"You will finish it," she commands.

"Then I will do so from memory," I reply.

"You will remember my face?"

"Yes."

Cassandra looks to me, then, and smiles ever so sweetly. She loops her arm in mine to guide me away from the chair and sculpture. At first I resist her touch, her pull, her sweetness. But, I am so wondrously comforted by all of it— all of her, that she succeeds in pulling me from the room and guiding me back to the front display where Winthrop waits, having returned from an errand he assured me had to be done on his own.

"Hello, my dear," he greets Cassandra with a smile. "You two seem to have become good friends."

My cheeks grow hot.

"She asks a lot of questions," I say, trying in vain to reclaim my arm, for she suddenly holds to it a bit tighter.

"He offers a lot of silence," she replies. Winthrop laughs.

"I regret that you will have to interrogate each other another day," he says. "We must make our preparations, and I regret, too, that we shall part ways again, so soon." He approaches Cassandra and lightly touches her chin.

"Me, too," she replies. "But you will return soon? Mr. Bailey has promised to finish this sculpture and I am quite eager to see how it turns out."

"I see," Winthrop looks at me with raised brows.

"So you will see that he finishes it, yes?" Cassandra asks.

"If he is to sculpt, then I am not so sure how much help I will be. A man cannot teach what he does not know. I will do my best, however."

"Oh! But he shall not go on as a cabinetmaker," she protests. "Can't you see he is ill-suited for the task?"

"I think he does fine work," Winthrop chuckles, amused by Cassandra's insistence.

"But he does not love that work."

"You are not wrong," Winthrop says. "I will do what I can."

"Yes, you will," Cassandra says. "You will see that he finishes my sculpture."

"Yes."

"And that he returns it here to me."

"Yes."

"And maybe he will stay a while longer before you ship him off to wherever your other apprentices go."

"I'm beginning to think that you aren't so sad to see me go at all," Winthrop chuckles.

"Oh, of course I am," Cassandra protests. She hurries from me to him and throws her arms around his neck. "And I will be ever so happy to see you when you return. With him."

Winthrop roars with laughter, and I am again grateful for my dark complexion.

"My dear, Cassy!" Winthrop says, "you have grown quite demanding, haven't you? Perhaps you have been here under Isabelle's tutelage for far too long.".

"And who is to blame for that?" Cassandra remarks.

"The universe," Winthrop says, his eyes glistening to behold the young woman before him. "The universe that erred in not making you my daughter."

"But aren't I, anyway?"

"You are, indeed."

I turn away from them then, for I feel once more that I have happened upon a moment to which I do not belong. On the next morning, I am quiet as we pack. Among my belongings is the meadowlark I have been carving. Its final touch is a hole in its wing through which I thread a leather string. I tie this string around my neck and tuck the meadowlark beneath my shirt. Perhaps it will be a gift for another time. As we ride back to Liberty, I am reminded of the story Solomon once told me about my mother's coming to Elysium Plantation.

Chapter 10: Words I Carry With Me

Miriam's Song of Solomon

My mother once told me the story of her coming to Elysium Plantation. She was always reluctant to talk about it, but I had caught her in a particularly pensive mood. She spoke the words to me with such a magic that it seemed the whole of the events were playing out before my own eyes. To this day, I find it hard to shake the melancholy that filled her in the moments before she gave birth to me.

Joachim Meets Miriam, 1839

"**A**in't no use in you crying," Miriam's mother, Abigail, said to her on the eve of her departure. She had considered it fortunate that Miriam, at the dawn of her adult years and budding beauty, be sent away from the wandering eyes of Master Benjamin Thomaston. Benjamin was somewhat reluctant, but being old and hampered by debt, was convinced to part with Miriam. He sought and secured a hefty sum as compensation for Miriam's sale to a young tobacco merchant named Joachim Bishop. The young merchant, praised by many in Fayette for doubling the value of his father's business only a year after he inherited it, came calling with great enthusiasm, greater still when he met the negress who would become his property. Benjamin thus became willing to send Miriam on her way, and Abigail, who would be emancipated in her old age once Miriam was gone, was willing too.

"He a good, God-fearin' man. I reckon he be mighty good to you." Abigail was kneeling and trying her best to halt the flow of tears from Miriam's large chestnut eyes.

"He a wealthy man, and he come all this way just for you," she added, smiling and hushing her tone to soften her daughter's sentiments. Miriam ignored the knowing smile, and when Abigail wiped Miriam's damp cheek with her coarse hand, Miriam withdrew from its touch. Abigail responded by snatching her daughter by the strings of her corset and forcing a gasp from her.

"You gonna have to learn to get along," she said sternly, "You can make it easy on yourself. Or you can make it mighty, mighty hard. Now, Master Thomaston can't do no more for you here. We down to our last pennies, and I can't be working no more. I need rest. Don't I deserve that? Ain't I suffered enough?"

Miriam avoided the gaze of her mother though she knew quite well how her mother had suffered, how her back and legs had grown crooked from the work. She knew that her mother had suffered in earnest. Before they had come to live with Benjamin Thomaston, Miriam and Abigail belonged to a master who coveted Abigail's body and a mistress who hated them both for it. She worked Abigail to the point of illness every chance she got. If she had gotten her way, the mistress would have worked Abigail to death. By comparison, Mr. Thomaston was much kinder, but by the time Abigail had come under his care, she had already developed the crook in her back, and much of her beauty had worn away. Thomaston admired Abigail greatly, nevertheless, and so Miriam knew very well what Abigail hoped to gain from her daughter's departure—or rather what Abigail hoped not to lose.

"Isn't it my turn now?" her mother pleaded, "Survive for me. Like I done for you. But let me be done. I can't do no more. It's your turn, now. Can't you do that for me?"

"Yes'm."

Her mother bore a strained and solemn smile, and she took these last moments to admire her daughter.

"My, but you are beautiful," she said, as she tied the laces of the turquoise frock she had fashioned from the garments of their master's dead wife. Abigail looked at her daughter's toned arms and legs and her narrow waist. She admired her cheekbones, curved like baroque pearls, and her lips, pouted forth like the soft petals of a gentian flower. With her rough hands, she petted her daughter's hair, which was as black as raven feathers and streamed in thick, tight, untamed curls down a neck as long and graceful as a swan's. For a rare moment, Abigail looked at her daughter and beamed with pride. Then she heard her master's steps outside the door.

"You stay in here until your new master comes," Abigail said before hastily leaving the room.

Ain't no use in Mister Thomaston losing his nerve, now, Abigail thought.

When Joachim came to claim his property later that day, he paused inadvertently in the parlor threshold. He had admired the slave on his first visit thinking she would make a suitable mate for one of his own prized slaves. However upon this second visit, he gazed at Miriam and had the most unsettling thought.

She will be my undoing. Yet, he had no intention of reneging on the sale.

"She's all yours now," Benjamin said. "I suppose I'm out of the slave business for good. I'm getting too old for such dreams."

"I beg your pardon?" Joachim replied curiously.

"Oh, I suppose there isn't anything wrong with dreaming," said Thomaston. "But they do have a way of wearing on a man, dreams do. Mine have just about worn me to pieces."

"Do you speak unfavorably of slavery?" asked Joachim.

"Not slavery but the southern way of life as a whole," replied Thomaston. "I'm just no good at it."

"I see," Joachim replied.

"No. No, you don't see. You're looking, but you don't see."

"Looking?"

"Oh, I know the lookers when I see them. I might not have all of the intuitions of you Southerners, but I know the lookers."

"I would hardly call us Southerners," Joachim opined. "We aren't so far south as other slave states."

Benjamin, however, waved his hand dismissively in response.

"Oh, don't let me bother you," said Benjamin. "I'm just an old crank, worn out by life as such. On to business, then!"

With a cumbersome limp, he led Joachim down the hall into the anteroom where he presented the bill of sale and they exchanged monies.

"What about your older slave?" Joachim asked as they headed back to the parlor.

"What older slave?"

"The girl has a mother?"

"Abigail? What about her?"

"I have found that a slave can be most disagreeable when separated from her family. Is the mother for sale?"

Benjamin at first seemed offended. Then he chuckled and winked at Joachim.

"Won't be anymore slaves here once you buy Miriam," Benjamin said. "My Abbie doesn't have any more working years left in her, and I figure I don't have many years left at all. I should fetch a sizable sum for the land. Then, we're just gonna head on north and die, I suppose."

"I could buy her, anyway," Joachim replied. "Make that trip up north a bit more comfortable."

"Well, that's why she's coming with me," Benjamin replied shrewdly. "My wife is gone. She didn't give me any children. Abbie is about all I got left. Perhaps I do not understand the Southern sentimentality, but I do think, perhaps, that I can understand your attachment to this institution. I got my own attachments."

Joachim narrowed his eyes, and Benjamin offered a weary smile.

"You look. Soon enough, you will see," Benjamin said.

Those last words lingered in Joachim's mind long after he walked through the door with his new slave, loaded his wagon, and saw the plantation disappear behind his carriage. The wheels clattered along the rock-strewn road, and the horses panted while their ironclad hooves kicked up dirt. However, these sounds failed to drown out those words.

The value of a slave is in her ability to work, he reminded himself. *No matter how beautiful she might be.*

Joachim tried to keep in his mind Miriam's intended purpose, which was to tend his house and serve as a wife for his most devoted slave,

Solomon. Nevertheless, a separate feeling of eagerness and excitement fluttered about in the pit of his stomach. He wanted to turn around to the back of the wagon and simply look upon her body. But he knew looking would give way to touching, and touching to ravaging. So, he kept his eyes on the road. The sound of his heart synchronized with the beating of hooves against the earth below them, and it raced along as the wheels turned and clattered across the rugged terrain, bringing them closer to home. It was only Benjamin's lingering words that compelled Joachim to take a deep breath and compose himself.

Miriam, meanwhile, sat quietly with her slumped head and downward looking eyes. Shadows lurked where tears might have flowed had she allowed herself to feel something about her departure. The hooves beat against the earth, and the wheels chattered against the stones in the dirt road, yet her heart stood still, and her teeth were clenched. She looked upon the distance that spread between her and her mother as a chasm that ought to swallow any sadness she felt, so with each passing acre between her and her mother, she told herself that she could bear their separation a little more.

After all, she thought, *I have been surrendered. Ain't I capable of surrendering, too?* So, she told her eyes to freeze her tears. She dared not look up at the quickly retreating path, and she dared not loosen her jaw. By sunset, when Joachim's carriage finally arrived at his plantation, Miriam thought that she had forgotten all of her past life.

As they turned from the main path and onto the stone-paved way to Elysium Plantation, the land that stretched out before them seemed perfectly serene with its immense yet well-manicured lawn and rows of ash trees, which seemed to have been lined and planted with mathematical precision. At the end of the paved way, just before the dirt road that led to the crops and slave quarters, a separate walkway ascended a hill upon which sat a regal, Georgian house. The pristine white of its wooden beams shone against the sunset and within the frame of its red brick quoins. The two chimneys, one one each end, stretching toward the sky to give the house a tall stature in spite of its width. The paneled, red door with its gold knocker completed the home's elegance.

"This is your home now," Joachim said with a sternness that he hoped belied all that he secretly felt for her. He did not look back at her when he spoke, nor did he acknowledge her before he descended from the carriage and removed his gloves. He approached a plump, oval-shaped, negro woman who emerged from the house along with a slender, male negro who had appeared at the side of the house, on the path where the cobblestone turned to dirt. Both of these negroes were immaculately dressed. The man wore new, dark-colored trousers and a periwinkle vest that had paisley embroidery all over the front. The woman wore a violet dress with elegant, bell-shaped sleeves and white, lacy ruffles around the collar. Joachim handed his riding gloves and coat to the woman before speaking to the man.

"Make sure she finds her way comfortably," he said.

"Yessir," said the slender man, who was looking at Miriam now with the overt enthusiasm Joachim had stifled in himself. The master and the housemaid disappeared behind the bright red door. The negro man jumped onto the carriage.

"You're going to like it here," he said with a smile as he grabbed the reins and directed the horses onto the dirt path toward the slave quarters. "Mr. Bishop is a fine man. He treats us better than most men treat their families."

There was something about the negro's tone that Miriam did not like though she did not yet know exactly what it was.

The dirt road bisected the land so that the fields were on the left side and the cabins were on the right. By the fading light of dusk, Miriam could discern the small patch of neatly lain rows of corn, tomatoes, potatoes, and other crops. These soon turned to an immense field of tall, leafy stalks of tobacco. Smoke billowed from the chimneys of the slave cabins to the right, and dim, orange light flickered in their windows. Ahead, there was a large barn and an enormous black pecan tree that spread its branches high and tall like a fan that shaded and cooled the entire field. Miriam noticed to the far right of the barn a row of ash trees that were not as straight as the ones in the front. Her eyes remained fixed there.

"That one belongs to Cyrus and Opal," the negro explained, pointing at one of the slave cabins, "They been married for a few years now, and she is with child. That one there belongs to Sarah and Zachariah. They were some of the first ones here at Elysium. They been together since Mister Bishop was a child, and their three children are all here—one big family inside an even bigger one. You'll meet them soon enough.

"Over there is Goliath's cabin. He's the overseer, a big redskin who can track an albino through a blizzard. He used to chase runaways. Nowadays, he don't do much but chase deer with Mister Bishop.

"My name is Solomon, by the way. They call me the preacher, or the teacher on account of my ability to read. But, I like to think of myself as a storyteller. Whether I'm preaching or teaching, I'm just telling the stories we all need to hear. Mister Bishop taught me the Bible when we were children, and I've just about read everything in his library except the French stuff. I don't know French. But Chaucer and Shakespeare, Milton and Hawthorne and Poe—I know all the best and important stories.

"Oh! That's my cabin there," said Solomon, "with all of the plants out front. They make me happy, the plants do. And at the end there is your cabin, right next to mine. We just finished building the roof on it this morning. I put the door on myself.

"In all there are fifty-three of us, but most are still children. Aunt Esther stays in the big house with Mister Bishop. She has her own room in there. Ain't that something? We ain't many but we get the job done. And we look out for one another."

Listening quietly to Solomon's monologue, Miriam soon discovered what it was that bothered her about his manner of speaking.

"Who's 'we'?" Miriam asked.

"All of us. Every soul who lives here," Solomon replied.

"You sound proud."

"Proud as can be!" Solomon declared as they stopped before her cabin. "We make this place run, and Mister Bishop, he's more of the brains of the place than our master. He does the important business, but he knows he can't get on without us. You get some rest, now. Tomorrow you'll see that you couldn't have prayed for a better place to be."

Miriam Beholds Elysium, 1839

The door to Miriam's cabin opened, and she squinted at his silhouette in the doorway. The sun shone a brilliant halo behind him, one that darkened him to a mere shadow before her. She could discern no features of his, and it was not until he stepped into the room and the sun could shine upon his face and wide, toothy grin that Miriam noticed how fair Solomon's brown skin was.

"You made it through the night," he said with a grin as he offered his hand to her. "Didn't sneak off or anything." She held her hand out to him, and he took it gently, holding it for a brief, almost imperceptible pause before helping her rise from the floor. He looked over to her bed, which was as neat as it was on the day he prepared it for her.

"You didn't sleep in your bed," he remarked.

"I did not like it," she uttered.

"Too neat, and comfortable for your taste?"

"I didn't think it would be comfortable."

Solomon tossed his head back and let out a loud, contemptuous laugh.

"You are something else, aren't you? I'll bet they had goose feathers for you to sleep on at your last place, huh? Talk about proud negros. Come along. Let me show you the property."

The sun shone radiantly just above the horizon and onto an idyllic scene. A pair of blue jays flittered about the apple orchards. A trio of squirrels in their chestnut colored coats and bushy tails chased one another around the black pecan tree and along the oak walls of the barn. Sunlight graced the large tobacco leaves, and caused them to shimmer with golden viridescence in their tall, neat rows.

"I told you yesterday that you'll like it here," Solomon remarked. "I don't think I'm wrong. But I suppose that all depends on how you adjust."

"I'm sure you all is good and happy," said Miriam.

"We're just waiting on the Lord like everybody else. But we're comfortable. Mister Bishop makes sure we're treated right. Everybody here has a full belly. Nobody has been whipped here since Mister Aaron Bishop died more than fifteen years ago. And no one has run away since Aunt Esther's boy around the same time—we call her *Aunt* Esther, by the way. I remember the old Master Bishop. He was a hard master—my master until I was a full grown man. His son and I grew up together. Mister Joachim was always different from his father, and we're all the better for it."

"So he don't whip you?"

"Why should he? He does good by us and we, by him. He's only ever mentioned one sin that will get you whipped, the same sin that'll get you whipped anywhere, and that's stealing. But there's no reason to steal. And, like I said, nobody has even thought of running away since Mister Joachim inherited the land."

They headed toward the fields where Solomon introduced Miriam to the other slaves. Cyrus, the slave foreman, gave her a friendly nod, and his wife Opal paused her work for a moment to wave and hold her protruded belly. Goliath, the overseer, trotted around on his horse and gazed sternly in their direction. Solomon stared back and offered a two-fingered salute.

"Don't mind him none," Solomon mumbled to Miriam. "He just likes to look tough. He ain't nothing but decoration around here. Ain't had anything to chase in years."

"Y'all getting on?" Goliath asked once he had approached. He wore his long, black hair in a plait down his back, and his sun-burnt face was made darker by the shading brim of his worn, brown gambler's hat. His shoulders seemed as broad as his mustang, and he wore a similarly long, unamused expression.

"Yessir," Solomon replied. "Miriam arrived last night. I'm just getting her acclimated. How's it looking, sir?"

"Same ol'," Goliath replied as he pulled a can of dipping tobacco from a pouch.

Solomon looked at Miriam and winked. "Ain't much for an old bounty hunter to do around here these days, is there?"

"Not unless you thinking about giving me something to do," Goliath said.

"Now why on God's green earth would I do that for?"

"Just to try out your wings, I suppose," Goliath looked away to the fields as he tucked a pinch of chaw behind his lip. He squinted a bit as he looked toward the rising sun. Then, he turned his horse and trotted away.

"He thinks that's a happy expression," Solomon said to Miriam, drawing her eye back to himself. "Ain't no whipping or hunting for the old wolf to do, so he don't know what to do with himself."

"So, he lets you forget you a slave. Must be nice," Miriam remarked.

"Hmph," Solomon grunted. He stared at her until she looked away. Then he continued. "You ain't no better than the rest of us. Just more bitter. You are acting all proud, self-righteous like I don't know what pride is. But I know it, and the pretty ones always have it. You can't tell me you haven't used all of that pretty to your advantage."

Miriam folded her arms and looked away.

"Or maybe someone else has, is that it?" Solomon asked. She looked back to him with fiery eyes.

"Ain't nobody ever taked me…"

"Took."

"What?"

"Nobody ever *took* you," Solomon corrected her. "You about as dumb as you are pretty and proud, huh?"

"I ain't dumb. And nobody never *took* me, neither. Mister Thomaston was just as kind as you say your master is. But we was still slaves. We ain't never forget it."

Solomon smirked.

"I have my work ahead of me with you, huh?" he said.

"You ain't gotta work on me," Miriam snapped.

"And what do you know about work, anyway?" Solomon asked. "You ever make a living? I'm not talking about pulling some tobacco from a land that was there before you were even born. I'm talking about scratching a whole life out of the dirt from nothing and watching it lie there struggling to breathe, begging you to keep working, keep digging and scratching to keep it alive. Do you know what it's like to fail and damn near starve for your failure?"

Miriam clenched her folded arms, but Solomon snatched them loose and forced her hands to her sides.

"Do you?" he demanded an answer.

Miriam looked back to him, but her eyes teared up, and doused the defiant flickering in them.

"You let me go," she said. But, Solomon did not surrender his hold of her. Instead he returned her glare until she looked away.

"That's what I thought," he concluded. "Drop all that pretty pretending. You only *wish* you knew the pride of a free man. And I'll tell you one thing: they wish they knew your leisure. You've never heard of real work. You know nothing of working for your own living. You work twice as hard out there for a quarter of what you'll get here. Except, you *will* eat here. You *might* eat out there."

He loosened his grip.

"Learn to get along here," he said. "Ain't no use in letting all that pretty go to waste."

He started toward the stables, but he stopped when he noticed that Miriam did not follow him.

"Time don't stand still!" Solomon shouted to Goliath. Miriam soon recognized this as the verbal signal for laziness in the fields, for she saw Goliath turn his horse around to face her. His hand came to rest on the coil of whip in front of him.

"If the slaves don't get beat, why does the overseer need a whip?" Miriam asked Solomon.

"That's a new whip," Solomon replied. "New whips aren't for old slaves."

He continued toward the stables and Miriam followed him there.

"These are my horses," Solomon said when they were inside. "I clean them and take care of them. They listen to me better than they listen to anyone."

"So that means they belong to you?" Miriam asked.

"I think it does," he replied.

"Will it listen to you if you tell it to ride you away from here?" Miriam asked.

"Why would I want to do that?" Solomon asked.

"Because they yours, like you say."

"Just because a thing is yours doesn't mean you can just do what you want with it. Mister Joachim has a gun, but he can't shoot any man who crosses him."

"That's different," Miriam said.

"Ain't no difference," Solomon snapped, his refined speech slipping away from him briefly. "Everyone abides by the law. Law says you can't kill a man just because you own a gun."

"Law says a slave can't even have no gun," said Miriam.

"Well," Solomon muttered, "everybody's a slave to something."

"If you can't do what you want with these horses then what's the point of having them?"

"There is no point. They are just mine. Things aren't a means to an end. They are the end."

"I don't understand."

"God did not create the heavens and the earth and all of its creatures so that they might go off on their own purposes. He created them just for the sake of having them, that they might worship him."

Solomon guided her over to one of the horses, a Missouri Fox Trotter, which became agitated when they approached.

"Shh." He calmed the horse and held his hand high and flat in front of its nose until it bowed toward him. "Good girl."

In spite of herself, Miriam was impressed by the calming effect that Solomon had on the beast. Part of her wished that the horse would remain ornery with him, but she was also awed by his manner with it.

"Nuki," he said to Miriam. "That's her name. But it's just a word, right? It doesn't define her anymore than if I named her 'Butterfly.' And, if she decided she wanted to rear up and stomp me into the ground, I'd suddenly become more dirt than man, wouldn't I?"

He guided Miriam's hand to the horse, and she felt its warmth. Nuki lowered its head a bit more and her ears hung to the sides. Miriam smiled, though she did not know it. She wanted to wrap her arms around Nuki's immense neck and feel the strength of blood flowing through the beast's muscles.

"She is mine because she heeds my command," Solomon continued, "and she does that because it suits her. If it did not, she could kill me with one blow. Instead she lets me take care of her and she obeys me in return. Hers is a beautiful strength. The man who understands this strength understands the will of all things."

"Is that what you want of me? That I obey?" Miriam asked.

"You'll do whatever you think suits you best. Hopefully you're smart enough to know what that is. Aunt Esther will show you the housework, which is what you'll do in the mornings. When that is done, Opal will show you the field work. You'll do that in the afternoons. Mister Bishop will return from his business in Hannibal in about six days' time. He'll want to be seeing you then. I'll take you to the big house now if you're ready."

Solomon led Miriam out of the stables and down the dirt road toward the Georgian mansion that was known to the slaves as The

Bishop House. Solomon, himself could not help but smile as he approached the back door, which was as elegant as the front. He knocked twice, not for permission to enter, but to hear the resonant thumps from the lustrous maple wood. He turned back to Miriam.

"Maybe we'll see each other again. Maybe at feeding time." He smiled. When Esther came to the door, he introduced the two, and headed back to the barn.

Miriam Meets Esther, 1839

Although she tried not to, Miriam began to admire this mansion belonging to Joachim Bishop. As she followed Esther through each of the rooms, each decorated sparingly but elegantly, she longed to touch every item in it, the flowers embroidered on every chair, the grain that ran along the lustrous, wooden tables, the velvety billows of the heavy curtains that adorned every window. When they entered the study, Miriam gasped at the sight of the many bookshelves that stretched along every wall and up to the ceiling. She could not read, yet she also could not help but wonder about the magic in each book of the multitudinous volumes that graced those shelves. She had always imagined that every book told some magnificent tale, but she was only allowed to hear the tales of one book: the Bible. As Esther explained the chores she was to do in the study, Miriam heard not a single word, for she instead wondered if every story in the whole world was not present with her in that room. She did not want to be charmed by this home, yet her hands betrayed her, and ever-so-lightly she touched the engraved wooden desk and chair, a quill and well of ink, and the leather bindings of an open book with the tips of her fingers.

Miriam then followed Esther into the dining room in which sat a long, stately table and twelve matching chairs. A cabinet made of the same dark wood as the table stood in a corner between two windows with drawn curtains, and paintings adorned the walls. Some were portraits—a large painting of Mister Joachim's father and several smaller portraits of grandparents, perhaps. Other paintings were of peaceful landscapes that held Miriam spellbound as she observed them. She stopped before one that depicted a gathering at a fancy ball. The people stood beneath a majestic structure supported by pillars that stretched as high as the trees in the distance. It depicted what seemed like a man courting a woman. It was this female figure that captured Miriam's imagination. The woman faced the man, so Miriam could not see her face. She stared, instead, at the shimmering silk dress that adorned her. Of all of the clothing depicted in the scene, hers alone seemed to capture all the sun's rays. Miriam only imagined that the woman's beauty was worthy of the dress she wore.

"Come along," Esther snapped at Miriam. "Ain't no time to be staring at pictures."

As they headed out into the foyer, Miriam saw that even this room, which merely served as a waiting area for guests at the front door, was daunting in its width and splendor. The staircase ascended to a bright and spacious corridor lined with the doors bedrooms an guest rooms. The kitchen was bright, for it was positioned back near the side entrance, across the hall from the dining room and though its only window was rather small, it had the benefit of light from the side entrance door, which faced east. It was fairly large and had its own staircase that led up to Joachim's study. It was into this kitchen that Esther settled upon her wooden stool and began the work of preparing the afternoon meal.

Miriam did not follow Esther's example nor did she even enter the room. She simply stood in the threshold and observed the heavy-set, brown-skinned negro as she sat snapping beans into a large wooden bowl in her lap. Miriam figured that Esther was about the same age as her own mother. Esther even had a few similar mannerisms—for instance how she would talk to someone without looking up from her task.

"Well, I can see why he so happy," Esther remarked, her eyes still fixed upon the beans in the bowl. Miriam meanwhile studied the elder woman's face, riddled with dark moles and deep creases, and her cloudy, hazel eyes. As Miriam observed the lines that ran along Esther's forehead and downturned mouth, as well as the wisps of hair that hung in thin grayish-brown tufts from beneath a knotted headscarf, she wondered if Esther might have once been very pretty.

"I don't reckon Mister Bishop done brung you here for your looks," Esther said, finally looking up at the girl. "This yo' first day as a slave?"

"No, I just thought— " Miriam began, but Esther interrupted her with a voice that shook the silverware in the drawers and the dishes in the cupboards.

"No? Just 'no'? Well I never met me a more disrespectful nigger in my whole life. I been on this here plantation since before even Mister Bishop was born. He may be master, but this here is my house. I nursed him from the time he was a babe, and he called me 'ma'am' until he was old enough to have chest hair. I been runnin' it all his life and half his papa's life, and I'll be damned if a little slave girl ain't gonna call me 'ma'am.'"

Miriam's eyes grew wide with surprise, but she replied, "Yes, ma'am."

"So this *is* your first day as a slave?"

"No, I—"

"No?"

"No ma'am."

Esther frowned and glared at Miriam with a deliberately drawn out silence.

"Well, the Lord forgives, but I ain't so easy. You do right by me and we'll get along good, you hear?"

Miriam looked down and frowned, but she nodded and uttered, "Yes, ma'am."

"Good. Now, God done gave you hands, didn't he? Use 'em to pick up that broom and sweep that there floor. You can finish snapping these beans here when you finished. Then I'll show you the way Mister Bishop likes his linens done."

Miriam finished every chore given her in resolute silence, and she did so in the efficient manner that once made Benjamin Thomaston proud to lend her out as his property. Esther could do naught but remain silent as she watched Miriam work. Every once in a while, she mumbled something about Miriam's being too thin, or she expressed surprise at Miriam being able to lift a heavy load.

"I might have some use for you, yet," she remarked snidely once Miriam had refilled the supply of firewood in the parlor and dining rooms, a job that was usually reserved for field hands.

"The real task is upstairs," Esther continued.

As they headed up the dark staircase, Miriam began to feel ill. She recalled what Esther had said earlier about Joachim being happy, and the walls of the corridor seemed to encroach, pressing in upon her.

"I done had to send many little girls back to the fields on account of they don't do Mister Bishop's linens right," Esther interrupted her thoughts, "He's very particular about his sheets and pillows. He likes them layered a certain way, and they always has to be the right kind of clean. They can't smell like the field or the tobacco. He wants 'em to smell like the breeze." She opened a closet and shoved several folded sheets in Miriam's arms. "Now you put these in there on the chair and then gather up the dirty linens."

Miriam turned to carry the items through the door, but when she crossed the threshold and gazed at Joachim's bed, she froze.

"Child, get on over there. You act like you done seen a ghost," Esther chided her, but Miriam did not move. Her lips began to quiver and her arms began to tremble as if the linens were suddenly a tremendous weight.

"Child, what is wrong with you?"

"I don't want it," Miriam said slowly and softly.

"You don't want what? Lord, the pretty nigger has preferences!"

But Miriam no longer saw Esther or heard her words. She just shook her head, her eyes fixed on the disheveled bed.

"I don't want it, I don't want it," she began to repeat over and over.

"Girl, get a hold of yourself. Here, give me the— " Esther reached for the linens but Miriam dropped them to the floor.

"I don't want it! I don't want it!" she bawled as tears flooded her eyes.

"Child, what done got into—"

"I don't want it!" Miriam shouted and ran from the room, but she tripped over the wooden threshold and tumbled to the floor outside the room. There, she curled into a ball, rocked back and forth, and sobbed as she clutched her hair and temples.

"You gon' get the devil on both of us, you keep carrying on like that," Esther hissed the words, though a familiar, motherly instinct had begun to creep into her body. Though she meant to strike the girl on the head, she could not help but pat her instead. Then she got on her knees by Miriam's side.

"I don't want it," Miriam trembled and cried, her voice becoming a tiny whistle. Esther gave an exasperated sigh and stroked the girl's hair. It had been many years since she consoled a child, and she gave in to the warm nostalgia of the tender, nearly-forgotten act.

"Ok, girl. Ok."

Chapter 11: A Sculpture of Torment

Solomon's Prophecy, 1839

Esther eventually coaxed Miriam back into her master's room under the false promise that she would never have to enter his chambers again if she did not want to. They cleaned the room together in silence, and Esther managed to teach Miriam a few of the bathroom chores as well. And, although Miriam performed these tasks well, she noticed that Esther looked at her warily.

It was close to noon, and Solomon was waiting for Miriam when she passed from the back entrance.

"I don't know if you learned to cook with your last master," he began, "but if you haven't, Opal is the best teacher. The only better cook we've had is Esther, but it's getting to where I can hardly tell them apart. Besides, you can't always trust Esther's food, especially when she's angry. I once made the mistake of breaking her favorite bowl. I was sick to my stomach for three days after that. I'm not saying she poisoned me, but—"

"You talk a lot," Miriam interrupted.

"I'm just trying to teach you about your surroundings. Stay off of Esther's bad side. She's a vindictive woman."

"She's already not too happy with me."

"She's never happy with anyone, so that doesn't mean much. But that's different from getting on her bad side. Stay on her good side and you may learn a thing or two."

Solomon turned away toward the cookhouse. Miriam, however, turned to her cabin.

"Food is this way," Solomon called to her.

"I'm not hungry," she called back without turning around.

"You need to eat. I can bring you some."

"Don't," she said with a resolute tone as she quickened her pace.

"You'll come around," Solomon shouted after her.

He was right after all. Miriam did come around, for it was difficult to resist the many comforts of Elysium Plantation. Their weekly food rations consisted of not only the usual meal, lard, and molasses, to which Miriam had grown accustomed, but also there were such luxuries as bourbon and sometimes brandy, cane sugar, an assortment of fowl and big game meats, as well. Clothing, too, was provided generously. On her second day at Elysium, Miriam received two dresses, both of which were handsomer than the frock her mother had made from their master's curtains.

For several days afterward, Miriam refused to wear her new dresses though she admired them where they lay upon the bed, which she also refused. Each morning when she left the cabin to tend to her work, she stole a glance at them before she closed the door behind her. Once she even touched the fringes of one before she went to sleep. It was Esther who convinced her to put on one of those dresses in anticipation of Master Bishop's return.

"Ungrateful slaves ain't worth the trouble," Esther warned her. "He'd just as soon sell a slave down river than let her disrupt his home."

On the day that Mister Joachim was to return, one week after Miriam had come to stay, she picked up one of the dresses and put on. It was so soft against her skin and much lighter on her frame. So light were these garments that when she departed her cabin and passed across the fields to the big house, and when it seemed to her that all the slaves' eyes were on her, she felt as though she were nude. Even the air seemed to pass through the fabric of the frock and touch her skin.

Miriam entered the house and headed upstairs to her master's chamber. Inside, she caught sight of her own beauty in the reflection of his looking glass. So taken was she by her own image that she knew she would never again wear the dress that her mother made for her. In her new garments, she took to her other chores with a heartier spirit. She did the laundry, the sweeping, and the dusting. She brought in the clean linens, but she stayed away from Mister Joachim's bed chamber, which had not been slept in for the entirety of his absence. She left the firewood for the male slaves and the tending of his room to Esther, thereby allowing herself a spell of contentment.

Why shouldn't I? she thought. *There is so much beautiful in the world, and none of us deserve it. But the ugly always take it. Why should they get it all and I get none?*

She did not see Mister Joachim that entire day, and when she made it back to her cabin just before sunset, she felt a sense of relief. Still fully clothed in her pretty dress, she took a moment to imagine herself as the lady at the ball, the one adorned in shimmering silk. Miriam did a half turn, causing the skirts of her dress to flare a bit before she lay on the bed of her cabin for the first time and drifted toward slumber. She did not sense the many hours that passed, so she was startled when she heard a knock at the door. In the middle of the night.

The steps were hesitant at first, shuffling to her window and then her door before shuffling away and then returning. There was a quiet tapping at her door, and a muffled whisper came through.

"Miriam, you awake?"

She was surprised to hear Solomon at her door. She froze for a moment before crawling from her corner to answer.

"What do you want with me?" she asked through the sliver of an opening she had offered him in the doorway.

"Oh nothing, woman. I just came to check up on you. You turned in so early, didn't you? That doesn't seem right for a young woman. You missed a feast, and I guess I was just wondering if you weren't feeling like yourself. Maybe you'd like someone to share your thoughts with."

"How do you know who myself is?"

"Well, usually I get the pleasure of talking at you while you ignore me. I didn't get to do that today. You aren't gonna leave me out here in the cold, are you?"

She opened the door wider but she herself slipped outside.

"It is so late for you to still be dressed," Solomon remarked. Miriam looked into his admiring eyes but quickly dropped her gaze and folded her arms across her chest.

"I don't reckon you supposed to be around here this time of night," she said.

"Oh, I don't think Mister Bishop would care none. He probably asleep by now, anyway. In fact, I rather suspect he'd be quite happy to know we were getting along." He placed his hand lightly on her shoulders, and she shrugged it off. "I see," he said, dropping his hand.

"What is it you think you see?" she asked.

"You. You think you're too good for me."

Miriam backed up slowly until her heels and shoulder blades were pressed against the door.

"I don't think I'm too good for nobody," she said.

"You do. I see it," Solomon said. "So proud, even still. Maybe you and I have more in common than you know."

Miriam now felt the cold that Solomon had complained about. She shivered as she stood before him, and she was angry at her body for its weakness in this moment. She was not afraid. Yet, there was something unsettling in the way he looked at her now, as if he knew some secret of hers. She was incapable of fully admitting this secret to herself, and thus she felt threatened by his knowledge of it.

"What do you want from me?" she asked.

"Everything."

"I don't have nothing to give you."

"You do. You only wish that you had nothing. Perhaps you will try to push it way down, but it's still there. You guard it with that rebellious spirit of yours."

"What do you think I have?"

"Love."

"Love?" she blurted out. "You think I could love you? I don't want you. I don't want nothing or nobody."

"But you want to," Solomon whispered, stepping closer to her. "You want to love something *and* somebody. You just haven't found the right thing or body. Yet."

"You don't know nothing."

"Yes," Solomon said as a light seemed to shine in the darkness of his eyes. "I do. There's something in you that wants to love this whole world, all of the beauty in it. But that's dangerous, isn't it? Because what is a slave permitted to love? That's why you'll push it down. That's why you rebel, isn't it?"

Miriam could feel the sting return to her throat, and she tried to hold her tears tight in her clenched eyelids.

"You see?" Solomon said, "I know you well."

In that very moment, she wished to tear her dress to shreds and burn her bed to ashes. She longed to enter the dining room of Bishop's house and tear that painting to pieces. She wanted to be away from the knowing gaze of this man who turned reverie to ridicule.

"I want to sleep, now," she whispered.

"Sleep then. But make good use of that bed in there. It belongs to you more than you want to admit. So does this place. You haven't been here but a week, and still it already belongs to you more than it belongs to any other living soul here. You might as well get used to it."

Solomon turned to leave her there in the darkness, but before he went, he spoke once more.

"No need to worry. I won't take anything you don't give me. But I know you will come to me. In your own time."

With her eyes clenched tightly, Miriam fumbled behind her until she found the doorknob. She turned it and quickly escaped inside.

A Symptom of Melancholy, 1839

When Miriam finally decided to sleep in her bed, she slept fitfully. She feared Solomon coming to visit her again at night. But more than his visits, she feared what she supposed to be an imminent visit from Joachim Bishop. Thus, the breeze did not calm her but awakened her when it rapped at her door, and the moonlight did, too, when it peered through her window. Raccoons and mice crept through the dried leaves outside and stole the solace from her dreams. And though she would never have Solomon's knowledge of Poe or Hawthorne, she lay tormented as if she were drawn by their pens.

What are those footsteps that I hear? she might inquire of baleful shadows. *Who peeks through my window? Who haunts me from behind that door? What do you wish to take from me? Please tell me, I implore!*

Why do you torture me in sleep? How can I rest in peace? Should I submit to hell's embrace? For yet, He'll come for me.

If I should yield the monster's grasp and kisses from demons, no howls from wolves, nor serpent's hiss shall stir my sweet dreaming.

What can you take when I'm awake, if I give up this realm? If I confess to love no thing, no man can steal the song I sing. No one shall find me overwhelmed. My soul shall some day soar!

At once, she awakened in the still of the night, for there he stood at her opened door. The moon shone a crown upon his head, and his silhouette filled the room with shadows that displaced every bit of air. She closed her eyes again. She exhaled a resolute sigh. She inhaled the violent darkness.

A Burden to Bear, 1840

Her breaths came in hurried gasps. Her eyes darted back and forth as she clutched her protruded belly; the contractions were causing her to double over in pain. She looked up to see the moonlight mingle with the branches. Silhouettes mimicked shadows that stretched like tendrils after her as she fled towards a river she merely hoped was out there. She only knew that she must get there. She stood and stumbled forward.

Where are you going? She heard the wind howl, but she dared not cry out to it, for someone would hear her and come for her. She will be beaten even as she labors birth to her son. She could not let this happen. She clutched her hands to her ears to shut out the sound, but the bushes still clawed at her belly.

You won't get far. She heard the low brush hiss and whisper as it tore at her clothing, raking her skin. She wrapped her arms around her unborn baby as if it were possible to hold it closer. She would keep it warm even as the cold encroached upon her.

How will you feed yourself? The wind nipped at her neck, and a sudden pain brought her to her knees. She dug her hands into the cold, damp ground.

How will you feed your child? She looked down at her belly and sobbed. Then gathering all of her strength, she took a deep breath and stood. She meant to press on, but a sharp pain shot from her womb through

144

all her bones. She collapsed, and she clutched her belly again, and she sobbed.

Life shall be impossible if you go. The wind hissed at her.

Love shall be impossible if I stay, she thought as the rain began to fall in torrents. She lay back against a tree trunk as the pain overtook her. She cried out and knew that she could go no further.

Percival Bishop was born during a storm, upon the cold earth, and shortly before dawn. He declared his entrance into the world with a cry that sounded all the way back to Elysium and when Esther trudged into the woods in search of her master's son, she discovered him rain and blood-soaked, in Miriam's arms, one-quarter mile past the crooked ash trees. She looked upon them both and shook her head.

"You done brought a whole lot of trouble to yourself, little girl," she said, "but I reckon you weren't running. Just lost."

Joachim, however, was not inclined to believe Esther. Perhaps it was out of pride for his dominion or anger over her insolence. Perhaps it was both. Whatever the case, Joachim ordered Miriam to receive the first whipping he had seen on his plantation since he had become its master. She would hold her baby as she suffered that torment, for no one could wrestle him free from her grasp. It was Esther who softened Joachim's sentiment toward the mother of his child, for she came running before the whipping, and she stood between that cowhide and Miriam's exposed back.

In that moment, Esther remembered the first and only time Joachim had whipped anyone: he whipped her. He was but fourteen years old at the time, and his father Aaron Bishop, had decided it was time Joachim became a man. Young Joachim did not have it in him then. He looked into the eyes of the woman who nursed him when he was a babe and cared for him when he was sick; the woman who bandaged his wounds and taught him his first prayer when he was afraid of the dark; the woman who scolded him when he did foolish things. But Aaron Bishop did not see a woman. He saw the slave who scolded his only son far too often as he approached manhood.

So, his father commanded Joachim to put the slave in her place. And, seeing that he did not have the heart to do so, Esther knelt before him and exposed her own back. When Joachim struck her the first time, she did not cry out. Nor did she cry on the second or fifth lash. Now, it seemed that she had saved her tears all these years for Miriam and her baby, for as Joachim raised the whip in his hands, she cried,

"No! She can't suffer no more tonight, not if you expect her to live." Esther had tears in her eyes. Joachim looked at them both, and he remembered. He looked at those tears, and he remembered Esther's limp body as it lay in a heap of torn earth and crimson streams. His expression softened then, and he shook his head with pity.

"You have made things very difficult for all of us today," he said as he looked down at Miriam clutching her baby. He looked at the newborn, at the color of his skin that was lighter than his mother's but much darker than he had hoped it would be.

"Very difficult, indeed," he said as he turned toward the house.

Esther then guided Miriam to her cabin where she built a fire and gathered a pail and water, rags, and blankets. With care and familiarity, she cleaned the newborn, wrapped it tightly in a blanket, and placed it in Miriam's arms.

"Scripture says a woman must bear her fruit in sorrow," Esther said, as she dabbed Miriam's forehead with a cool, damp cloth. "You ain't have to go and give yourself or anyone else more sorrow than you was already meant for. You would've killed this child out there all alone. Is that what you were trying to do?"

"No," Miriam said.

"Then perhaps you meant to kill yourself," Esther said. "But you'll put any kind of foolishness like that out of your mind now, won't you. You has too much to live for now, don't you? I had that once, too."

"You had a child?" Miriam asked.

"Three of 'em," Esther replied softly. "All boys."

"What happened to them?" Miriam asked.

"They was all taken in some way or another. The old master took one. The world took another. And the third took hisself."

"How do you go on living, losing three sons?" Miriam asked. Esther smiled weakly.

"I suppose I'm just waiting on God," she said. "Maybe he'll give them back to me some day. Somehow."

"So I must be his mother," Miriam said, looking at the baby in her arms. "But how? How can I be a mother to a boy who mustn't grow to be a man? What joy can be found in first steps that must lead nowhere? What pride can come from the knowledge that any strength he gains is not for him? What satisfaction can I have for first words that must never speak his dreams?"

"You did the birthing," Esther said. "You done enough."

"No, I haven't," Miriam replied. "I want to do the hoping. And the dreaming."

"You can't do none of that," Esther said sternly.

"Why not?"

"Because that's when they take him from you," Esther said. "As soon as you get to hoping and dreaming? That's when you lose your child."

"Then what am I to do?"

"Love him," Esther said. "You won't be able to help loving him. But don't let him be anything they can take from you."

"They won't take my son from me. Nothing or no one will take him."

"You're so full of hope already, aren't you?" Esther remarked. "Solomon told me about you when you first came. He told me how proud you were. Said that if there is any good in this place, it ought to belong to you."

"Solomon is a fool," Miriam said. "He is in love with me, but he thinks he needs permission to be. I think that I hate that most about him."

"Hmph," Esther snorted with a derisive grin. "This place does belong to you, Miriam. More than you know."

"A place like this doesn't belong to anyone," Miriam responded. "I belong to this place. But this child belongs to me."

A Depiction of Torment

My mother's torment was always apparent to me. My father's was a later revelation. Though I am certain that naught but the most depraved form of love can take place between a master and his slave, I cannot help but consider what he would have permitted himself to feel for us if not for the dreadful evil with which slavery imbues the heart of any man who takes its rightness for granted. Perhaps it was simply lust that brought him to my mother's cabin that night and a monstrousness of spirit that permitted him to exert his proprietorship. Perhaps it was earnest sympathy that made him hesitate to whip me but sovereign pride that made him proceed until I was rendered unconscious. Or perhaps it was something more that brought me into this world and inspired me to reach my present state. Whatever the case may be, I cannot help thinking of the price my mother had to pay in the wake of my father's intermingling of lust and commerce. And it is her tragedy that I have in mind as I work on my next sculpture.

I pierce the bark of the tree with the chisel and it cracks a bit before it falls away, revealing the pristine and fragrant wood beneath. I press my fingernails beneath this page of bark and pull it away, rubbing my calloused fingers against and then along the log's grain, imagining the form I might yet discover in its depths. Painstakingly I remove the rest of the bark with my hands and chisel. When I finish, there is, at once, a moment of elation mixed with dread.

As I hold the chisel in my hand and look at the bare trunk, I have the sudden paralyzing thought that I am inadequate to the task of carving any sort of appreciable image. I shall mark this virgin surface and scar it terribly. Or worse, perhaps I may scrape and scour only to find nothing there— that I am incapable or unworthy of finding it. I think of my mother but remember her anger the first time I showed her my work. I could almost see the blood at the tip of my finger again. Then there is Solomon's sneer and Cassandra's hopeful eyes, neither of which stir my hand. Only one thought, one memory spurs my hand to work. It is the face of a man, a look of contempt and angst and dread. It is the coil of cowhide in his hand. I pick up the hammer and with the chisel begin to hack away at the flesh of the tree before me, remembering at the same time the whip that once tore away at mine. I remember, too, the woman who cried out in the distance. The anguish.

She had shouted, "But he's your own flesh and blood!" She had meant, *He's my flesh and blood!* I could hear the demons wrought forth in her feverish protest as the flesh of her only child split open. Feverishly, I begin to carve her story into the wood.

The splinters fly; the wood breaks along the grain and falls away until an oak box emerges like a sealed coffin before me. I pick up the chisel to cut her rounded nose and baroque pearl cheeks. I try to carve somber eyes, but a prideful visage peers forth nevertheless. Peels of wood flutter to the ground like so many dried leaves piling about my feet, giving hushes and gasps as I shuffle through them. First they hush when I move left and right to chisel her delicate chin. Then they gasp when I begin to raise her bust from the fibers that so firmly hold her. The neck strains upward, but her shoulders slump from the weight of the shackles on her wrists. She kneels upon the trodden earth, but her head is raised toward the heavens.

"A slave girl?" Winthrop asks when he sees the completed work.

"But she wasn't supposed to be," I reply.

Chapter 12: Away from Havens

November 26th, 1858

A crack of thunder splits the silence of the night, and I rise from my bed to look for the rainstorm that ought to most certainly accompany it. But, there is no storm and no more thunder. In fact, there is not a cloud in the sky. In the distance there is what seems to be a pitter-patter, not of rain but of hooves. The sound fades quickly and the night becomes still once again. The next morning, Winthrop seems a bit more agitated than usual.

"You must travel to Quincy alone," he says to me though his mind seems to be elsewhere. "I will join you there after I make arrangements for your safe passage to Chicago."

"Must I go so soon?" I ask.

"Yes. I will send your unfinished sculpture there, but you must deliver the finished one to Isabelle. She has lined up a buyer for you. The money you receive for this sculpture should be all you need to get settled. In the meantime, visit with Cassandra. Finish her sculpture. She will appreciate this. When I arrive in Quincy, it will be safe for you to leave for Chicago. Do not go until then."

"You are afraid," I say, suddenly realizing that I had never seen Winthrop afraid.

"Slave catchers are stalking the railways," he says. "Until you hear from me, stay put in Quincy. And keep your head down. I will meet

you there soon."

Seeing fear in Winthrop is unsettling. The look is familiar, and I had hoped to leave such familiars on the plantation. Instead, it stays with me, causing me to look upon every shadow between Liberty and Quincy with wide-eyed suspicion.

I arrive in Quincy on a Friday morning when the streets do not yet bustle with the sounds of activity, and for the moment, I have all of the town's splendors—the streets, the buildings that frame the horizon, and the river that rages behind it all, to myself. Nevertheless, the stillness creeps upon me. I imagine that lurking eyes peek from the windows and discover me as I ride the one-horse wagon into the town alone. And yet, it is also true that my heart flutters with the anticipation of seeing her again. It is therefore to my great dismay that she does not greet me when I hitch my wagon outside Isabelle Maertz's shop.

"It is most inconvenient that you should require two deliveries," Ms. Maertz says in a chastising tone. "Have you and Mr. Goodfellow grown busier since our last meeting?"

"Did Mr. Goodfellow not mention his delay in his telegraph?" I ask.

"He did. But, that does not make the arrangement any less convenient. I do not expect to become accustomed to late deliveries."

"But I am here."

"And he is not. I shall now have a partially vacant storefront. But I suppose that is better than a wholly vacant one. Come along."

I lift one of the chairs and follow her inside the store where I encounter a familiar face.

"I have been told that you have met Mr. McAllister?" Ms. Maertz asks, gesturing to the man before the counter.

I remember this Irishman's face. I had seen it by the port on my second day in Quincy. He had concerned me then, but his having not recognized me set me at ease. Learning his name, however, makes my veins run cold.

"That's not him," the Irishman says, "The Abraham I knew was a bit taller. But I do know this young lad. He helped me at my store.

About a month ago, I reckon."

"Yes," I reply. "The tobacco store."

"Yes," he says, offering his hand to me. "I don't think I properly introduced myself, then. Aideen McAllister. You and your friend were very kind."

"Mr. Goodfellow," Ms. Maertz says.

"Yes, his reputation precedes him," Aideen says.

"We were just being neighborly," I add.

"Of course," Aideen smiles.

"Well," Ms. Maertz says, "we were just conjecturing on the name 'Abraham Bailey.'"

"Yes," Aideen adds, "but as I was saying, the one I knew was taller. A bit darker, too."

The Irishman smiles warmly then and offers me his help.

"Please," he says, "allow me to return your favor." He takes the chair from me and places it by a crate of cigarettes. He then follows me out to my wagon to help with the other items. He stops to admire the sculpture when he sees it.

"Ah!" he declares. "Ms. Maertz does not tell a lie. We are in the presence of a great young negro artist!"

"I wouldn't say 'great,'" I reply.

"Nor did I," Ms. Maertz adds.

"Ah, yes," Aideen concedes. "I believe you said, 'promising,' but I cannot help but be excited nevertheless. Everyone has inquired about the sculpture there in her storefront window. She had refused to part with it. It took a pretty penny to pry it from her possession, I must say, and I have been eagerly awaiting your return."

"You sold my sculpture to him?" I ask.

Ms. Maertz smiles a bit sheepishly, "It was not my intention. But Mr. McAllister here was quite persuasive."

"How much?" I ask.

"That is hardly proper—" Ms. Maertz begins.

"One-hundred dollars," Aideen interjects.

"I sold it to Ms. Maertz for ten," I say.

"Then congratulations! Your talents have already appreciated ten-fold," he chuckles. I do not.

"I thought that it was meant for Cassandra," I say.

"A one-hundred dollar gift for a shopkeeper?" Aideen asks incredulously. "And a negro one at that! That is nearly a year's wages for someone in her station."

"It was not meant to be a one-hundred dollar gift," I reply.

"She was understanding," Ms. Maertz says. "Besides, what would she have done with such a thing?"

"What will he do with it?" I ask.

"I have a buyer in Missouri who is interested," Aideen replies. "And I hear you have something new in the works? He may be interested in that as well."

"And who is this buyer?" I ask.

"Oh?" Aideen says with raised brow. "Could it possibly be someone you know? I don't imagine you know the art collectors or anyone else in St. Louis, would you? I will only assure you that he is a man of deep pockets."

"Then you must know that I will expect far more than ten dollars for it," I say.

"Of course," Aideen chuckles.

"Then let us see it," Ms. Maertz says.

As we head back to the wagon, Aideen questions me.

"So you are a native son of Quincy?"

"Missouri," Ms. Maertz interjects. "But he has made his home here. Well, close to here."

Aideen turns to me with surprise.

"Missouri!" he says. He studies me for a moment before flashing a shrewd smile. "Then perhaps you do know my buyer. Wouldn't that be a perfect coincidence? I suppose we ought to make you feel at home lest you go in search of this patron of yours."

"Oh, we most certainly want him to stay here, of course," Ms.

Maertz replies.

"And how did you hone your craft in Missouri?" Aideen asks. "The only negroes I ever heard of from there are slaves or common sharecroppers—which is pretty much the same thing."

"Well, he certainly wasn't a slave," Ms. Maertz says. "Mr. Goodfellow will vouch for him."

"And he is perfectly trustworthy, isn't Mr. Goodfellow?" Aideen snidely remarks. "Nevertheless, I imagine that opportunities for negroes to indulge in the arts are not found easily in these parts. Or Missouri. Or anywhere else in this wide country for that matter. Have you ever heard of a negro artist, Ms. Maertz?"

"Indeed I have not," Ms. Maertz replies. "But I suppose that makes him all the more special! His is a natural talent, I suspect."

"A veritable genius then!" Aideen declares. "How remarkable your story must be."

"I assure you it is not a story worth hearing," I reply.

"Nonsense!" Aideen declares. "I must some day learn all about the negro artist."

"There will be time for that," Ms. Maertz says. "Let us move the wares indoors, first."

"And then we'll get a closer look at your newest masterpiece," Aideen grins, baring stained and crooked teeth.

When we have moved the pieces of furniture inside and finally arrive at the muslin-covered works, Cassandra has returned from an errand. She smiles when she sees me.

"You have come back to us," she says.

"I have," I reply, after clearing my throat.

"And where is Mr. Goodfellow?"

"He will join us a bit later."

"Later?" she asks, a bit concerned. "Where is he?"

"Camp Point," I lie, remembering the only other town in Illinois I know besides the two where I have been.

"Camp Point," Aideen says, rubbing his chin. That is a curious little village.

"And how long will he be?" Cassandra asks.

"Just a few days," I reply. "He has to see a shipment off, and then he will be straight here."

"With the rest of my wares," Isabelle remarks.

"No matter," Cassandra says hastily, "This just means we will have Mr. Bailey all to ourselves for a while."

"While he works on my commission," Aideen chides.

"A commission for you?" Cassandra says. "Only if he has finished my sculpture."

"A commission for you?" Aideen jeers. "I wasn't aware that shopkeepers were so wealthy."

"We must be at least as wealthy as shop merchants," Cassandra quips.

"Hmm," Aideen utters through pursed lips, "You are a charmer, aren't you. If only I were in possession of such currency."

"That is enough," Ms. Maertz says, "Cassy, I am sure there is a shop to be kept. As for you, Mr. McAllister, I imagine Mr. Bailey could use your help up there." Cassandra curtsies but does not leave Ms. Maertz's side. Aideen, favoring his knees, climbs laboriously aboard the wagon. He rubs them once he is beside me, but his attention quickly shifts to the sculptures before him. He tears the first muslin away, looks down upon the wooden figure, and curls his lips into a wanton grin. He walks around it once to survey it. Then, he fingers the details with a jagged finger, its joints swollen into bulbous knots.

"It is as though she kneels before me in flesh and blood," he marvels. He circles it twice and then sets his gaze upon the carved shackles.

"This work is quite a statement, indeed" he says. "If one did not know better, one might think you were an anti-slavery sympathizer."

"Not necessarily," Ms. Maertz interjects.

"Oh, relax!" Aideen adds. "That is not such a terrible thing to be these days, is it? Quincy has harbored fugitive slaves—still does. Some people care nothing for the law..." He trails off, becoming a bit more pensive about the sculpture.

"Perhaps she is Irish?" Ms. Maertz suggests, though even she is not convinced of the idea. Aideen replies without looking at her.

"Definitely negro," he replies. "In fact, I can't help thinking that she is quite familiar."

"Do you know many slaves?" Cassandra asks.

"Not so many," Aideen replies. "My people were indentured servants when we came to this country, and worked our way from the fields to… well, I suppose we stayed in the fields. My brother was a foreman and then a catcher. Hunted slaves until his death just over two fortnights ago."

"Oh! My sincerest condolences," Cassandra says.

"Died alone in the woods. Seems appropriate, though."

"My condolences as well," Ms. Maertz adds. "That sounds awful."

"How did he die?" Cassandra asks.

"Gunshot to the chest. I suspect he got into a row with someone just as inclined to violence as he was. Only that feller was a faster, better shot."

"How dreadful!" Cassandra says.

"Oh," Aideen replies, "it is like I said: seems appropriate. He was an ill-tempered man. I tried to get him to come live in the town. Not the life for him." Aideen turns to me. "But I suppose some people are just better suited for plantation life, right?"

I hold his gaze for a moment before responding, "I suppose this sculpture is painful to look at."

"No, quite the opposite!" he replies. "I will pay you the same price I paid for the horse. Is that agreeable?"

"And a bit of commission for me," Ms. Maertz chimes in.

I look to Aideen and then to Ms. Maertz, certain that I court my own undoing with the transaction. However, having no inconspicuous reason to decline, and hoping to be ready for Winthrop's arrival, I agree to the sale.

"Wonderful!" Aideen says. "Bring it down to my shop before sunset.

I shall pay you straight away so that Isabelle here may receive her share. And then you can bring the art by later and we can find a nice display area for it."

"That sounds agreeable," I say.

He retrieves his wallet from his belt and produces a few billfolds from it. He hands eighty dollars to me and hobbles down from the wagon to hand twenty to Ms. Maertz.

As he mounts his horse, I remark, "I agreed to one hundred dollars."

"Yes," Aideen replies, "but Ms. Maertz gets a commission."

"I do not care what you give her," I say. "I agreed to one hundred dollars on my end."

Aideen grins wryly. "Bring the art by my shop later. I shall give you the rest of your money then." With that, he mutters inaudibly and rides off. I follow Ms. Maertz and Cassandra inside for lunch whereupon they proceeded to discuss various matters of casual importance. I, however, cannot take my mind off of Aideen McAllister.

As evening approaches, I ready the sculpture in the back of my wagon and head toward Aideen's tobacco shop. I rein Moses to walk, not trot down the road though my mind races. Certainly, I am approaching an impending doom. I do not know if the tobacco merchant knows my true identity, and the only things keeping me from turning eastward and fleeing are Winthrop's warning to stay put in Quincy, and the idea that such flight might remove all doubt for Aideen as to who I am.

I arrive at the tobacco shop, and as I climb down from the wagon, I find myself reaching for the pepperbox inside my coat. I rest my palm upon its handle for a long moment, and in this moment, a peculiar sort of courage comes over me. I have never had a realization such as the one dawning on me. The epiphany is this: I have never killed a man. But the opportunity is holstered at my side, and only I know of it. Emboldened by this thought, I head into the shop.

"Ah, you are one of the trustworthy ones, then," Aideen remarks when I enter the shop.

"Did you not expect me to come?" I ask.

"You might have ridden off with the money and the art," Aideen says.

"Why would I do that?"

He laughs uneasily, "Oh, I have heard so many stories. No offense. You understand, I'm sure."

"I don't," I reply.

"Well, I suppose you aren't like most negros. I should expect you free-born types to be more of the agreeable and trustworthy kind."

I nod though I do not agree.

"Good," Aideen says. "Ornery men often meet with unfortunate ends."

"Like your brother," I remark. Aideen's smile fades.

"Like my brother," he says. "On to business, then. I think between the two of us, we can get the sculpture from your wagon and set up in my shop."

"Yes," I reply.

Our task is impeded by his achy knees, but soon we have completed the task. He retrieves the notes, but before he gives them to me, he seizes my hand and pulls me close.

"You know," he says, "you and I are in a unique position. in Missouri, it is not very common for a white man to hand a nigger money."

"Well, I suppose we are both grateful that we are not in Missouri," I reply.

"Both of us?" he asks.

"I imagine it is just as uncommon for a nigger to shoot a white man over a matter such as money," I say.

He smiles politely and releases my hand. Then he counts the money. I notice his tight grip on the notes as I take them and tuck them in my coat near the pepperbox.

"Why don't you stay for supper?" Aideen suggests as I turn toward my wagon to leave.

"No thank you," I reply. "Ms. Maertz is expecting me. Besides, I must awaken early to complete my work for Cassandra."

"Ah yes," Aideen says. "If there is something that slavery gets right, it is that work is best done at the first light of dawn."

"I'm sure you would know better than I," I reply. As I climb aboard the wagon, Aideen remarks.

"I very much admire your horse."

"The sculpture?" I ask.

"Sure," he replies. "That one, too."

November 27th, 1858

"Who are you?" Cassandra asks sweetly while she practices Chopin at her piano. I work from behind a rather ornate room divider, peeking out every so often to catch a glimpse of long, elegant neck, the curve of her shoulders, and her serene expression.

"Nobody," I reply.

"Nobody is nobody," she says. "Everybody is somebody, even if they're just pretending to be somebody."

"Not me," I say.

"Or maybe you're just pretending to be nobody."

I do not respond, choosing instead to listen to the melody while chiseling away at the wood. She abruptly stops playing.

"So," she says, "are you?"

"Am I what?"

"Pretending to be nobody?"

"Why would I do that?"

"Because you're afraid of being who you are. Or of becoming what you will be."

"Why would I be afraid of that?" I respond.

"I don't know. Some are afraid of becoming anything. They think the world will destroy them along the way. Or when they get there."

I have been indulging her in this conversation, but now I am sure I have lost her meaning. She plays the final note, and then we sit in silence. When I place the chisel down and peek out at her, she is staring in my direction. I wonder how long she has been doing that.

"Aren't you going to ask me?" she says.

"Ask you what?"

"Who I am."

"I already know what I need to know."

"Do you?"

"I think that I could not sculpt you if I didn't."

"Or maybe your sculpture says more about you than it does about me," Cassandra remarks.

"How so?"

"That is what art is. It always says far more about the artist than it does the subject. I suppose that is why you don't want me to see it yet. You are afraid that you have been answering my question to you all along."

"That is not it," I say. "I only want to get it right."

"Then show me, and I will tell you if you have gotten it right."

She stands suddenly to approach me.

"It is not done," I say, standing as though I might stop her from seeing it though I know that I would not dare to touch the real her, the *flesh, blood, and bone* her.

"I am sure it is not so bad," she says.

"It is not that, it's just—" I stammer.

"I am not talking about the art," she interrupts. "I am talking about you, whatever it is about you that you wish no one to see."

She stops before me the same way that she did when I first heard her play the piano. I close my eyes the same way, too.

"I won't hurt you," she says.

"Nothing hurts me," I reply.

I open my eyes and she has moved past me to stand before the sculpture. I wait for her to say something, but she remains silent. After a long, heart-wrenching moment, she saunters back to her piano.

There, she begins to pluck out a song with a furious tempo. It reminds me of a hummingbird beating its wings.

"I've met quite a few of Mr. Goodfellow's apprentices, you know," she says without looking up from the keys. "You're all very much the same: quiet on the surface; reserved; terrified, even. And yet, I can never help but think that there is a far more interesting person hiding beneath. Some gentleman, perhaps. Or perhaps not. Perhaps you're all just runaway slaves masquerading as cabinetmakers."

"You think I am runaway?" I feign disbelief. "You think that I am pretending to be his apprentice?"

"Maybe not the first part, but yes," she replies. "And terribly at that. You've all been terrible. I've seen your chairs. You should drop the charade at once." She stops playing and looks at me. "Maybe you're not some fugitive, but you're definitely no cabinetmaker."

"That is rude of you to say," I reply.

"It is not my fault that Mr. Goodfellow can only find terrible apprentices," she says. "Perhaps that is why none of you ever last. I suppose I was hoping that you would."

"What makes you think I won't?" I ask. She stands again and walks away from the piano.

"Because," she replies, "Mr. Goodfellow is not here and for some reason, you are. It is the same pattern every time. When he shows up, you will leave and be gone forever." She approaches the door to leave. There is music even in her steps. She pauses in the doorway.

"Come along," she says. "I may as well make use of you while I can. I would like some company on a walk about John's Square."

"Wait," I say. "Are you not going to tell me what you think of the sculpture."

"Oh, Mr. Bailey!" she remarks. "But I have said so much already! And if you shall accompany me to the town square, I will tell you some more. Not that you need me to tell you. I think you know perfectly well what I saw in that sculpture. You only lack the courage to see it yourself."

Jeremiah Cobra

November 30th, 1858, Morning

F our days pass in Quincy without word from Winthrop. Cassandra and Ms. Maertz have spent much of their time fretting over his absence, but I find myself preoccupied with the presence of a most troubling kind. Whenever possible, I have taken to following Aideen McAllister furtively through town, for I am certain that he knows who I am and is only biding his time until he can catch me off guard and claim the bounty on my head. Although he has not seemed in any way suspicious since our last encounter at his shop, I cannot set my mind at ease. At times, he comes into Ms. Maertz's shop to inquire about some goods or wares, and when he leaves, I shadow him all the way back to his tobacco shop. By the third day, I began to wonder if I had not gone mad with guilt. Guilt for being a fugitive. Guilt for lying to everyone but especially Cassandra about my identity. Guilt for harboring a most nefarious idea of firing my weapon into Aideen McAllister's heart, watching the life drain from his eyes, for with the ending of his life, the threat he presents to mine also perishes. And yet, after three days of following him, I was no longer sure that he posed such a threat. The fourth day was different.

It began with my noticing him outside Ms. Maertz's. When I saw him from the window of the attic, where I was occupied with the storing and counting of inventory, I noticed that he was studying my horse, Moses. By the time I descended the stairs and made my way outside, he was gone. I did not see the direction in which he went, but I decided to head toward his shop nevertheless. I did not get far before I caught a glimpse of a familiar face. And a single black plait. I held my breath as I ducked into an alley by the gun shop. When I peered out from my hiding space, he was gone.

Now, I huddle in the shadows of the alley, wondering if my mind has played a trick on me. Before long, I abandon my trip to the tobacco shop and head back to Ms. Maertz's shop. There, Cassandra greets me with a concerned look.

"I think Mr. Goodfellow is in trouble," she says.

"You've heard from him?" I ask.

"No. But I've heard from the bounty hunter who is looking for him."

It is as I thought.

"Who is this bounty hunter?" I ask.

"I don't know, but he is a redskin. With a long braid down his back and a mean look on his face. He told Ms. Maertz he was looking for a slave named Jasper."

"What does that have to do with Winthrop?" I ask.

"Well, the way he described him. He said that a gunman found him in the woods and killed his partner. He also brought these."

She unfolds two posters. The first is much older, has a lot of writing, and features a blurred and aged image. The other has much less writing and no picture, only a few words of description and two more that stop my heart.

Percival Bishop

I swallow hard and try to seem unperturbed.

"I still don't see what these have to do with Winthrop," I say.

"The bounty hunter confirmed what Ms. Maertz has long suspected about Mr. Goodfellow: that he has been helping runaway slaves escape to Illinois and hide."

"And if he is?" I ask. "This is a free state, yes?"

"Yes," Cassandra replies, "but that does not stop bounty hunters from tracking them here. And there is plenty of anti-abolitionist sentiment here, too. Mr. Goodfellow has brought us a lot of trouble if what the bounty hunter says is true. And, that is to say nothing of the trouble he has brought himself." She hands the posters to me and begins to wring her hands.

"Did this bounty hunter have a name?" I ask.

"He wouldn't say. However, perhaps Mr. McAllister, the tobacco merchant, will know."

"Why is that?"

"The bounty hunter's partner was Mr. McAllister's brother. And I fear that it was Mr. Goodfellow who shot him."

I can feel the small hairs rise at the nape of my neck.

"Did he mention me?" I ask.

"Why would he mention you?" Cassandra asks. I look up to hold her gaze. Looking into those eyes, I think that I shall tell her everything: my life in bondage, my escape to freedom, my wicked father and solemn mother, the heroic deed by Winthrop Goodfellow that may have saved my life though it has endangered his.

"They wouldn't," I say instead. "I must go."

"Go where?"

"If Mr. Goodfellow is in trouble, then perhaps he may need my help."

"Do you know where he is?"

"I will check Liberty first."

"And if he is not there? What will you do?"

"I don't know. Not yet, anyway."

I return to my wagon and unhitch Moses from it. Having no saddle, I hoist myself upon her bare back, feeling the warm hide beneath my palms and through my breeches. It occurs to me in this instant that I might flee this town and head to Springfield. Perhaps my passage there will be safer than Winthrop suspects. Perhaps I can hide there...

Hide? Why must I hide? Am I what they think I am? A fugitive? When a man does wrong, he must run because he should be pursued. Have I done some wrong?

I place my hand on my waist to feel the gun that is holstered there.

I am right to be here, I think. *And I am free. Is it not I who belongs here and they who ought to flee?*

I ride down the main road, and a certain strength swells in my chest. I bring Moses to a trot, and I watch each of the passersby carefully, expecting that at any moment one of them may look at me and recognize a fugitive among them. Only a few of them even notice me, and when they continue on about their business, I become more steadfast in my earlier conviction.

I never saw a free man who shouldn't boldly stand and declare his righteousness.

I sit taller in the saddle as I get nearer to the road that will take me toward the docks. The sun has set behind the great river, and the shadows behind the shops are as dark as the night shall soon be. It is only when I look into that darkness that the reality of what I am going to do fully dawns on me. I am going to confront Aideen McAllister. And if he objects to my freedom, I am going to kill him. So caught up am I in this idea that I nearly miss a most important sign of my own demise. Several paces ahead of me, and yet several hundred yards from the tobacco shop is a saloon. And into that saloon walks a mountain of a man upon whose head lies a raven-black plait of hair. My courage crumbling into the pit of my stomach, I yank Moses's mane, causing her to halt, whinny, and throw me from her back. There is a flash of light before my eyes, and I hear her gallop away. In a moment, a few strangers, both of whom are white, hurry to my aid, but I scurry away before they can reach me. I head for the shadows of an alley, and for a moment, all I can hear are my breathing and heartbeat.

Perhaps he did not see me. But certainly he heard the ruckus.

I take a moment to catch my breath. Then I peer out from the shadows to see that a bit of calm has been restored although the man and woman who had tried to help me are talking with someone who appears to be the sheriff. They talk for a bit before the woman points to the shadows into which I am seeking refuge. I duck and head farther into the alley. It is only when I reach the rear of the buildings, one brick and one wooden, that I hear a voice call out behind me.

"Ay," it says in a thick accent. "You okay fella?"

I hesitate for a moment when it occurs to me that the man will pursue if I do not offer him some assurance.

"I'm okay!" I call back.

"You had a pretty nasty fall," he says. "Let's have a look at ya."

I recognize the accent. It is much thicker than Aideen's, but it is certainly Irish.

"I'm fine," I try to assure him as his footsteps grow louder.

...but I am no criminal. Not yet...

I sit and rest against the building, allowing him to approach me in the darkness and feeling, rather suddenly, a great throbbing in my head. I reach back to feel that a large and tender knot has formed there. When the sheriff arrives, he seems sympathetic and friendly enough.

"Ay son," he says, "You don't look too good."

"I'll be fine," I say, closing my eyes. "I just need a moment."

"I don't think that is wise, son. Let me help you back to your horse."

"You have Moses?" I mumble as the world begins to fade away.

"Open your eyes, son."

The sheriff helps me to my feet. He tries to guide me back to the road, but I resist.

"Bring my horse to me," I say as I steady myself.

"Y'know your horse has no saddle. I don't think y'can ride it in your condition."

"Just bring it to me," I reply. "I will manage."

I open my eyes to see the concern on his face.

"Please," I say.

"Alright, son. Wait here. And keep your eyes open!"

As he turns to leave, I lean against the building and take several deep breaths. When he steps onto the road, I turn and head behind the brick building, stumbling in the darkness until I reach another alley. I pass it and several others before I arrive at the rear of the saloon. I creep up to one of the windows that is ajar, and before I peek into it, I listen to two familiar voices inside.

"I never thought I'd find him again," one man says in a low rumble of a voice.

"And to think that he had been under our noses all of this time," says another. I work up the courage to look in the window, and there at the bar is Goliath and a man I do not recognize. The bounty hunter tosses his head back to empty a glass of whiskey down his throat.

"Are you sure he does not know that I have been asking around?" Goliath asks, gesturing to the barkeep for another pour.

"If he does, he plays the perfect fool."

"Most of them do."

"And he certainly looks the part," the man says, seeming to admire the subject of their conversation.

"I should have recognized him in those woods. At this point he done probably fooled himself into think he was never a nigger."

"Nearly thirty years, you say?" the man asks. "My God! Do you think he has been here the whole time?"

"He was always a crafty one. Even as a boy."

I duck down from the window and huddle in the shadows, clutching the pepperbox inside my coat.

Run!

I try to command my body, but it does not listen. My head throbs and the world spins beneath my feet. Slowly, I move my hand to the meadowlark around my neck and press the wood to my chest. I can hear that a spirited group is gathering inside, and it is hard to discern any particular sound among the conversations, laughter, and boots thumping against the creaky, wooden floor. The throbbing in my head grows until I must slump to my knees. I clench my eyes closed. And the world fades away.

November 30th, 1858, Evening

When I come to, there are several eyes looking down upon me by the light of a lantern: the eyes of the sheriff, those of the man and woman who tried to help me earlier, and those of Winthrop, whose smile is most welcome.

"Where were you?" I ask.

"It seems every time I find you, you have managed to find some kind of trouble," he chuckles. I try to rise to my feet, but he stops me.

"Rest, my friend," he says. "These folks tell me you had a bit of a fall."

"You fell so hard," the woman explains, "we were surprised you got up at all."

"And then I went for his horse," adds the sheriff, "But he up and took off."

"Did you find her?" I ask.

"Luckily," the man replies, "this gentleman—uhh, what is your name again sir?"

"Winthrop."

"Yes, Winthrop here came along and helped us calm your horse, but you were already gone."

"It seems you know this young fella, Mr. Goodfella," the sheriff says to Winthrop.

"I do," Winthrop replies. "I would imagine you know Mr. Bailey, too.

He works for Mrs. Maertz."

"The German?" the sheriff asks.

"The shopkeeper, yes," Winthrop says. "Surely you have seen the furniture in her shop?"

"I have bought a few things from her wares," the sheriff replies. "I suppose we all have bought something."

"We bought a lovely table from her, isn't that right, Emmitt," the lady says to the man.

"That's right," he replies.

"Well that table was made by the young Mr. Bailey, here," Winthrop says, much to my befuddlement. "Or perhaps the sculptures in her window. Your merchant friend, Mr. McAllister has taken a liking to it."

"McAllister?" the sheriff asks. "With his dependency on alcohol and debt, I would figure art to be the last thing on his mind. Speaking of McAllister, he has been looking for you."

"Me?" I ask, alarmed.

"Me," Winthrop says, holding the sheriff's gaze. "Did he mention why."

"Nope," the sheriff says. "But he's but riding around with a big Indian fella. Calls himself Goliath."

"Well," Winthrop sighs, "I should see what they want. Come on, Mr. Bailey. Let's get you to your horse. I'm sure Ms. Maertz will be worried about you if you don't get home soon."

I stare at Winthrop with bewilderment as he helps me to my feet. He seems to notice my confusion, for he winks at me in response and takes me away from the others, across the road to Moses's hitching post. Evening has set in and the only light comes from the gas lamps placed here and there along the sidewalks. As Winthrop helps me mount Moses in the shadows between the gas lamps, I notice that she has a saddle, one that Winthrop usually uses.

"Get on to Chicago," he says. "I'll handle things here. You will be safe at Ms. Maertz's home for a short while, but move on as soon as you feel capable enough."

I open my mouth to speak only for Winthrop to clasp it closed with a gloved hand. He uses his chin to point behind me to the saloon. I look to find Goliath speaking with the sheriff outside.

"Get gone before he recognizes the horse."

"What do they want with you?" I ask.

"I don't know, but it is most important for you to get away right now."

"I heard him say something about hunting a slave for many years," I mention. "A slave named Jasper. That can't be me."

"And yet, I am certain that you don't want him to find you here instead."

"I shouldn't leave you here," I say.

"We'll talk soon. Talk to Cassandra. I left a message with her."

"You should have shot him," I whisper.

"Maybe I'll get another chance," Winthrop says with a wink and a grin. He turns toward the saloon, and I command Moses in the opposite direction.

"Ay!" I hear the sheriff shout behind me. "This is that big Indian fella I was telling you about, the one that wants to talk to you."

"Good!" Winthrop shouts back. "I want to talk to him, too."

Their voices fade away behind me as Moses canters up the road toward the general store. When I arrive, the store is closed, and Cassandra is waiting for me outside. I dismount and approach her. In the light of the street lamp, her wet eyes glisten.

"Mr. Goodfellow was here," she says with a trembling voice.

"I know," I respond. "I saw him."

"You saw him? What did he say?"

"Not much. Only that I must go to Chicago."

"Is he going with you?" she asks, her eyes lighting up with hope.

"He is not."

"Why?" she cries, stepping toward me as if I must provide her with an explanation. "Why must he face those bounty hunters? Why must he be so stubborn?" She raises her fists as though she will strike me, but instead she collapses in my arms and buries her face in my chest. Bewildered, I place my arms around her as she sobs.

"Why doesn't he run away?"

"Why should he?" I ask. "Has he done something wrong?"

She steps away from me and wipes her eyes.

"No," she replies. "I suppose he has not."

"Then perhaps he is doing the right thing?" I say, looking toward the river.

"He left this for you," she says, removing an envelope from her apron. I peel away the wax seal and unfold the letter.

Ride west to Fowler. Meet a negro pullman by the
name of Not George. He will see your passage to
Springfield. From there, you must ride on your own to
Chicago.
Godspeed,
Winthrop Goodfellow.

"What will you do in Chicago?" she asks.

"I don't know," I reply.

"Then why are you going?"

"I'm not," I say, looking back toward the river. "Not yet."

I mount Moses and head toward the dirt roads behind the store, keeping my eye toward the river that will lead me to the tobacco shop. At the riverfront, I find a hitching spot for Moses and make the rest of my way on foot.

By the time I arrive at the port, night has fully enveloped the town. Most laborers have retired to their homes, and those who remain have commenced the drinking of ale and other spirits. I consider that perhaps it is too late to find Aideen in his shop, and I am right, for when I arrive, every window is dark. In fact, the entire building is dark but for the nearby street light, its flame flickering an orange glow upon the drunken faces that pass by the storefront. In that light, I recognize the face of Aideen McAllister.

Sticking to the shadows, I follow him, venturing back onto the main street as he heads west toward the saloon on Third Street. He stops to speak to an acquaintance, then turns to stumble down an alley. Placing my hand inside my coat, I unholster the pepperbox and follow him onto the darker, narrower path. He hums what I gather to be an Irish folk song. A few steps farther, and I shall silence him. A few steps further, and I shall be halfway to freedom. A few steps further...

And, he tumbles to the ground. I stop in my tracks as he turns upon his back to see my silhouette against the night sky.

"Wh-who is there?" he stutters, not from fear but inebriation.

He does not know who I am.

I slowly raise the gun in my hand until it is aimed at his chest.

"Y-yes my dear lad," he says. "Help me up."

My hand begins to shake.

"Well? Don't just stand there," he continues, struggling upon his back to sit but slipping upon the mud beneath him. Finally he stills himself and peers into the dark. A look of familiarity passes across his face.

"Do I know you?" he asks.

I am silent, yet I feel my resolve weakening.

"If so, don't just stand there, my boy!"

He struggles to his feet, and when he turns away, I aim my gun at his back. My hand trembles on the trigger.

"McAllister!"

I hasten to return the weapon to its holster.

"McAllister, you down here?" I recognize the voice of the sheriff, and I see the flicker of the lantern he holds.

"Ah, if it isn't my old friend," Aideen mumbled.

"How many times have I warned you against drinking and wandering into these alleys? You wandered into the cemetery last time, for Christ's sake!"

"Oh, Eamonn relax! I have a friend with me this time," Aideen replied. "He shall keep me out of trouble, ain't that right, Mr. Bailey?"

"Yessir," I reply softly, hoping the sheriff does not approach. Aideen stumbles forward and leans on my shoulder.

"See? All is well, Eamonn," Aideen says. "Mr. Bailey shall see to it."

"Mr. Bailey?" the sheriff asks, coming forward with a raised lantern. "You're back?" he seems incredulous. "I take it you're feeling better? Mr. Bailey fell from his horse not more than an hour ago."

"I am feeling better," I say.

"Good!" Eamonn says. "Mr. Goodfella will be glad to hear it."

"Ah, yes!" Aideen interjects. "I must speak to Mr. Goodfellow."

"Well," Eamonn chuckles, "he is in a most fortunate place, for you: the saloon. It appears that he has a most troubling allegation against him, if your Indian acquaintance is to be believed."

"And you say he is in that saloon?" Aideen squints off in the dark.

"He is," Eamonn says, retrieving a piece of paper from his breast pocket and waving it. "I am just returning with this telegraph from the sheriffs in Fayette, Missouri. It corroborates the Indian's claim. And yours."

"Well," Aideen says grinning drunkenly at me. "It is just so fortunate that Mr. Bailey here has come along to help me." Eamonn turns to lead the way, and Aideen uses me as a crutch to make his way back to the main road. I endure the stench of whiskey and tobacco as he breathes heavily on me.

"Perhaps you should help him, sheriff," I say to Eamonn. "I do not think that I am yet well enough."

"You're doing fine," Aideen says as we approach the wood-framed glass door of the saloon. Just as Eamonn reaches for it, I feign a stumble and Aideen falls to the ground.

"Goddamnit!" he cries as Eamonn turns to help him. As they struggle with the door, Winthrop comes crashing through it, reeking of whiskey.

"Ah! Mr. McAllister," he declares with drunken glee, "I have been expecting you!" He looks at me with a briefly sober expression before grinning widely and dragging the two Irishmen clumsily through the door. In that moment, I slip away, but curiosity and conviction will not let me flee. I find the window at the side of the saloon and once again, I peer through it.

"Yes, from Missouri," Eamonn says as he waved the piece of paper. "It says here that a slave named Jasper went missing from there back in 1830!"

"Good for Jasper," Winthrop quips.

"Not so good for you," Goliath says. "It has been many turns around the sun, since we last saw each other, hasn't it? Jasper Bishop."

"I do not know that name," Winthrop replies. "And I do not know you. However, if you have a problem with me, I am happy to resolve it."

"You are stolen property!" Goliath declares, "And so is the slave you helped when we met across the river. He was my bounty—our bounty. Do you remember? When you killed my partner?"

"My brother!" Aideen shouts. "If you are indeed his killer, I will see that you are brought to justice."

"Well," Winthrop chuckles, "it seems your Indian friend is very imaginative. I am but a simple carpenter."

"You are a radical abolitionist!" Aideen cries, spittle flying forth from his lower lip. "We have laws against that here. Eamonn, tell him the law!"

"Well…" the sheriff begins.

"What law?" Winthrop interjects. "This is a free state."

"A law," Aideen begins, "against bringing niggers here that don't belong here."

"It is true," Eamonn says. "We are a free state, but that does not mean we harbor fugitives."

"What fugitives?"

"You!" Goliath shouts.

"Me?" Winthrop scoffs. "A fugitive slave? Of course this is demonstrably false."

"What about your apprentice?" Aideen says.

"Which one?" Winthrop smirks. "I've had so many. There could be one in Chicago. Or New York. Or even California by now."

"This Abraham Bailey," Aideen says, gesturing behind him and realizing for the first time that I am not with him.

"Mr. Bailey is no fugitive," Winthrop says. "He has his papers."

"Even if he is no fugitive," Eamonn interjects, "it is against our law for him to be in this state if he is not from here."

"He has lived here his whole life," Winthrop says.

"Not according to Ms. Maertz," Aideen says. "She says he told her himself that he is from Missouri."

"Ah," Winthrop says. "So she is mistaken."

"I will be the judge of that," Goliath says. "Where is he?"

"Well, he must be at Ms. Maertz's residence by now," Winthrop replies.

"I will check with her in the morning," Eamonn says. "For now, Mr. Goodfellow, I believe you better come along with me."

"Why?" Winthrop asks. "You have no reasonable charge against me."

"Because you no longer have a place to go," Goliath says with a smirk. Winthrop looks at him sternly.

"What do you mean?" he asks the Indian.

"When I look for a fugitive," Goliath says, "I do a thorough job."

"What have you done?" Winthrop asks, his jaw and fists trembling.

"Justice," Goliath replies.

"There is no such thing as justice where you are concerned, unless it is your body hanging from a gallows."

"I am a bounty hunter," Goliath grumbles. "I am the justice."

"You are a hunter of just men, a violator of justice," Winthrop says, no longer showing the effects of inebriation. He stands tall and resolutely. "You ought to hang!"

"And I suppose you mean to do it?"

"If the Lord allows it."

Goliath smirks. "And how do you propose that be done?"

"A duel," Winthrop says.

"You have had your chance with duels, and a most unfair one at that. Besides, duels are a white man's game—with a white man's weapons. Let us settle this like men—with our hands. If I win, I return you to Missouri."

"No," Eamonn says. "A duel is permitted. A prizefight, of course, is not."

"You would prefer a dead man to a badly bruised one?" Goliath asks.

"I would prefer that we uphold the law," the sheriff responds.

"A duel will serve my purposes well," Winthrop says, his gaze steady on Goliath.

"If I win," Goliath says, "and you survive, I shall see you brought to justice in your place of birth, Jasper Bishop."

"And if I win, you will die," Winthrop says coldly.

"And if you both miss?" Aideen asks.

"Then we both lose and go about our business," Winthrop says to Goliath. "But lose or draw, you must leave Abraham Bailey alone."

"That is fine," Goliath says with a smirk. "I'm here for Percival Bishop, after all."

Goliath heads out of the saloon first. He is followed by most of the bar patrons, the sheriff, and the tobacco merchant. Their exit forces me to retreat further into the alley so that when the duelists take their places, I can only see Winthrop.

There is, at first, a murmur among the crowd, but soon it settles into silence I watch Winthrop prepare his weapon.

"I will serve as the seconds," Eamonn says. "You get one shot. Any more is murder. When I drop this handkerchief, you may fire." Again there is silence, and I watch Winthrop stand still, holding his gun with the muzzle down. Then suddenly he lifts his gun and fires—a misfire. I hear one shot after his, but he does not fall. Instead, his hand begins to shake, and he drops his pistol.

"The victor!" Eamonn declares as the crowd resumes its murmuring and returns to the saloon. My eyes well with tears as I watch the sheriff tether Winthrop's hands together. I want to run into the road and declare my own challenge to duel Goliath. However, I know that he must not see me. I hurry away, behind the shops toward the Main Street where I then turn toward the river. I retrace my steps until I find Moses hitched where I left her.

I mount the horse quickly and gallop off, hearing only its hooves beating in sync with the frenetic pounding of my heart. We race down the dusty road until the city and its horizon is far behind me. Only then do I relent in my command, but as the horse slows, I hear a second set of hooves in the distance behind us. I look back to find no one there. Perhaps my ears deceive me. I bring the horse to a stop. I turn my head here and there, but I hear nothing. I bring the horse back to a trot, and I hear a second trot behind me. I bring her to a canter, and I hear a second canter. I bring her to stop, and I hear nothing. Finally, I command her to a gallop, until we reached our destination.

It is the middle of the might when I arrive in Liberty, and there is a peculiar yet familiar smell. It is pungent and distinct, reaching me long before I find its source. As I come upon Winthrop's home, the silhouettes of the house, the shed, and the barn look the same. But as I get closer, I discover that these shapes are the remnants of what I had looked forward to. I approach and the smell of burning wood grows stronger. I enter a haze through which the moonlight glimmers. I stop and dismount the horse in the middle of the dirt road leading to the soulless bones of a place that I ought to have called home. I kneel in the powder of ash that covers the soil like snow. I know that it is useless to continue forward or to look for any remains.

I clutch the small, wooden meadowlark that still hangs from my neck by a string, and I look around. I hear a distant sound like the galloping of a horse, but exhaustion and hunger and hopelessness have settled into my body. My grip loosens from the carving and finds the gun in its holster. It remains there as I lie down in the ashes and close my eyes.

You wonder don't you, my father asks me. I look into an ethereal mirror, and he is my reflection. I do not respond.

They say you look like me. Is that what bothers you? I consider his question, but I do not have an answer for it.

You know, he says, *We have the same eyes.*

I look at those eyes. Black like obsidian. Born from the fire. I sometimes wonder if they are not more like my mother's.

"No," I say to him. "They do not bother me. They are my eyes. I'd like to keep them. My mother gave them to me."

She could not give them to you by herself.

"I should thank you, then?"

It would be the Christian thing to do. Honor thy mother and father.

"Should I thank you, too, for the color of my skin?"

Like it or not, you have me to thank for your life.

"And whom should I thank for being a slave?"

He looks back at me silently. Solemnly.

"Have you no answer for that? Who should I thank for the fact that I lie here dying in the ashes?"

Son, is that what you're doing there? Waiting for death?

My eyes shoot open. I am shivering. A light snow settles upon me, and the cold has soaked through to the bone. It is dawn, and the moon has given way to thick tufts of white clouds. Seemingly from those clouds, I hear a familiar voice and a most dreaded question.

"You are Percival Bishop, aren't you?"

PART TWO
WINTER OF 1858

Chapter 13: Follow Moses

December 1st, 1858

*H*is fires have burned and behind them left ashes...
I cannot help but think of my father as the snow turns to
rain and washes away the ashes of Winthrop's home. I let
its cold sting my face and am reminded of the turmoil on
the Mississippi when I crossed it. I thought I would find freedom there.
Some happily ever after. Now, I wish that each icy drop that falls from
the sky will return me to those tepid torrents and dash my raft to bits.
Then, those torrents might seize the breath in my lungs and drag me
down into the depths of the river. I want hell or torture for what I am
about to do. As I lie still with the sky falling into my eyes, I wonder if
any part of him ever loved me as a son. I wonder, too, if I am not like
him, doomed to a love I can never have. With this thought, I know that
I must lie still when she again asks:

"You are Percival Bishop, aren't you?"

This sweet voice has uttered my name twice. I ought to be relishing
this moment. Instead, I loathe myself for what I am about to do. I sit
up to look upon her pretty face, and I utter, "I do not know that name."

"Certainly you must," she challenges. "It is all over town by now. If
you want to claim that it is not yours, that is fine. But do not claim not
to know it. And if it is yours then claim it. Don't be a coward. Now is
not the time. Mr. Goodfellow may have died protecting that name."

I am wide awake now, and look into the eyes in which my soul may

185

burst into a million pieces.

"It is not my name," I say.

"I see," she says. Her gaze drops from mine as she turns toward the horse she rode here. I search desperately for something to say, something that will keep her from going away.

"He is not dead," I call out to her.

She stops and turns back to me.

"At least I don't think he is," I continue.

"How do you know?"

"I was there when the bounty hunter took him."

"Took him?"

"Yes. They dueled outside of the saloon.

"Dueled!?"

"The bounty hunter won."

"Why didn't you stop them?" she asks.

I pause.

"Why didn't Abraham Bailey stop them from taking a good man?" she cried.

"I could not. I mean… It was the conditions of their duel."

She turns away and mounts her horse. I hurry to my feet.

"I did not know that Winthrop was a wanted man," I say.

"He was a good man," she replied. "In an unjust world, that makes you a criminal."

"Do you know what he is accused of being?" I ask.

"I do not care what they accuse him of!" she declares, pointing to the cinders and ash behind me. "They are on the wrong side of it all. And look at what they'll do in the name of their villainy. I hope that whoever this Percival Bishop is, he knows the cost of his freedom."

She turns to ride away then, and I call after her.

"Will you go back to Quincy?"

She replies, "I am going wherever they took my father. They'll give him back to me. Or they'll have to take me with him."

"Your father!?" I shout, but she has ridden too far. I hurry to ride after her. I do not know what I must do or say when I catch up to her, but it seems I will have plenty of time to think of something.

She hurries through the forest. As I strive to match her pace, I recall my first days learning to ride on the plantation, a rare treat afforded to me by Solomon who had done and said much to convince Mister Joachim. I was not allowed a saddle, so I had to learn balance as best as a child could. I imagine that Cassandra had many more advantages in her lessons, for she is a much more graceful rider than I—and a mich faster one.

Cassandra and her steed tear around the winds and binds of the road at a furious pace, and I soon feel that my body will fall apart before I ever catch her. That I know not her destination makes me at once agitated and wary. I suspect she simply means to outlast me.

Soon, my body begins to ache unbearably. I fear that I cannot go on much longer. I stop commanding Moses to go faster, yet she persists, and I know that she moves by her own will. I simply try my best to maintain my balance and hold on to her mane and reins.

Hold on for dear life.

Before long, we open upon a wide plain, and as Cassandra guides her horse along an arching path westward, I steer mine onto a straight path that I hope will intersect hers. Then suddenly she breaks north, and I nearly tumble from my mount when Moses changes her course. With great effort, I steady myself and strain for balance.

Cassandra breaks westward again, putting greater distance between us. Nevertheless, I persist. Before long, the Great River comes into view, and I notice that she is losing speed. Grateful, I command Moses to a canter. When Cassandra comes to a bluff, she does not break north again. She stops. Soon I am beside her again. She is silent for a long while as she stares across the river, toward my old home. She seems to be discerning a great many things over a great distance. In our silence, I imagine that she holds my mother's gaze over that distance.

"You are from there," Cassandra states.

"I am," I say.

"Show me."

"Show you? Show you what?"

"The farm you grew up on. Your mother. Your father. Show me the land that made you, Abraham Bailey."

"Are we actually going to ride across the water?" I try to say ironically but say sheepishly instead. Perhaps she actually intends to cross this violent river on horseback, if only to leave me behind.

"Do you think my father is across those waters?" She looks to the horizon beyond the river as if she might catch a glimpse of him.

"Who knows that he is your father?" I ask.

"You," she replies.

"Anyone else?"

"No one else."

"Why not?"

She looks askance at me and then back toward the horizon.

"I hope you are much brighter than that question suggests," she remarks. Then I can see it. I do not know how I had missed it, the resemblance between the two.

And he is…

"Is Winthrop Goodfellow who the bounty hunter says he is?" I ask, turning my gaze to the horizon as though the answer to my question lies upon it. Or beyond it.

"Is Abraham Bailey who he says he is?" she asks in response. I have never seen her more serious. The furrow in her brow. The tightly drawn mouth. I cannot imagine her curtsying or even fretting over her piano technique.

"I am who I am," I reply.

"Well, I must say I was hoping you were Percival Bishop," she says. "Freeborn negroes take their freedom for granted. They think life is free. Slaves who buy their freedom legitimize the system. Their life is only worth what they paid for it. But a runaway was born a slave and took his freedom. He knows the true value of his life and everything else in it. He was ready to lose his life for freedom. If he wins, how can you ever take anything from him? He will fight you for everything he holds dear. And that's who I need right now. Because Mr. Goodfellow is someone I hold very, very dear."

She turns her horse northward but looks back once more.

"If you can't understand what I mean," she says, "then you should go back and keep watch over the ashes." She rides off, and my tongue is stricken. For Cassandra, my soul longs to be Percival Bishop. But to remain free, my body must for now remain Abraham Bailey. They cannot act in harmony, and I sit upon my horse in a stupor. It is most fortunate for me that Moses carries me after her.

Chapter 14: Solomon's Song

Solomon's Song, 1839

Miriam was meant for Solomon, but Joachim would not let him have her. This deprivation broke Solomon up inside —more than he would ever admit. I only suspected his broken heart later, when I would recall the spiteful manner in which he retold the circumstances of Miriam's coming to Elysium. His story did not differ much from that of my mother, but there was one key element toward the end of his tale that reminded me of another story he once taught me. As I became more advanced in my studies, and perhaps with the intention of explaining to me the history of my name, Solomon presented me with the story of *Prometheus Unbound* by Percy Shelley. It was the only story he shared with my mother that wasn't from the Bible, and it impressed her such that she named me for the author. I, myself, took to the reading of this story most enthusiastically, for not only did the rhyme and rhythm of the work impress greatly upon me as it did my mother, but so, too, did Prometheus's attitude toward Jupiter. Solomon presented me with this book in secret—the way he taught me to write; the way he once snuck water to me when I was meant to be deprived of it as punishment for some misdeed; and the way he taught me to ride horses when I was a child, long before Mister Joachim permitted me to. At times, it seemed that Solomon regarded me as his own son. Perhaps he coveted fatherhood, too, and it broke him up that Mister Joachim had also deprived him of that.

That I was allowed the privilege of applying my growing abilities to secular literature did not at first strike me as sacrilege, for Solomon assured me of its purpose in making me useful to my master. Prometheus, who had been punished by Jupiter for bringing the gods' fire to man, became virtuous in his ambition to love in spite of his torture. And Jupiter, according to Solomon, fell from the heavens because of his pride, thereby freeing Prometheus. It was only when Solomon would later conclude his story about Miriam's arrival at Elysium that I saw on his face a rage that recalled that of the enslaved —Prometheus at the outset of his torture, when he wished upon his god an infinite agony and omnipotent pain.

When Solomon spoke of Joachim's refusal to betroth Miriam to him, he was not the same self-assured storyteller that he usually was; in his tale, he was not narrator for the sun and willow. Unlike his story of the sun and the willow. Certainly mother was the willow, and my father was the sun. But Solomon was the river, the water alongside whom the willow ought to have grown. When Solomon spoke of Joachim's ascent to master over the property that was Elysium Plantation, he spoke with the understated solemnity of a man who did not expect his fervor to be understood. After all, I, his audience, had only recently become a man, and a slave one at that. What reason had he to believe that I might fathom the hatred he felt for his master? So, he told me all that he knew, and I listened as attentively as I did when he taught me the story of Prometheus, and I saw many parallels with one exception: unlike Prometheus, Solomon did not repent the curses he wished upon his lord.

Joachim Bishop's father, Aaron Bishop, died in 1834, leaving the new lord of Elysium Plantation with an inheritance of twenty slaves and one-hundred acres of fruitful tobacco farmland. Mister Bishop was eighteen years of age at the time, but his father had begun grooming Joachim in his own image four years prior.

Aaron Bishop was a cruel master and he ruled with a steel whip that mutilated bodies and withered away spirits. It took one generation of slaves for him to strip them of all hope for a merciful existence. The children of those slaves did not even argue with the whip. They only wished it to be used with some semblance of reason. So, they prayed for a benevolent master. It was Solomon, a cunning and perceptive slave even in his childhood, who vowed to bring them one.

Solomon watched Joachim grow to be a man with sentiments quite different from those of his father, and Solomon sought to foster those sentiments as best he could. In their discussions on religion, Solomon observed a pious young man who lacked the bloodthirstiness of Aaron Bishop. Whereas Aaron saw the whip as a tool for compliance, a weapon against unruliness, a method for motivation, Joachim would see the whip as an instrument of God. He intended to use it, not because he shared his father's thirsts but because he shared his father's Bible.

Joachim aspired to do what the law of man and the Word of God commanded he do, and he found that if he could motivate his slaves in other ways, he could use the whip fairly—and sparingly. Furthermore, and much to his father's dismay, Joachim had too much of a fondness for these slaves with whom he had grown up. Solomon and Jasper were among those he prized most. And Esther was the most highly prized. For this reason, Aaron Bishop commanded his son to beat Esther, to assure that power would not be simply something that the young Joachim Bishop took for granted.

It is true that of the many who know servitude from birth, it is the talented few who ever question his own oppression. The same is also true of one who knows power from birth. Joachim was the one for whom the power and burden of being a slave master was his by birthright. It was no more unnatural than the plants and flowers that grow. Solomon, on the other hand, was the one from the many. He was much more concerned about the pots in which those plants and flowers grew. Joachim wielded his power as justly as his ignorance allowed. Solomon was the rare slave who took neither power nor servitude for granted. So, when he watched Esther's beating and Jasper's escaping as a consequence of that beating, he knew that he had to gain the ear of his future master right away.

"Of course he ran away," Solomon said about Jasper. Joachim was fourteen years old when this happened, but Solomon was older—closer to twenty, though exactly what age he was, even he did not know. The runaway, Jasper, was somewhere in between, older than Joachim but younger than Solomon. The three of them were something like friends as children, but this changed when Jasper had to watch the beating of his mother. Then it was just Solomon and Joachim.

"But you did what you had to do," Solomon said to a distraught and pensive Joachim.

"But did I really have to?" Joachim asked as he sat on the porch of Solomon's cabin and looked away to the scattered ash trees.

"In the eyes of your father, yes. You must become a man, and that means doing those burdensome things that men must do."

"But Esther was— is like a mother to me."

"But she is not, Mister Joachim. She *is* Jasper's mother."

"Why couldn't he understand that I did what I did out of duty?"

"I reckon he did. That's why he left. No one wants to see their mama be whipped on when he can do nothing about it. Maybe we aren't men like you and Mister Bishop, but we feel the same things."

"Do we?"

"Don't all of God's creatures? Even a wild dog will attack if you abuse his mama."

"But a dog is loyal to his master."

"Have you never seen a dog attack his master?"

"Are you suggesting that Jasper would be justified in attacking me? And for following my father's wishes?"

"I'm saying he did the only thing he thought he had power to do."

"What power can he have? He's a fugitive, now. Bounty hunters will bring him back to us. Or kill him."

"Then he has that power, at least. The power over his death and life."

Joachim looked away from the ash trees and into Solomon's solemn eyes.

"But who would choose death?" Joachim asked.

"Someone with nothing to live for."

They both looked away to the trees, then.

"So, he has chosen death?" Joachim asked.

"Not if he gets away and survives."

"What if the bounty hunters catch him? He can come home."

"To what kind of life? Your father is not a forgiving man."

"He'll come home and get what he deserves."

"A beating worse than his mother's."

"There are consequences for..." Joachim began.

"He dies, either way then," Solomon interrupted him.

"What ought my father do?"

"What would you do?"

"I am not the master of this plantation."

"But you will be, sir. By and by."

"A long time from now."

"Such things are always closer than you think. Best to think about them now."

Solomon did seem prophetic in those days, for not more than a year later, Aaron Bishop came down with what the doctor's determined to be cholera. Joachim became the master at Elysium on his eighteenth birthday, and in those early years, he found that he could rely on Solomon to be his eyes and ears among the slaves. He taught Solomon to read when they were children, mostly as a dare from Solomon, and so in their adult years, Joachim could rely on Solomon to spread the good Word of loyalty and piety. Joachim might have even made Solomon the slave foreman had he not met an ambitious Irishman by the name of Chester Albert McAllister. Chester brought Goliath along with him, and these four, two white, one negro, and one redskin saw to it that Elysium became the most productive tobacco plantation in

Fayette. Elysium Plantation supplied Joachim's tobacco company well, and for this, the slaves at Elysium enjoyed more privileges than others elsewhere.

"They seem happy," Joachim remarked to Solomon on the day that they had repaid the last of his father's debts.

"They have full bellies, clean drawers, and warm cabins. What more could they live for?" Solomon remarked.

"How would you answer that question?" Joachim asked.

"The same as they would," Solomon replied. "The Lord said that the meek shall inherit the earth. I live for that." He smiled. "Until then, the food and shelter shall hold me over. What about you?"

"A wife," Joachim replied. "And a son."

"And you shall have them," Solomon said. "By and by."

On the day that Joachim arrived at Elysium with Miriam in his carriage, both Solomon and Esther knew something had change in him. He had never taken a stern tone with them, but he did on that evening. He was also not known to be away from the plantation for very long, but he embarked on a week-long journey almost as soon as Miriam had been settled in her cabin. He oversaw a delivery of tobacco to his merchants across the river, another unusual undertaking. Then, when he returned to Elysium, he vowed not to be alone in Miriam's presence whenever he could help it. He could not.

On his second day home, he happened upon her as she cleaned the study. He hesitated at first, but she turned and saw him standing in the doorway. He remained austere, though his heart fluttered at the sight of her in her new dress. In fear, she dropped the book she was holding, and he rushed over to retrieve it for her. He opened to its first page but clasped the book closed when he saw the title page.

Notre-Dame de Paris, it read.

"Do you know what this says?" Joachim asked Miriam without looking away from the book.

"I do not, sir," she replied. "Maybe Solomon..."

"No. He has no talent for French literature."

"It is true then? You learned him how to read?" Miriam spoke quietly, staring at the book in his hands.

"*Taught.*"

"Sir?"

"I taught him how to read."

"Do all of the slaves know how?"

"Only the ones for whom it is useful."

"I will put it back, now," Miriam said, reaching out her hand. Joachim held it away. Then he stepped past her and placed it on the shelf himself.

"Would you like to learn?" Joachim asked.

"Would it be useful."

"It might be useful to me." He looked up at Miriam, then, but she looked down at her feet.

No, that shall not do, he thought.

"You must look at me when I speak to you," he said. When she looked up, Joachim admired the way her eyes caught the light streaming through the large windows and gave them an almost golden quality in spite of their otherwise dark color.

"It's settled then," Joachim said, "You'll find that Solomon is a very good teacher. I taught him myself."

Miriam nodded and looked down at her feet, again.

"Otherwise, I take it you are getting on well?" Joachim asked.

"It is very nice here."

"And your cabin, it is comfortable, yes?"

"More than a slave should hope or pray for."

"That is good," he said. "This is your home, now. You ought to be happy in it."

"Yes sir."

Joachim placed a gentle hand on her shoulder, and Miriam did all she could to keep from shrugging it off.

"What would make you happy?" he asked.

"I don't know. I reckon it ain't my place to say so."

"I suppose you have never had to think of it," Joachim replied. "Well, think of it, now. Perhaps I shall call on you some time. You'll have an answer for me, then?"

"I shall do my best, sir." Finally, he withdrew his hand from her shoulder and she expelled a slow, relieved sigh.

"I should be getting back before I am missed," she said.

Miriam departed quickly then, down the stairs and into the kitchen. There, Esther glanced up at her, but seeing the tears in her eyes quickly returned to preparing the master's supper.

Later that evening, Joachim called Solomon to his study.

"You may teach her," Joachim stated, his eyes peering over the gold, wiry brim of his spectacles. He then removed the spectacles and placed them upon the open pages of a large volume.

"Well?" he said. "Aren't you pleased? You will have a new student."

"I ought to be, sir. Only, I think she has not taken a liking to me."

"A pupil need not like the teacher to learn from him," Joachim said.

"Mister Joachim, was she not also meant to be..."

"Your pupil, only."

"I'm sorry, sir?"

"She ought to learn to read. She will be better conversation for me then."

Solomon was speechless.

"I trust you understand me?" Joachim said as he picked up his spectacles and perched them upon his rounded nose. "You are to teach her, but you are not to— ."

"I understand you well," Solomon interrupted with a tremor in his voice.

Joachim glared at him.

"Never interrupt me again," Joachim said.

"I humbly beg your pardon."

"You'll start tomorrow after the morning work."

Joachim looked down at the volume and turned to the next page. Solomon turned to leave the study, but he could not step forward. He looked back at his master, and his lower lip quivered just a bit. He looked away, again, to the tapestry that adorned the wall and the books upon the shelf. He looked to the curtains that draped the windows. Yet, he did not really see these things; they blurred before his eyes. It wasn't until he looked again to his master, who sat complacently at his desk, that he could see clearly again.

"You're still here," Joachim remarked without taking his eyes from his book.

In silence, Solomon then found the strength to depart the room. He descended the stairs, walked down the hall, past the kitchen, and out of the house. He looked to the crooked row of ash trees, and a thought occurred to him.

The meek shall inherit the earth, he thought. *Don't trouble the water.* He looked away to his slave cabin and allowed his feet to carry him there.

Chapter 15: Return to Quincy

December 2nd, 1858

"I will find him," I find the nerves to say to Cassandra as we arrive in Quincy. She does not respond at first, and I wish to further assure her.

"We have a mutual acquaintance in Chicago. If I can meet him there, perhaps he can help me."

Still, she is silent.

"The letter," I say. "It says…"

"You wanted to kiss me," Cassandra interrupts me.

"W-what?" The word catches in my throat.

"That morning by the piano," she continues. "I played Bach, and you listened with your soul. Then I stood in front of you, very close to you. You closed your eyes like you were making a wish. And I think you wished for a kiss."

This time, it was my turn to be silent. She did not seem to mind, however.

"Mr. Goodfellow once had an apprentice named Caesar. He was a free negro from Kentucky, though he would not talk about if he was born free or freed later. He did love to talk, though. He talked about blue grass and magnolias; cedar wood and rosewood; dovetails and bird-mouths. He loved wood and making things out of wood. He told me the only thing he loved more than wood was me. He loved the way I played the piano. He loved that I could read. He loved that I talked like white folks. So, I told him I was a runaway slave."

"You're a runaway?" I ask.

"Doesn't matter what I am. When I told him that, he told me what I needed to know about him. I never saw a man change so fast, and I never even had a white woman look at me with more disdain."

"I'm sorry," I say.

"I'm not," she replies. "He wanted to kiss me, too. Or at least he thought he did. He really just wanted property. Until he thought that I was stolen property. Turns out he didn't know what he wanted."

We ride on for a while in silence before she speaks again.

"What do you want?" she asks.

"Must I want something?"

"Yes. You just told me that you're going to ride to Chicago. For what? Everybody wants something, or else they lie down and die."

"What do you want?" I ask.

"You know what I want. I have been very clear about it: I want Mr. Goodfellow safe and sound. You haven't been very clear, though, and I don't know why. Maybe you're scared to say what you want aloud."

"Words have power," I reply. "You tell people what you want, and they will figure out how to keep you from having it."

"Who taught you that?" she asks.

"Doesn't matter. I believe it."

"Hmm," she says. "And here I have told you exactly what I want. Do you mean to ensure that I don't get it?"

"No," I reply.

"So it seems that the person you entrust with your words makes all the difference."

"Perhaps you're right," I say.

"I usually am," she replies. "So?"

"So what?"

Cassandra brings her horse to an abrupt halt.

"I feel better when I know people's intentions," she says sternly.

"Maybe I want the same thing that you do," I reply.

"If you did, you would have rescued Mr. Goodfellow when you had the chance."

"Perhaps a chance did not present itself," I say.

"I don't believe you," she argued. "Opportunities always present themselves to people who want them badly enough. We'll even make them if we have to. I certainly think that you would."

"And what makes you so certain of that?" I ask. "Are you saying I didn't want to save Mr. Goodfellow?" I ask.

"I'm saying that you are making an opportunity for what you want right now," she replies. "So what is it?"

She stares so intensely at me with those dark eyes that I feel as though I am falling into a night sky. I can no longer resist her gravity, and so I simply reply, "You."

She smiles and rides onward.

"I knew it," she says as she passes me. Then we proceed to Ms. Maertz's residence.

Isabelle Maertz is in a curious mood when we arrive after dusk.

"It seems Mr. Bailey has brought us quite a bit of luck hasn't he?" she says, greeting us at the door.

"Pardon?" I reply.

"Your sculptures," Ms. Maertz says with a smile that doesn't quite reach her eyes. "Mr. McAllister is on his way to Missouri as we speak. He will meet his buyer there, and if all goes according to plan, he and his buyer will return here to discuss a new commission with you." She looks at us expectantly before the smile fades from her lips. "I would expect you all to be happy," she says.

"Did you not hear about Mr. Goodfellow while you were in town?" Cassandras asks.

"What about him?" Ms. Maertz replies.

"He was shot!" Cassandra cries. "In a duel!"

"Dear!" Ms. Maertz responds. "I did not hear this most unfortunate news. Is he dead?"

"Mr. McAllister did not tell you?" I ask. "He was there."

"No," says Ms. Maertz. "He did not mention it. I suppose he was more concerned about his business in Missouri."

"Than a man being shot?" Cassandra scoffs.

"It is dreadful," Ms. Maertz says. "But what is Mr. McAllister to do? Mr. Goodfellow is always finding himself in mischief. Perhaps he is fortunate enough to some day learn his lesson?"

"He is alive," I say, "but I do not know if he is well. I do not know where he is at all."

"Well," Ms. Maertz says, "this is most troubling news for the both of you, I imagine. Of course, Mr. Bailey, you may stay here until things have settled."

"Thank you," I reply. "However, I would very much like to get going and find out the wellness of Mr. Goodfellow."

"But you said yourself that you do not know where he is," Ms. Maertz says.

"Then I ought to set off to find him."

"I understand," Ms Maertz replies. "But I urge you to stay until Mr. McAllister returns. It could be a most fortuitous circumstance for you."

"And what of Mr. Goodfellow?" Cassandra asks.

"Perhaps we ought to let the sheriff handle it."

"He did," I reply. "He was there when Winthrop was shot. He oversaw the duel."

"Then it is done, yes?" Ms. Maertz says. "What more do you think you can do?"

"If he survived the shot," I say, "and I think that he did, I must know if he is recovering."

"If he survived the shot," Ms. Maertz reasons, "he must certainly be okay."

"Not if the bounty hunter that shot him has anything to do with it," I reply. "When last I saw Winthrop, he was being led away by the bounty hunter."

"Then it is as I have said," Ms. Maertz says. "I know this is troubling to you Mr. Bailey, but it seems the law has done its work. I won't ask how Mr. Goodfellow came to be in the presence of a bounty hunter, nor how he came to be dueling said bounty hunter. It seems to me that he has gotten himself in deeper trouble than even he can manage, and the wise thing to do, Mr. Bailey, is to leave well-enough alone. You have your own circumstances to consider."

"If it weren't for Mr. Goodfellow," Cassandra interjects, "Mr. Bailey would have no circumstances to consider!"

"Now Cass—" Ms. Maertz begins, but Cassandra interrupts her.

"How can you be so nonchalant about this?" Cassandra cries.

"I know what he meant to you," Ms. Maertz replies, "I am only thinking of things as reasonably as I can. If anything, these circumstances are no different from the past: Mr. Goodfellow often carries a good deal of misfortune with him wherever he goes."

"I know that he has brought you a great amount of fortune," Cassandra counters.

"Listen," Ms. Maertz approaches Cassandra with outstretched arms, but Cassandra recoils. "Tomorrow, when we head into town to open the market, we can discuss things with the sheriff. You have to know that this is all that any of us can do."

"No," Cassandra says, "I do not know that." With these words, she leaves the room. Ms. Maertz turns to leave as well, but before she goes, she speaks to me with a somber expression.

"I do hope you will stay with us for a few days," she says, "at least until Mr. McAllister returns.

"I will consider it," I reply, though I have no intention of ever seeing him again.

Chapter 16: To Break a Mother's Heart

Stowing Away, 1851

At the dawn of his life, a slave does not know he is a bonded child. His entire world is the plantation, and its confines seem quite natural to him. And, every child, whether enslaved or free, has within him a light that is his by birthright, a kind of beacon that signals life's potential. He is involuntarily drawn to this light just as he is to the breath that fills his lungs or the heart that beats in his chest. It is therefore natural for him to love, to desire, and to dream. Soon, however, he will become aware only of their corollaries; he will learn to loathe, to despair, to dread. When he encounters men and circumstances that will teach him these things, he will either hide and safeguard what he can of his light or he will surrender it to those unfortunate circumstances.

The greatest evil of slavery, is this: that it seeks to snuff out that God-given human birth-light, long before the child is old enough to defend himself, long before he knows how to or even that he must. It is only the hard-headed that resists this darkening of body and soul. I suppose I was, as my mother sometimes put it, as hard-headed as they come.

There is no other way to describe the drive I had to create, to shape something lasting, to help counter the process. Every mark I made on paper or cut from wood kept the spark flickering in me. I was like the neanderthal then who ventures beyond the lit wall of his cave and returns to scrawl upon the rock walls those things of beauty which he hoped to remember during dark hours.

I sometimes think that curiosity in children comes from that same, natural light. Curiosity is a strange kind of hope; there is no fear in it. If there were, I never would have stowed away on Goliath's carriage when I was ten years old. I was filled with wonder by the things I might discover in town, things I might be able to see or even some day draw if it left its mark on my memory. As I curled up in the cloak of an old blanket that was often kept beneath the seat inside the carriage, I delighted in the rumbling of wheels upon the ground below. Knowing that Goliath sat atop the carriage, I often ventured to peek through the dusty window at the world that passed by. The first time that I heard the bustling sounds at the center of Fayette, I think that I fell in love.

The many buildings of brick and wood lined the road on either side. They were close together and the men and women sauntered to and fro before them. I marveled at the many signs, all painted in different script, all neatly lined across the tops of the buildings, all inviting my curiosity to discover what was inside. The noises and smells, too, were captivating. I could hear the low murmur of the many privately held conversations about me. The sound of iron-clad hooves beat against the ground. The fresh and pungent smell of horse dung mingled with the sweet aromas of ladies' perfumes, gentlemen's bourbon, and fresh bread from some nearby bakery. I could not help but imagine an abundance of majestic horses and splendidly-clad people just outside the door of the carriage.

I longed to throw open that door and greet the world, to greet the people and contribute to their conversations. But alas, when I imagined doing so, I imagined, too, that I might be a pitiable sight before them, and that the color of my skin would offend them. They would not have me among them, and I loathed them for this. However, I was still enamored by them, by their existence, for it suggested that there were other towns and other people elsewhere. Perhaps among those elsewhere people, I might find mine, whoever they were. I buried the idea of them deep in my mind when I heard footsteps approach the carriage. I ducked down beneath my blanket and hid under the seat of the carriage. My heart raced until the wheels turned, and we returned home again.

Things were not the same for me after I had traveled to town, and I tried my best to keep this new thing for myself. I tried to hide it from my conversations, my laughter, and even the expressions on my face. However, there was one time, the last time in fact, when I could not hide the entirety of my secret. Goliath had stopped the carriage just behind the Bishop house but before the dirt road and slave quarters. I tried to creep from my hiding space to see if I might steal away to the cabins. That is when my eyes met hers. I quickly ducked beneath the carriage seat, but it was too late.

"I seen you," Serafina said later as she strolled over to my nook. "I seen you sneakin' away to town. Maybe I'm fixin' to tell yo' mama 'bout it."

"Don't you tell her nothin'," I cried as I hastened to hide my carvings beneath me.

"What do I get if I keep your secret?"

"Whatchu want?"

"Somethin' pretty. Next time you sneak into town, bring me back something that's sweet or fancy."

"But I ain't got no money for nothin' sweet nor fancy."

"You figure out a way 'less you want your mama to find out about where you been."

With these few words between Serafina and me, paradise became purgatory. I vomited on the morning when I next meant to steal away. Nevertheless, steal away I did, and when we arrived in town that afternoon, my actions became what are now mostly a blur in my memory. I remember that I crept from the cabin of the carriage to hide in the shadows between the large wheel spokes. The townspeople themselves seemed as tall as the buildings. I could not see the joy on their faces as I had imagined from my hiding place in the carriage, nor could I hear the excitement in their voices. I felt small and insignificant, yet it was only in this state of insignificance that I could gather the courage to scurry clumsily into the shadows between two shops.

From there, I crawled among the footsteps of other negros through the back door of a general store. It was rather crowded with people and full with the shouting of orders and prices, yet I only heard the loud footsteps and the creaking of the wooden floorboards beneath me. My eyes darted back and forth as I struggled to view the shelves between the knees and legs of the many patrons. When at last I saw the leaves and flowers of a basil plant, my heart nearly seized up in my chest. I reached among the knees and legs to obtain this prize, but another hand seized mine first.

"That's mine," said a stranger's voice. "I need that for Master Wilkes's dinner party." I withdrew my hand— and indeed my entire self— to a place under a table. There, the entire room swirled around and around until I lost my orientation. I stood in a daze and ran through the shop, and it was only as I spotted a door that I noticed a pretty, wooden comb on a table of other small trinkets. It was within my reach. However, as I ran by that table, I resisted the urge to grab it and leapt empty-handed through the door that opened before me. I tumbled onto the dirt road to the outraged gasps of two white women in brightly colored dresses. Their green eyes glowered at me, and their looks of astonishment quickly twisted into looks of indignation. I scrambled to my feet and ran without direction though my eyes searched the road frantically for the carriage that would carry me home. I only ran for a few seconds longer before I realized that I was lost. Panic-stricken, I fled from the road and into the brush. The sound of a carriage rumbled behind me and passed on down the road. Then another. And another. A dog barked in the distance. A solitary horse rider galloped by. I curled my knees to my chest and sat as quietly and as still as I could.

I remained in the brush for what must have been several hours, for when I dozed and awakened, the sun was gone. I might have stayed there but for the grumblings in my stomach, which caused my wits to return to me somewhat. I remembered that I knew this road from my previous escapades, so I stood a bit apprehensively and followed the road away from town. Though the moon squinted a bit of light down upon the world, it was true that the darkness disguised my otherwise familiar surroundings. The blackness of the trees stretched ominously to the sky, and every critter and creature became indiscernible among their menacing sounds. I became all but certain that I would walk through this darkness eternally, but at last Elysium stood illuminated in the distance.

As I approached her grounds, I found her silent and still. The lights flickered in every window, but not a soul stirred. Foolishly, I walked up the cobbled-path, past the big house, and onto the dirt road toward the tobacco fields. The large barn loomed tall before me, and the eyes of the other slaves peeked from the windows of the cabins that lined my path. As I walked toward the last cabin, I saw the crooked row of ash trees and wondered if I could not retreat to my nook beyond them.

A door opened before I arrived there, and my mother scowled down upon me.

"Where you been?"

"Lost."

"Damned right, you were lost!" She yanked me toward her by my ear. Then, she grabbed my collar and dragged me toward the barn. She huffed as she was hastening or impeding my stride. Inside the dark barn, I could not see her, but I heard her sniveling as she stripped me bare and began to lay into my hide with the braided branches she often took from the willow behind our cabin. When a mother beats her child, he may have two responses. Either he repents his sins wholeheartedly, or he laments an unjust act. Mine was the latter.

"No remorse? No repenting in you?" Miriam huffed between strikes. She spat epithets and curses at me until her voice ran hoarse. The welts rose upon my arms and chest. I felt them when I instinctively sought to protect myself. Nevertheless, I wept not. Soon, my mother grew tired and left me alone in the darkness. When she returned, she brought two large buckets of water, which I was meant to hold in either hand while standing on one foot. If I faltered in balance or strength, she knew by my footprints in the moistened earth, and she beat me with the switch again. During these times, too, I did not weep.

Only when I was alone did I cry, not from the pain of the strap nor the heaviness of the buckets. I cried because I was alone and in the dark. I had never known such a darkness as that which closed around me in that barn. My eyes could not adjust to it, and it seemed futile to leave them open. I could see nothing. I smelled horse shit. I heard snorts here and there but silence otherwise. Only once did I hear a kind whisper in the darkness.

"Percy?" it said. "You sure did something awful, didn't you?" I did not respond.

"I shouldn't even be bringing you water," the whisper continued. "What were you thinking?"

Still, I did not answer though I discerned Solomon's laughter in that whisper. I did not wish to acknowledge my presence here to anyone, not even him.

"Next time your mama beats you," he said, "at least pretend to cry. I ain't never seen that woman so mad." I heard him place the water by the door, but he did not leave. My tongue immediately turned coarse in my mouth, and I gagged, my throat too dry for swallowing. Yet, I would not drink that water, nor would I steal sips from the buckets in my hands. I accepted my sentence but denied my guilt. If there was any justice in the world, perhaps my suffering would teach the unjust a lesson.

"You mother did not want to beat you, do you know that?" he said. "It hurt her more than it hurt you, yet she still chose to do it herself. Do you know why?"

I don't care.

"Because it would have been worse if Mister Bishop had done it," Solomon continued.

No. Nothing could have been worse.

Miriam Pleads for Her Son, 1851

Joachim placed the ledger on his desk and folded his hands across them. He looked at Miriam sternly over the rim of his spectacles.

"It is good that he be broken," he explained to her. "For your part, you beat him, and he did not cry out, did he?"

"No sir," Miriam replied.

"And he ought to have the fear of God in him, ought he not?"

"Yes sir."

"And the Lord says that we must cry out to him."

"But isn't God not merciful, as well?" Miriam reasoned as she looked at the floor beneath his desk.

"Only to the obedient. Percival has not been so deserving. Not with this latest act of his."

"But that is only because he is a child. He can learn."

"He will learn. This is how."

"But the barn is so dark. It is terrifying for a child. He has learned his lesson."

"Has he cried out?"

Miriam lowered her head more.

Joachim slowly removed his spectacles and held them loosely in his palm.

"What would you have me do with such a wily and unruly slave?" he asked.

"I only think that there must be some other way."

"This *is* some other way. The much more common punishment for a slave is far crueler. Or perhaps I should hug him and firmly chastise. How ought a slave child be treated?"

Miriam hesitated, "I only hoped for…"

Joachim closed his palm into a fist.

"What?" he interrupted her.

Miriam knew that Joachim had set a trap with this question. She did not say the words *mercy* or *favor*, and she ought to have uttered one or the other, for what she said instead was far worse. She looked up, away from the floor and into his eyes. Her stare was indignant as she spoke in a trembling whisper.

"How ought a white child be treated?"

She flinched when she heard the wire snap and the lens crack in Joachim's tightened fist. He walked over to Miriam and slowly took her hot cheek in his bloodied hand. He caressed it with his thumb. Then, with the other fingers, he traced a circle under her chin, brushing her neck with his fingertips until he held her jaw in his palm. He held her there firmly. But he did nothing more. He did not tighten his grip. He did not shake her. He simply felt the frantic beat of her pulse against his index finger. He said nothing to her, yet he forced the tears loose from her large, brown eyes. When Solomon knocked at the open door, Joachim let his hand drop to his side.

"How wrong you are to ask such a favor of me," Joachim said to her. "You should be getting back to the fields." He walked back to the ledger at his desk. "Before you are missed."

She dropped her gaze and departed. She tried to keep her head high, but when she passed Solomon in the doorway her chin tilted toward her chest, and she closed her eyes. She did not see his sympathy. She could not bear it. Solomon waited until she passed down the hall before he addressed his master.

"Everything okay, Mister Bishop?" Solomon asked.

"She tempts me, Solomon. She tempts me, and I fear I shall have to do something awful with the boy. Something I never thought I would have to do. Something it would pain me greatly to do."

"Sir?"

"Or perhaps I will have to sell him. He distracts her so."

"Oh, Mister Bishop! I don't think you will have to do all that. Besides, imagine how distracted she'd be if he were not here."

"I suppose you're right. But what else is there to do?"

"Indulge him. Just a little bit. He is but a child, and as it turns out, he has just a bit of, how you say, wanderlust. Like any child..."

"But he is not any child," Joachim interrupted. "He is a slave. And slaves do not forget their place."

"He will learn in time."

"He should already know it! He will learn in my time. He does not have his own time."

"Yes."

"Nor does his mother."

"Of course."

"See to it that they know this."

"I will, sir."

"Good."

Solomon cleared his throat.

"Well?" Joachim asked.

"An idea, sir, if you will hear it."

"Go on."

"I was thinking that we might lend the boy out."

"To do what?"

"To build, sir. He has shown himself to be quite capable, and it will satisfy his— well, his wanderlust, sir."

"I am not here to satisfy him."

"You are not, sir. But you might turn his will to your advantage."

"His will?"

"Excuse me, his desire."

"His desire?"

"What I mean, sir, is his inclinations."

"Inclinations! What do I care of a slave's inclination?"

"Nothing. Only you do care about the harmony of this plantation. Or am I mistaken?"

Joachim suddenly felt the sting and throbbing of blood in his wounded hand. He looked down at it and retrieved a handkerchief to tie it up. Solomon rushed over to help him tend to the cut. Joachim let him.

"Of course, you have been here for me all of these years, haven't you, Solomon?" Joachim said.

"Of course, sir. I try to fulfill my duty."

"Ah, but you do more than try, Solomon. You succeed."

"You know I'd do anything to keep this plantation," he paused as Joachim winced from the pain, "up and running."

"I know, Solomon. I know. Is there anything else you needed?"

"Nothing, sir. Nothing at all. You of all people know how little I need."

"And I am grateful for it," Joachim replied. "Perhaps there is some merit to your idea. Give notice to Goliath that he is to take Percy into town tomorrow. Introduce the boy to a few of our merchants there. I'm sure they will have some work for him. In the meantime, tend to Miriam. Perhaps I was a bit harsh with her."

"Right away, sir."

Solomon turned and hurried from the house and into the fields. He was suddenly very excited to tell Miriam the good news. But, before he did, he went to Goliath to tell him his new assignment— and to give him an important message.

"Make sure that nigger knows where his ass belongs and who it belongs to," he told the Indian.

A Nigger's Sin, 1851

"You gonna get me something this time?" Serafina whined on the morning of my first ride with Goliath into town.

"If I can."

"Boy!" she became suddenly brusque. "You not supposed to answer like that. You supposed to say 'yes.' Don't you know nothing about being a boy? Say 'yes' to a girl. Then if you can't, you make something and lie and tell me you got it just for me."

I looked back at her with a confounded expression.

"Say 'yes,'" she reiterated.

"Yes."

"Good."

She kissed me on the cheek, and my cheek grew hot.

"Except, now you really must get me something 'cuz I'll know if you use my lie." She winked, a kind of sassy expression she had mastered in her dealings with the older boys and men. Then, she ran off just as Goliath arrived with the wagon. He smirked when he saw us.

"Come on boy," he muttered. "Ain't no time for that stuff. Get up here. With me." His invite felt like a threat. Upon the bench, I found that I was closer to Goliath than I had any desire to be. He was quiet for most of the ride, and his presence loomed beside me. Furthermore, I was surprised to discover that we did not head westward on the road into town but eastward toward the Mississippi River. The grim expression on Goliath's face did not invite questions, and so I did not ask him where we were going. I would discover our destination soon enough when we turned onto a narrow path that led to a worn-down log cabin. The willow trees sulked low over the path and the critters became quieter the closer we approached.

"Yeeeeeoouu!" Goliath called out with a screech, and before long, a tall but scraggly man appeared at the front porch. He wore a tattered, brown hat, and there was a lump in his jaw from the snuff that was lodged there.

"Ready to go hunting?" Goliath shouted.

"Yeeeeeoouu!" Chester Albert McAllister called back and grabbed his rifle from behind the door before proceeding with his gangly gait toward our carriage. He sat beside me so that I was beset on both sides by the repugnant stench of tobacco and beer, and I became acutely aware of Chester Albert McAllister's jagged elbows and shoulders.

We rode for nearly an hour away from Elysium and away from Fayette. Soon the road beneath us narrowed to a mere strip of dirt in the grass. Our bodies jerked to and fro as the carriage traversed the rocky terrain. Before long we stopped and Chester Albert McAllister climbed down first. Then, leading me with a strong grip on the back of my collar, Goliath forced me down from the carriage.

"Stay close," he said sternly. I followed the two men as they quietly searched the woods around us. Goliath kneeled close to the ground to examine some prints that led to a large oak tree.

"They settled here, away from the sun," Goliath said to the scraggly man. "Must've rested here early in the morning."

"Umhmm."

"Come on."

We followed the prints until we came to some low hanging vines and brush that grew past my waist.

"Shh!" Goliath said, bending to touch the broken branches and torn leaves that made up the path through the high brush. He rubbed his fingers together. "Still damp," he said. "Not far."

Chester Albert McAllister was becoming giddy. He grabbed me by the scruff of my neck and drew me close so that I could smell the stale snuff that browned his teeth. He spit at the ground in front of me and hissed into my ear.

"Y'all probably don't know why they call this man Shadow Wolf. It's 'cause his prey never sees him coming. And I just love it. He's got 'em by the throat before they even know he's onto 'em." He wheezed from laughter, and Goliath hushed him vehemently.

"Shh! I need your gun, not your mouth. Listen. You hear that?

"No."

"Exactly. No birds. Look there. All that flattened grass before that tree. You see it?"

"No," the scraggly man whispered.

"He's up there. Shoot into that tree. But don't hit him."

"Now how I'm supposed to miss what I can't see?"

"Give me the gun."

"Okay, okay, I got it."

The scraggly man pointed his gun into the tree and almost as quickly as he raised it, he fired. The leaves rustled and settled and became quiet."

"Again."

The scraggly man fired into the tree and there was a loud groan.

"There he is," Goliath grumbled. He ran to the tree just as a scrawny negro hobbled down from the branches and collapsed to the ground. When he saw Goliath, he tried to scramble to his feet, but he grabbed his leg and cried out before collapsing to the ground again. Goliath brought only a rope with which he quickly hog-tied the negro and hoisted him upon his shoulder. Though the captive wriggled and writhed, Goliath carried him calmly past us and toward the carriage. I followed in silence, but Chester Albert McAllister was aroused by the successful pursuit.

"Ain't we undefeated!" he boasted to Goliath who did not respond.

"With my gun and your sense for catching niggers, we'll make a fortune. Probably have our own plantations before it's all said and done."

"Shut up, Skunk," Goliath warned as he tethered the runaway to the carriage. He stopped a moment for a drink of water before we boarded, and the runaway struggled to keep his feet beneath him as he was dragged closer to Fayette. Along the way, Wolf and Skunk hunted and captured two more runaways in the same manner as the first.

The sun was setting by the time we finally saw the town on the horizon, and the dust of that often busy road had settled in amongst the cluster of lowly risen buildings around the town square. The pedestrians ambled about, some with a drunken gait. We rode just beyond a public house to a large gallows where four ropes hung. Waiting.

"Get to work, then," Goliath commanded me as he pointed to a pile of worn, rickety, wooden planks. A hammer and a box of long nails lay beside them. "Four chairs. No backs. No one will be sitting in these."

Both he and Chester Albert McAllister watched me while they chewed their wads and spit occasionally into the plodded road.

"What if he makes 'em too good?" asked Chester Albert McAllister.

"Then I guess you'll just have to shoot 'em out from under them," Goliath replied.

"I'll just kick 'em."

"What? Losing faith in your sight?"

"Hmph," Chester Albert McAllister sniffed. "Leave all the work to me, then."

"I figured you'd have fun with it."

When I finished the four stools, Goliath took each and placed them upon the gallows, one under each rope. Then, the two of them led each runaway to a rope. By the time the last one was bound by his neck to the gallows, a small crowd had gathered from the various buildings in town. The sheriff soon appeared to read the list of offenses for which the three negros were to be hanged.

"Albert Jeffers, caught in the unlawful possession of a firearm. Winifred Banks, perpetually lying out and deluding of slave to runaway. Obadiah Wilkes, instructing in the knowledge of poisons. All three shall be put to death by the will of the court and their masters— err," he paused and looked at the fourth rope. He then looked to Goliath.

"What's that one for?"

Goliath nodded toward me. "Teaching a lesson." Chester Albert McAllister then grabbed me by the scruff of my neck and pushed me toward the gallows. I resisted at first, but then he lifted and carried me there. I stood in terrified silence as he slipped the rope around my neck and stood me upon the stool I had myself made.

"What are these stools for?" the sheriff asked, looking again to Goliath.

"Another lesson."

The sheriff nodded. For a long while, we stood with our necks in nooses and our feet upon the rickety, makeshift stools. The crowd before us stared with expectant eyes. When one of the stools gave way under the weight of its bearer, I felt my soul fall away from me. I lost all control of my body as I nearly swooned to my own death. At once, I struggled to regain my footing, and upon doing so, I looked around at the many eyes that were wide with excitement. Only, they were not looking at me but instead the unfortunate negro to my right whose voice gurgled in his throat and whose body shook violently until it was suddenly still, dangling from the rope. Then he was silent.

In the moment before the next stool snapped, I realized that my pants were warm and wet. And the warmth rose to my nostrils, carrying with it the stench of urine. I might have died from humiliation if my actual mortality were not imminent. The sudden bristling of the stool to my left startled me, and my heart pounded as I listened to the sound of another negro's voice choking in the warm, dusk air. When he was silent and gone, Chester Albert McAllister took aim with his rifle and blew a third stool to smithereens. The crowd cheered, and the

Irishman waved, his rusted and crooked smile spread wide across his face. Then he and the Indian walked away to the public house which had come alive with bourbon and laughter. Only a few men stayed behind to watch me, but soon they, too, entered the public house. And, I was alone, my neck throbbing in the noose, my feet trembling upon this crude and sturdy threat beneath me, my body trembling from the evening cold and the piss which had spread to all of the threads in my britches.

Every few moments, I heard the stool creak beneath me, and a yelp would burst forth from my throat. I wanted to give shape to that sound, to cry out for someone to help me. Or someone to comfort me. Or someone to care that I was living my last moments, that my short life was coming to an end. I would perish and I could not say a final word, not even to my mother.

But I was alive, mama…

I heard a final creak from the stool, and my knees buckled so that I lost my footing. Then, the rope grew tight and I tried to call out to someone. But, the only sound that came was a croak like a bullfrog from my throat. And the night grew darker. And darker.

I did not remember falling asleep. I only knew that I awakened after what seemed to be many hours. I was no longer on the gallows. Indeed, the whole world had changed, for the town of Fayette had disappeared, and there was only darkness before me. As I struggled to stand up, I immediately realized that my arms were bound behind my back and to my ankles, which were also bound together. I writhed with all of my strength. I tried to wriggle forward. I cried.

"Mama?"

Silence.

"Solomon?"

Silence still.

"Mama! Somebody? Where am I?"

"Shut up!" an unfamiliar voice shouted at me through the darkness. I wriggled forward until my head banged loudly against a metal barrier.

The pain shot through me, and I became aware that things crawled all over my body. But, I could do nothing but writhe in the hopes that they would leave me alone. I strained my eyes to see if it was spiders or cockroaches around me. I heard spectral echoes that I could not distinguish from my own wailing. And wail, I did. For the emptiness in my stomach and the bitter taste of hunger in my mouth. For the men who had no reason to care for me. For the slaves whose inevitable capture I had to witness. For the world that had suddenly grown darker around me. I wailed until I fell asleep. When, I awakened my feet were being dragged across a rugged terrain, and my arms were bound to the side of the carriage. My face was pressed against the window so that I could see inside, and sunlight poured through the adjacent window and past the undrawn curtains, blinding me. I strained my neck and face against the carriage until I could see his familiar, lumbering body. Goliath was bringing me back to Elysium.

Chapter 17: The Remnants of a Slave

December 3rd, 1858

I
t is most curious to me that on the morning of my departure to Chicago I should happen to see Aideen McAllister lurking around the stables on Ms. Maertz's property. He has either made an extraordinarily fast return from Missouri, or he was never there at all. I am inclined towards the latter conclusion. Both, Ms. Maertz and Cassandra have gone to town to tend the shop. I had intended to be on an eastbound train when Ms. Maertz's house servant, Louise, summoned me to the front entrance. As I looked at the tobacco merchant's stained and crooked grin, I could not help but be reminded of his brother.

"They called him Skunk," Aideen says to me. "I suppose the name fit him, though. He smelled like hell, but otherwise he was harmless— all bared teeth and no bite. But, I suppose you knew that."

"Why would I know that?" I ask.

"Oh, you don't have to play dumb with me," Aideen remarks. "In fact, you can dispense with all of your niggerish wiles. I don't have the patience for it today."

We stand alone in the parlor of Isabelle Maertz's home. Neither she nor Cassandra is home, for they are minding the store. I had expected Aideen to visit sooner or later, but because I had taken to keeping my pepperbox close, I was not inclined to run when I saw him from the upstairs window. Still, I was also not inclined to let him in the house.

Louise must have. He was in the parlor when she informed me of my visitor. Now, I hope she is far out of earshot along with the rest of the house servants. As I stand before the brother of Chester Albert McAllister, I cannot help but see the resemblance, in spite of the vastly different ways in which each carried himself.

"Is there a reason you have come here?" I ask.

"Just a social call," he replies. "As I said, I have a commission for you."

"I have not been particularly inspired to do any work lately."

"Oh, I think you will find a way of motivating yourself."

"Why is that?"

"Because you have been enjoying this little taste of freedom. Because you don't want to lose this life. Because you don't want to lose her."

"And you're so sure I can lose these?" I ask. "Who will take them from me? You?"

"You may find that I am as ruthless as my brother," Aideen replies, "only far less careless."

"I know nothing of either of you," I say. "I'd prefer to keep it that way."

"Oh, I suspect you know a little something."

With these words, he reaches into his coat and reveals a small wooden thing. I immediately recognize it as the carving of my father's face—my face. It is filthy and weathered. But, it is unmistakably mine. Aideen dangles it before my eyes as though he taunts a caged, wild animal.

"Our Indian friend found it in those woods where your friend killed my brother," Aideen says. "But do you know who confirmed it? I did. I was in the parlor that day when Joachim bragged about it. You know who else confirmed it? Your mother. She was most pleased to know that you were still alive. Your father, too. He might have expressed it with more vigor if he were not slightly under the weather during my visit. Luckily, Jasper is there to take care of him. Just like he did when they were boys."

"Exactly who is it you think I am?" I ask.

"Well," Aideen begins. "I went on down there to Elysium Plantation. I talked to the niggers down there. I showed them this little charm. Then they all got to talking about a runaway named Percy."

"I do not know that name," I reply.

"Hmm. Some of them even seemed a bit broken up about the missing slave. Especially this one pretty wench there. Martha or Mary. That's your mother's name ain't it? She just cried and carried on about her missing boy. Pretty thing, she was. Especially in her despair. Kinda like looking at a deer before its slaughter."

"I see you share your brother's taste for cruelty," I remark.

"Cruelty, no. Reality, yes," Aideen replies. "No one can escape the reality into which they are born. You have tried, and I am like a harbinger of sorts for your failure. When Goliath arrives you will learn that we must all adhere to reality."

I do not mean to avert my gaze from him, but I cannot help it.

"Ah," Aideen notes, "you know the name?"

"I have seen him," I say. "Who hasn't seen him? He is a giant."

"But you know his name," Aideen remarks.

"I was with you in the saloon that night. You remember don't you?"

"Only slightly," he replies. "But, that is no matter. He will be here in a few days, and you shall meet him then. If you are who you say you are, it will be no more than a chance encounter. If not... Well, you know how Mr. Goodfellow ended up."

"You are so sure that I am a runaway."

He smirks. "I am."

"Why?" I ask.

"Because a nigger is never in the company of Winthrop Goodfellow if he is not up to some scheme."

"That is no reason at all."

"Then how about this: I have met your mother. And, I have met your master."

"I have no master. And the other is your word against mine. Unless you mean to drag someone's property across Missouri, I think your visit is done."

"You are not afraid to meet Goliath?" he asks.

"I am not," I reply. "But something else you have not considered is this: the reality of the matter is that we are in Illinois, a free state. And I am free. I do not have to be anywhere you are for any reason."

"Even if I ask politely?"

I clear my throat.

"Is there anything else?" I ask.

"No," he replies. "I suppose I should be going, now. I do, however, look forward to your visit when Goliath is in town. Otherwise, we may have to come looking for you. And, oh won't that be fun."

"I may be in Chicago at that time," I retort.

"Which time?"

"Whichever time is inconvenient."

I smile wryly and we head to the front door. Once the door is open, he pauses and turns back to me.

"You cannot stay in Chicago forever."

"Why is that?" I ask.

"Because *she* is not there."

I look away and reply, "Good day, Mr. McAllister."

He continues, "That is to say, I don't think she will want to go with you. Not once she knows who you really are."

"Good day, Mr. McAllister!" I place my hand on his shoulder to firmly guide him, but he does not move through the doorway.

"You would do well to get your hand off of me, Percy. I do not know who would win in a scuffle, but I do know that I would try my best to succeed in seeing you as Miss Cassandra has seen you."

"And how is that?"

"Without your shirt."

I quickly remove my hand from his shoulder and a wide, awful grin breaks across his face.

"Come by when you are ready to hear my offer for that commission.

Or come by when Goliath is in town. Or see if you can outrun the wolf. Either way, I'll be seeing you, Percy."

I close the door and expel an exasperated sigh. Then I turn around to see Louise looking at me with a sympathetic expression.

"He really is a nasty man, isn't he?" she remarks.

"You know him well, I suppose," I say.

"We all know him," she says. "Henry, Caleb, and I, we keep an eye on him for Mr. Goodfellow."

"Do you?" I ask with raised brow.

"You don't think he'd leave his daughter in just anyone's care, do you?" Her smile sets me at ease in a way that no other smile ever has.

"So she is his daughter?"

"Close enough," Louise says. "He raised her when her mother, Eunice died. Mr. Goodfellow was in love with Eunice. He's usually that way about the folk he helps find freedom. I'm sure he's that way about you, too. Anyway, Eunice had just given birth to a little girl when they decided to run away. Eunice didn't make it. Typhoid got her. So Mr. Goodfellow was raising Cassandra on his own when he met us."

"So, who are you?" I ask.

"Nobody," she replies, her sympathy turning to amusement. "Just house servants for Ms. Maertz."

"And she is—?"

"Just as nasty as Mr. McAllister. Oh, she pretends to be an anti-slavery sympathizer, but she and her husband were up to all kinds of dirt before he passed away. Once they passed those fugitive slave laws, she started playing a hand in many a slave being returned to their masters. Now, her house is on the Underground Railroad, and she don't even know it." Louise stopped to chuckle a bit.

"She agreed to have me in her home," I remark.

"Of course!" Louise says. "And not long after, Old McAllister found his way on our doorstep. You think that's a coincidence? She just wants to know where you at."

"But Cassandra, she—"

"Also wants to know where you at. Fortunately, that works out for us, too. We don't tell her everything for her own protection. But she figures things out. She certainly has you figured out. And she wants you here. If you haven't figured out why yet, you're certainly a bigger fool than you appear. And I certainly wouldn't have pegged you for one of those. You made it this far, didn't you?"

"So, you know who I am?"

"We all do. You probably wouldn't be alive if we didn't."

"I suppose I owe you my life, then."

"No!" she exclaimed. "You don't owe anyone that. Ever."

"Yes. I suppose I mean that I am very grateful. I don't know how to repay you."

"Oh, you're about to."

"How?"

"Well, you see there's this matter of a missing person. He's very important to us." Louise smiles warmly again, and I understand.

"Mr. Goodfellow," I say.

"You see," Louise explains, "I was born free. So was Henry and our only son, Jacob. But Winthrop, he was not."

"Jasper?"

"Jasper Diggs. He's been doing all the rescuing over the years. Now it's he what needs rescuing. We know where he is. It seems you do, too. And there is no one better suited for the task."

"I can't," I say.

"You can."

"I cannot go back there."

"Only you can. Love it or hate it, that is your land, and those are your people. If you made it here, you can make it back and then here again."

"And what if I fail?"

"We don't ask those kinds of questions around here. Such questions do not matter where freedom is concerned. Come. I will introduce you to more of your chosen people."

"My chosen people?"

"There are people you are born to, and you have no choice who they are. Then there are people you choose."

"When did I choose them?"

"When you chose the kind of life you wanted to live."

"I was born a slave. Slaves don't get to choose. Not anything."

"And yet, you chose anyway."

She leads me through the parlor and into the kitchen where Henry and Caleb are eating.

"Good day, Mr. Bailey," Henry says.

"He knows," Louise says.

"Good. It's about time," Henry remarks. "So, you're going to bring Mr. Goodfellow back to us?"

"I reckon so," I admit.

"Then you're going to need a few things," Henry says. "Do you still have that pepperbox he gave you?"

I reach into my waist coat and reveal it.

"You're done with that," Henry says. "You need a real gun." He reaches into his waist coat and reveals a Colt revolver. "You know how to shoot one of these?"

"Winthrop taught me," I say.

"Good. That's usually the first thing he teaches runaways. You can use this one. I have another."

"Thank you," I say. But as he palms the pepperbox, I stop him. "If it's all the same to you, I'd like to keep this one, too." Henry hands it over to me and grins.

"I suppose you'll be needing a boot holster, too," he remarks.

"I suppose so," I agree.

"So you were born a slave?" Caleb asks in a voice that belies the youth in his face. The clean-shaven face and long eyelashes make him look no more than sixteen years of age, but when he speaks, he seems much closer to thirty.

"I was," I reply.

"You done being one?" he asks.

"I suspect so."

"That's good to hear," Caleb says. "A lot of folks ain't ready for freedom. Even the ones who were free to begin with."

"He looks ready enough," Louise tries to steer the conversation, but Caleb continues.

"That's why Old Black Moses carries a pistol with her when she rescues slaves, just in case one of 'em wanted to turn back," he says.

"This one ain't need no rescuing," Louise remarks pointedly to her son.

"Like I said," Caleb continues, "I seen many slaves come half way. They get a little taste of how hard freedom is and they wanna go back to their masters. Some of 'em never stopped trusting their masters to begin with."

"Caleb—" Henry tries his hand, but Caleb goes on.

"Freedom is in the doing. It ain't in the waiting or the sitting or the praying. Did Mr. Goodfellow tell you that?"

"He did," I say.

"Good. You heed those words."

"Caleb!" Louise finally insists. "Look at him. He's doing the doing. Let him be."

"I know," Caleb says. "I sees it. Just make sure when it comes down to a choice between freedom and anything else, you ain't afraid to put freedom first." He holds my gaze for a long moment, and I see the fire in his eyes. I decide then that I want that fire.

"I won't," I say, returning his gaze.

"Good," Caleb says before standing to clear his plate.

"Don't mind him," Henry chuckles. "He just wishes he was going to Missouri, too. We got word that Old John Brown is fixing to start a war that way. Caleb don't know how crazy that old man is. His mama forbids him to go, and he thinks he's choosing his mama over freedom." Henry leans in close to me. "Between you and me, she's right. She's never wrong."

"There will be better fights to be had," Louise interjects. "Pick our battles and win them. That's the goal. That ain't what Nat Turner did, and it ain't what the Old Captain is doing. I have a feeling he's gonna end up in a bad way before the right battles can even get started."

"Ain't no battle gonna get started if men like John Brown don't start 'em," Caleb remarks.

"Ok, Caleb," Henry says firmly. Then turning to me he says, "You ever ride on a boat before?"

"No," I reply.

"Well, you're gonna need to sneak onto one in order to get into Missouri. I imagine Mr. Goodfellow has told you about Not George?"

"Yes. I was supposed to meet him in Springfield."

"You'll still meet him. Only he'll meet you on your way to the P&H Railroad."

"How will I know who he is? How will I even find him if I'm sneaking around?"

"Don't worry. In three days time, take the first cargo train heading to Sterling from Fowler. You'll have to sneak on, but he'll find you before you have to switch trains. He'll see you through to Douglas, and you can get into Hannibal by steamboat. He'll have a uniform to help you pass as a porter."

"Must I leave so soon?"

"Yes. McAllister will be back with his bounty hunter friend soon. They will be here. You won't be. They'll try to track you to Chicago, but you won't be there, either. When you get to Hannibal, you'll be on your own, but I'm sure you'll manage. We may be able to arrange a horse for you. That should make the journey easier. From here on out, when you travel, you'll need to be unseen. When you ride in Missouri, stay off the main roads. They ain't stopped looking for you. Not yet."

Chapter 18: Between Parent and Child

A Memory of my Mother, 1851

Solomon had once told me of a swamp in Louisiana so murky and desolate that it reflected no light, and no life could exist in its waters. Slaves dared not wade through it, not for the monsters that lurked there, but for the swamp itself, which might consume them before they had a chance to reach the other side to freedom. They would just as soon remain slaves than chance those waters. Solomon once told me that he saw those same waters in my mother's eyes on the day when Goliath brought me back from prison. She wandered about the plantation with my limp body in her arms. She did not cry. Her face held no expression. She simply held her son's scrawny body in her arms and paced the path between the cabins and the tobacco fields. Perhaps she looked forward, but not toward any place or thing in particular. Solomon feared how she might react to his presence, but he hid this fear deep down, even from himself.

"Let that boy down," he scolded her. "Let him eat. Let him sleep. He'll return to normal before long."

"He won't," she said in a monotone and without looking at Solomon. "He won't never be the same again."

"He will. Give him here. Let me get some food in him."

"You were supposed to take care of him."

"And I will. But you have to let him go, first. Go back to work."

"They're liars. My boy wasn't supposed to be in no jail. They tried to kill him."

"But here he is. Alive and well, if you just feed him and let him rest."

"Well?" Miriam cried. When she finally looked up at Solomon, he felt that her eyes might swallow him up. "You call this well? They might as well have killed him down there. They broke him, is what they done. And what about you? You said you were going to take care of him. How'd you let this happen?"

Solomon took a deep breath and waded into the murkiness.

"For sure you are right," he said. sympathetically to her. "They are lower than the dirt and even the hell beneath it. Look at what they have done!"

"They have broken him!" Miriam cried and dropped to her knees. "They have taken every bit of him from me and left only his corpse."

"Yes! Yes, it seems that way. And this was your greatest fear, wasn't it? When he was born, you came to me afraid to love this child. But look at you. How you have loved him."

Miriam became eerily silent when he said these words. Solomon was terrified then, but he waded further.

"Haven't you, Miriam?"

But Miriam was no longer aware of the man in front of her or the child in her arms. She was seeing herself in Joachim's bedroom for the first time. She stood before the threshold with an arm full of clean linens. She looked toward the bed, and when she saw the darkness there, she dropped the clean linens to the floor. She mumbled four words that Solomon could not make out, but the darkness heard her and replied.

"Give it here, then!"

Miriam's eyes filled with tears and she curled into a ball on the ground. It was Esther who saw her on the ground before her child and Solomon who picked him up. She rushed over to Miriam.

"What in the world have you done?" Esther said to Solomon.

"The right thing," Solomon replied as he lifted the child and walked toward his cabin. "Make sure she gets some rest. She is in no condition to work today."

When Miriam's son was asleep in Solomon's cabin, Solomon returned to Joachim's study.

"She will cause no further disturbances, today," Solomon began.

"Today?" Joachim replied. "What about tomorrow? What about any time when something happens to that boy?"

"Doesn't that question bring us to the bigger issue, here?"

"And that is?"

"Goliath and Mister McAllister. What happened to that boy should not have happened. Those two are the true source of the discontent, here. Have you no curiosity as to how they came to be dragging Percy across the town?"

Joachim did not look at Solomon, but Solomon could see the veil as Joachim continued with his work. He adjusted his spectacles on his nose and dipped his quill once more into the ink.

"They brought their discontent to your doorstep, sir."

"He ought not to have been in a jail," Joachim said with feigned nonchalance.

"It was impertinence!"

"Your tone, Solomon."

Solomon sighed as quietly as he could.

"My apologies, Mister Bishop. But when I think about all of the work we have put into this place— " Solomon paused to clear his throat. "What I mean to say, is that it is hard not to be passionate about this land, and every living thing on it. I love this land. And I know that I am not alone in this."

"You are not."

"Then, you must be livid. It is clear that they defied you. You had a request— indeed, an order that they took exception to. They punished poor Percy for it."

Joachim returned his quill to its holder and folded his hands upon the ledger before him.

"Is it clear?" he asked.

"Perhaps I am wrong. But I cannot for the life of me imagine what the boy could have done to warrant being dragged through the roads. Imagine how that must have looked. If anyone would have seen the spectacle, they would have to consider that one of your niggers was being unruly."

Now, the veil dropped from Joachim's face, and he contemplated in earnest. Solomon did not fail to notice.

"At the very least," Solomon continued, "they should have brought him back here for your judgment. Not theirs."

"You are not wrong in this regard," Joachim said.

"What do you think ought to be done?" Solomon asked.

"How is the boy?"

"He's fine," Solomon replied. "Miriam has let him go. She has seen her error, I think."

"You did well," said Joachim.

"I did what I could, but I do not think this will leave a good impression on the others. They have seen defiance in a slave. And they have seen the cruelty of their overseers."

"I will have a talk with Goliath. And Chester."

"I think this will do, sir. Only I was thinking you ought to talk to someone else."

"Miriam?"

"Percival. Talk to him. Let him know who you are, that what happened to him wasn't your will."

"And what, my dear Solomon, would be the purpose of this talk?"

"To keep him still. Let him know that his place is here. With his... master."

Joachim's expression softened a bit and he asked aloud but almost to himself, "What shall I say to him?"

"Say what we both know will come naturally to your heart. Be guided by that inclination that any lord with a good heart has toward his servants."

"What know you of my heart?"

"I know that it is good, sir. Since we were children, it has always been good. And it has led you straight all of your days. Why should it grow cold and cruel, now?"

"You think that I am cruel?"

Solomon looked upon his master's face. He saw the remorse there. He responded to it.

"Not at all, sir. But the boy does, perhaps. Such cruelty as Goliath and Chester have shown— he must think that this was of your doing. You must convince him that it is not."

"I will do this."

"And don't worry, Mister Bishop, about Miriam. She will be as right as rain before long."

When Solomon visited Miriam in her cabin, he found her curled in the corner, where she had slept on her first night on the plantation. He walked slowly to her and knelt down beside her and whispered in her ear:

"I think I figured out how to give you everything you've never wanted."

A Memory of my Father, 1851

"They say you look like me," my father said to me in the middle of the night. "Does that bother you?" I searched his face, which glowed in the light of the lantern he had brought into our cabin. I wondered what he meant by the idea that I looked like him. I did not think that we could be more different in that regard.

"What would you do," he asked, "if you were me? What kind of master would you be?"

"I don't know, sir," I replied. "I never thought about it. I don't think I'm supposed to."

"Why not?"

"Mama would get mad," I said.

"And why is that?"

"She always gets mad at me when I get to imagining strange things."

"Well what if it weren't so strange?" Joachim asked.

"If what weren't?"

"Here," he said, handing me the lantern. "Hold this." Then, he lifted me from my bed and carried me across the cabin floor. As he opened the door, I looked back to see my mother sleeping soundly. Leaving the door open, he carried me away, from the slave quarters and into the Bishop House. It was so dark inside that I could see nothing. Nevertheless, Joachim carried me with surefooted steps up the staircase and into his bedroom where he laid me in his bed.

"What if you could sleep here every night?" he asked me.

"That would be very nice," I said with a broad grin.

"Wouldn't it be?" he said in a soothing voice that I had never heard before. I closed my eyes and drifted away. When I awoke, I was in my own bed again. The sun shone needles into my eyes, and a silhouette, crowned by that sunlight, was dragging me from my slumber. My breaths came then, in hurried gasps as the silhouette lifted me into his arms, and I could see that it was Mister Joachim. He carried me into the fields and stopped among the tall stalks of tobacco leaves. He did not speak to me, but instead, rolled up his sleeves and began cropping the ripened leaves near the bottom of the plant.

He moved quickly, his pale, yet sinewy forearms darting between the stalks as his unweathered hands snapped leaf after leaf and bound them up in the crook of his elbow. He moved quickly down the row before returning to me and laying a large pile of the golden-green leaves at my feet. He stared at my with a raised eyebrow before it occurred to me that I ought to be doing something. I scrambled to my feet and grabbed as much of the pile as I could fit in my arms. Then, I carried the pile to the wagon to be bound. When I returned to Joachim, he had another pile ready for me. We worked like this for half an hour before the other slaves joined us.

Most of the slaves' eyes widened in awe as they looked upon their master toiling in the fields. Miriam frowned. Solomon seemed slightly amused. From morning until noon, we worked with our master alongside us. When Esther rang the bell for lunchtime, we hurried to her kitchen. Joachim, wiping his brow on his sleeve, returned to the house.

Chapter 19: Into Slave Territory

December 4th, 1858, Morning

I hope today is not the last time that I will see Cassandra, but I am aware that it may be. So on the morning, when she finished her piano practice and I had indulged in listening, I invited her to go riding east toward Springfield. We stopped at a meadow just short of Fowler station. Then I broke the news to her.

"I am going on a short visit to Missouri," I say.

"But haven't you heard?" Cassandra responds. "There is war there. You want to go to Missouri now? When radical abolitionists are tearing the place apart and every white face is terrified of every black one?"

"Winthrop is there," I reply.

"How can you be sure?"

"Because maybe I am not who you think I am," I say.

"But I know exactly who you are," she says.

"Do you?"

"From the moment you first walked through that shop door. I know who you are because I know Winthrop Goodfellow."

"Then you know about this?" I turn my back to her and remove my shirt. She sees then the Pecan of Elysium, its branches and leaves, its roots that dig deep into my brown skin. Its bark shines, inviting the touch of her hands and the caress of her breath as she gasps audibly at the sight of them. I hardly feel her touch. As if the skin there is not my own. As if the scars are an armor. As if some part of me had been removed. I think that some part had been. I hope to reclaim it now.

"Yes," Cassandra says. "But it is good to see."

"Then you know truly who Winthrop is? What he was?"

"I have had my suspicions," she says. "But it is better to know."

"We come from the same place, Winthrop and I. So I must go back to get him from there. Same as he did for me."

I turn back to look at Cassandra, and I see a light in her eyes that has never been there before. No star has shined brighter. No sunny day has been warmer. She gives me a strength to do something I have never done before. And perhaps I do the same to her, for she steps forward to be embraced. As I put my arms around her waist, she ascends upon her toes and touches her cheek to mine.

"Bring him back to me," she whispers. "Bring yourself back, too."

I hand her the reins to Moses.

"Take care of her," I say.

"I will."

I hesitate to walk away.

"Watch Isabelle Maertz," I warn. "I don't think she can be trusted."

"I know," Cassandra responds with her usual self-possessed smile. I smile back. Then I walk the rest of the way to the station.

December 4th, 1858, Noon

"Wait a minute, I know you," a man says as he looks askance at me from his adjacent seat. "Maybe I've seen you somewhere, or maybe I know the name?" He searches his memory for the source of familiarity, and seemingly finding it, smiles to reveal two rows of jagged teeth.

"You said your name is Bailey?" He has heard the reporter read my passport aloud.

"Yes, Abraham Bailey," I reply.

"The abolitionist," he smiles broadly, clearly proud of having arrived at the correct answer.

"I believe you are mistaken," I say.

"Oh, you're well known around these parts," he says. "The scar gave it away. Besides, I make it my business to know all the talented negros that come through Springfield," he replies. "Of course, that's where you're headed now, then?"

"I suppose I must pass through," I say. "That is not my final destination, however."

"Well, where are you headed?" the man with the jagged smile asks. Suddenly, the train seems so very far from Chicago and not close enough to Hannibal. I shift in my seat and assume an air of indignation.

"I don't believe I caught your name," I say.

"Oh, you wouldn't know me. I'm nobody," the man replies. "Just making conversation."

We ride on in silence for several moments, and I realize that I much prefer his talking to his silence. I would rather know what is thinking than imagine it.

"So, what have you heard of me, then stranger?" I implore.

"Oh not much besides the fact that you have spoken all over the state anywhere that will give you an audience. You're beloved in some parts." He leans closer to me. "And hated in others."

"I see," I say.

"Yes, indeed, if you are returning there, I'm sure that you have been missed by your patrons who are all but sullen since your sudden disappearance. But, that is all I have heard, about the great, young Abraham Bailey," he smirks.

"You have heard quite a bit," I say, becoming aware of the revolver holstered inside of my jacket.

"Oh, I have heard only a bit," the stranger retorts. "You see, my business is much less concerned freed men like you. Sure, you make my business hard, but I have more pressing concerns."

"And what is that?" I ask. He leans forward to whisper slyly to me.

"Slaves."

My heart contorts in my chest, and my face goes blank. The man laughs and he leans back, tilting his head backwards to reveal his crooked, rusty teeth.

"Oh relax," he says. "You look as if you have seen a ghost. Of course, I'm not in the business of capturing free and respectable Negros like yourself. No, my work is honest work. I'm interested in returning the runaways. There is quite a bounty for them down south, and I have made myself quite a business of finding them." He leans forward, a humorous glint dancing in his eye.

"You haven't seen any around here, have you?" he asks in a hushed tone. My face is blank, still.

"Oh cheer up, young man!" he guffaws. "You look as if I ask you to betray your kind. The slave is not your kind. You do yourself and this great country a service to–" he pauses as his laugh and smile fade. He sobers up a bit.

"Well," he continues, "I shouldn't expect you to understand so subtle a distinction. Look, if you should find a fellow by the name of Percival Bishop, just know that he is not like you. He is a criminal, a thief and a runaway."

He reaches into his breast pocket and unfolds a piece of paper. He hands it to me before standing. As the train screeched to a halt, he resumes his jovial spirit.

"Don't let him wile you with his niggerish charms. They're a cunning sort. You just build your cabinets and stay out of trouble." He departs the train car, but not before a warning.

"And keep away from the bounty hunters," he chuckles. "You never know what kind you're likely to run into."

As the train departs, I look down and read a description of myself. I crumple the paper and toss it out of the window to be taken away by the winds outside the moving train.

The rest of my train ride is uneventful, though I remain on guard at every train stop, and I must keep myself from staring conspicuously at the passengers who come and go from the seat before me. At first, my car mates seem to ignore, though a few scowl at my presence. By the time I have passed through Pennsylvania, I have been moved, against my wishes, to the porter's car where I must sit on a small stool that is not anchored to the floor. The porter, however is kind, and perhaps sympathetic to my position.

By the time I reach the Mississippi River, my body is exhausted from the floor, which shifted constantly below me as we passed the many miles. Nevertheless, this stop was where the work began. Keeping my head low, tucked beneath my hat, I debark the train and head for a hiding place between two freight cars. Quickly, I strip my neat clothing for soot-covered overalls, cap, and worn boots. I stuff my knapsack quickly and hustle over to the train connecting to the Hannibal line, where I seek out the porter. We make eye contact and I approach him.

"Don't call me George," he smiles.

"I ain't no George, neither," I reply.

He points to a freighter car filled with cargo, and I board it quickly. Before long, I feel the sudden jerk of the car as the engine pulls us forward. The wheels sing in a low, heavy bass as they crank forward beneath me. And slowly, we make our way toward the River. Toward my father's land.

December 4th, 1858, Evening

I t is a strange feeling to sit upon a floor that rumbles and moves beneath you. My first train ride is not nearly so spell-binding as I had imagined it would be. The car is so dark that I cannot see my hand in front of my own face. I am sure that my clothing is already tattered and filthy from having to crawl about the floor. I wreak of my own sweat and soot that has made its way onto every part of the train. While I was nevertheless thrilled to ride my first train, after what I surmised to be hours of tumbling toward Springfield, I am relieved when the train grinds to a halt.

The voices and the low patter of footsteps can be heard outside of my car. I wish to peek outside, but I know that I cannot possibly be far enough away to risk it. One stop. Just one away from the place I cannot see in the way that other inhabitants there see it. Perhaps my mother is simply like the others who live at Bishop Plantation. Perhaps she is merely trying to preserve the only notion of home she has ever had.

The train jerks forward, and my face is pushed forward into the steel wall before me. So, too, does my chest and stomach, and I suddenly feel the void in both. I do not know how I will reach my destination. Connecticut is a very far distance for a stowaway– for that matter, so is the river. If I am discovered before I cross the river, a slave again, I shall be. The train jerks to a stop, and my back is pressed against the crate such that I remember the scars there.

This time, the murmuring voices and pattering footsteps draw close enough to raise my guard. The car door open slides, and a sliver of daylight peeks in. Then, too men in dirty coveralls board the train, and my heart crawls down into my stomach where it seems that its frantic, rhythmic beat seems to vibrate the wall before me. At least that is how it seems to me, for I am afraid that the dirty men can hear me heart. What blasphemy would it be if I should be betrayed by my own heart.

"He wants these two crates, here," one of the men says indicating two crates adjacent to mine. I can hear them struggling to lift the crates one at a time and carry them off the car. They returned again and lifted the other crate. When they boarded a third time, I sensed that they were looking toward the crates that hid me. Beads of sweat formed at the nape of my neck and crawled down my spine. A few steps came toward me before the second voice interjected.

"That's that," he declared and hopped off the car. His partner, knowing he could not lift the crates alone, and therefore departed with him, sliding the car door closed with a loud screech behind him. The train jerks forward again.

Slowly, I peek out from my hiding place to find that the car is dark everywhere. I drop to my knees and begin to crawl, both to familiarize myself with the surroundings and to rest my suddenly weary legs. Suddenly, my body seeks to betray me with its weariness and its hunger. My stomach aches with emptiness, and my muscles longed for sleep. I begin putting out my hands to feel the crates as if my hands might somehow conjure knowledge of what is in them as I pass. This is to no avail, however, and I am just as ignorant as I was before. However, just as I am ready to give up, my hand rubs across a coarse, metal object on the ground. I pick it up to discover that it is an old, metal file. Quickly, I tuck it into my trousers as the train once again screeches to a halt. I stumble clumsily back to my hiding place and squeeze myself into it.

The murmurs and footsteps return, and before long, the door squeals open again. However, for a long moment, no one enters. My heart races frantically in anticipation of someone's existing there, but all I can hear are the murmurs and footsteps outside the train. Before long, the door closes again, and the train lurches forward. At first, all I can hear is the low rumble of the train and my slow, methodical breaths. But then, I hear something else.

The snap and hiss of a match cuts through the silence, and a glimmer of dim, orange light flickers against the ceiling of the freighter. I smell the scent of kerosine and something else.

"You can come out from there. I don't bite," says a deep and rather friendly voice. However, I do not move.

"It must be mighty hot and uncomfortable behind them crates," he reasons. "It's a long ride to Hannibal. You might as well come out and rest your legs."

Feeling that any attempt at pretense is futile, I slowly peek out from hiding place. I see a ball of orange, glowing fire and a massive shadow behind it. Then I see the brilliantly white teeth.

"Y'all runaways pick the worst places," he chuckles, and as my eyes adjust, I can see that he is my complexion.

"I ain't a runaway," I say, and he laughs more loudly, a large, booming laughter like thunder against the walls of the freighter.

"Then what you hiding back there for?" he asks.

"No ticket," I reply.

"Well, now that ain't so bad," he says. "You could be in a worse predicament." He stares suspiciously at me. His clothing, a worn-white button-up with brown vest and charcoal-colored trousers, is old but well taken care of. I think he does not look like a slave.

"You sure look suspicious, though," he says, raising the kerosine lamp to get a better look at me. My clothing is not old, but it is filthy so as to make their age and condition indeterminable.

"You got papers, or something?" he asks. I reach into my waistcoat pocket, feeling the handle of the revolver as I do so. I retrieve the papers and raise them up to the dim, orange light.

"Abraham Bailey?" he says with a further chuckle. "Ain't you fancy? I ain't never met no free nigger before. By the looks of you, it ain't much better than being a slave, I suppose." He laughed his thunderous laugh, and I find it infectious. I laugh, too.

"No, I guess not," I reply. "You got a name?"

"People on the railroads call me George. It ain't my name, but I suppose it is as good as any name."

"So, not George?"

"Not George. Nice to make your acquaintance," he bows low and deep with a twinkle of humor in his big, brown eyes.

"So what's a free nigger doing in a cargo train car?" he asks.

"Trying to get to Missouri," I reply.

"Strange," he says. "I ain't never met a nigger trying to get into Missouri. Met a whole lot who was trying to get out, though."

"I have an important matter to take care of," I explain.

"Well, it must be important to make you sully your fine clothes up like that. But hey, that's none of my business."

"I was thinking I'd fit in better," I jest.

"Hah!" Not George guffaws.

This time, I laugh a long, light-hearted laugh. When I do, a weight lifts from my shoulders.

"It's a long way to Hannibal," Not George says. "You play poker?" He reveals from his breast pocket an old and worn box of playing cards.

"Poker?" I ask.

"I'll teach you," he replies. He places the lamp on the floor and we both settle on our haunches. He spreads the cards across the floor with his large hands and picks a few to explain.

"This here is a king," he begins, "You can tell by its beard. This here is a queen. And this, a Jack. I call them the nobles of Africa. You see this King? What white king you know use a spear or an axe to fight?

"Now this here," he picks up a card with a solitary spade in the middle. "This card is called 'Master.'" He looked across at me with that twinkle of humor in his eye.

"Master?" I ask.

"Sure! It ain't got no nobility. It's suppose to be the lowest number, not worth the ass's shit it shovels. But this card here, is higher than all them there Africa cards!" he guffawed and slapped the card down on the pile. I smirk, but I do not laugh. He picks up the pile and begins shuffling them.

"So were you born free, or did you have a master once?" I ask.

"This train is my master," he replies. "I belong to the railroad. I reckon I got a master somewhere, but I ain't never met 'em. Nope. I been working on these railroads since I grew hair on my chest. And I can go anywhere I want in Illinois. I've been showing up for so long, the people that run this train probably think I work for them!"

"Sounds like you have the good life," I say.

"Sure!" he replies. "I got food in my belly. Nice clothes on my back. I feeds my chilluns. And my lady don't talk no smack." I chuckle at his poetry. Perhaps it was done on purpose.

"You ever wonder what's on the other side of the river?" I ask.

"Nope. Nuthin' for me," Not George replies. "I'm only concerned with bringing things onto this side."

"You ain't worried about the fighting happening over there?" I say.

"What war? I fight my war every day on this railroad." He slants his eyes at me briefly before waving his hand at me and chuckling.

"Pick up them there cards, free man. Let me show you how to play."

December 5th, 1858

At Douglas, we detrain and crouch low in the brush by the river shore, hidden by the foliage of the trees and bushes and the night that fell a few hours before.

"Over there," Not George whispers, pointing to a pathway that led to the cargo hold of the steam boats. "All of the freight gets stored from there. You'll have to be quick getting there. And quiet. One move and the hounds will be on you in a hurry."

"Hounds?" I ask.

"They been keeping that area pretty guarded on account of all the slaves that like to sneak aboard the ships and sail away to freedom." He winks at me.

"What do I do about them?"

"Avoid 'em."

"What if I can't."

"Die. Or, if you get away try again another day. Ain't much more you can do. Just don't get caught." I look over the pathway once more before I lay eyes on a patroller.

"Best to go when you don't see one of them over there," Not George says. "If you see 'em, they done probably already seen you. It's probably best we go, now, too."

"Why is that?"

"Do you see any hounds with him?"

254

"No."

"Where you think they at?"

Slowly we turn around. I try to peer through the darkness.

"You think—"

"Shh!" Not George whispers quickly. He looks around for a long period of time.

"This way," he gestures to me. I follow him slowly back toward the train station. The vegetation is dense such that I must step high to keep from stumbling. The trees are many so that they appear like menacing shadows before my eyes.

"How will I know that it's safe to get on the boat?" I ask.

"There's only two times it's safe. Lunch time and supper. Them guards don't never miss a meal."

I expect him to laugh, but he doesn't even crack a smile. He moves determinedly with large, careful steps. In brief moments, he pauses to listen, and satisfied with the silence that echoes back to him, he continues on.

"I reckon supper is the best time 'cause it will be night. You can hide in the shadows."

I nod. Then I freeze when I suddenly hear a violent rustling behind us.

"We gotta go," he says with apparent trepidation. The rustling suddenly seems closer, and he breaks out in a full run. I follow.

"The hounds. They found us."

My heart suddenly races as I try to match his stride. Soon I can hear the panting of the hounds behind us. Over the deep brush. Past the menacing trees. His steps are high. Mine are merely high enough. Then suddenly, they are not. A terrible pain shoots from my ankle to my thigh. I wince. I reach down in pain. I cry out.

"Keep going!" Not George said. I try to keep up with Not George. I can feel that my pants leg is becoming wet. I no longer hear the rustling or the panting. I hear only my heart beating. Finally, there is a break among the trees, and I can see the station's small, wooden building.

When we finally reach that building, I can hear the outside world again. My leg throbs with an immense pain. I can also hear Not George's thunderous laughter.

"Boy! You sure can run!" Not George guffawed as he caught his breath. I never saw a free man run that fast. Not if they wasn't no slave first."

I struggle to catch my breath. The pain throbs in my leg.

"Why were we running?" I ask.

"Oh, I just needed to see how badly you wanted to be free. When them hounds run up on you, it's easy to lose courage. That's what a friend once told me. He tried to run. They got him. Chopped off his foot. He don't run so good no more."

"So there was nothing behind us?"

"If there was, they had no chance against you," Not George laughs. "Come on. Let's get you cleaned up."

I am surprised to learn that Not George and his wife Elizabeth live so close to the river. Elizabeth has prepared a large meal for us, as if she knew I would be coming. Before I can eat, however, she insists that I bathe.

"You really need to get in this bath," Elizabeth remarks, guiding me to the washroom. I hesitate.

"I don't look so bad, do I?" I ask.

"You looks mighty terrible to me," Elizabeth replies. Not George nods.

"Relax," he says. "Get a load off that ankle. You gonna need to get that cleaned up. Especially if you looking to be in good running shape tomorrow." He laughs, but seeing my continued hesitance, he remarks, "Look, we can leave the room if you're bashful. You free niggers really need your privacy, don't you?" Not George and Elizabeth leave the room. I wait for the click of the doorknob and their retreating footsteps before I undress and step into the basin. The pain in my ankle subsides almost immediately upon entering the bath, and I lean forward to rub the slight swell in my ankle. When the door suddenly swings open behind me, I sit back quickly though not quickly enough. Not George stares at me. He does not seem perturbed.

"I got these porter clothes for you. You'll need them tomorrow." He places the clothing beside the basin but before he departs, he removes a loaded revolver from the folds of clothing.

"That tree on your back just saved your life," he remarks far more seriously than his previous demeanor has been. Then he chuckles. "I couldn't be sure you was who was supposed to be. You been acting so proper, I was beginning to think you was never a slave at all." He left the washroom, then and chuckled all the way into the other room.

Chapter 20: Arriving at Home

Prodigal Son

The moonlight lights my way, and I welcome its gaze upon me. Perhaps it will reveal my existence to men who would see me made a captive again, but I hold firmly to two things: one is the conviction that my life is my own; the other is the handle of my gun.

My passage across the Mississippi and into slave territory was calmer than my passage the other way into freedom. I would have considered my ride through the thick Missouri forests to be tranquil were it not for its purpose. When I clear those woods and stand before the open plains, as I look in the distance at the sprawling hills of my old home, I take a moment to revel in this truly beautiful land. The clear crispness of the night. The silver hue of the crystal moon that colors everything beneath the cloudless sky. Perhaps some day I may pass through Fayette and she will not threaten me.

As I along the road leading to the plantation, I remember the moment when my mother found me in the darkness and chastised me for my imagining myself free. I remember the promise she would have me make to her, I promise I dared not keep. I remember the scars like tree roots carved and intertwined along my back. I remember the cowhide, and the drunken stare. I remember my father. He is my master no longer, and I have come to tell him this. I pray that I shall not have to convince him with bullets.

In the still of night, the cabins in the slave quarters are like ghosts in the darkness, for they hover there with no life in them. Even these seem smaller than they did in my memory of them, and I am suddenly unsure of the one that housed the dusty floor upon which I had been born. I can hardly imagine that my mother sleeps on that floor, now. Perhaps she sleeps so peacefully that if I were to awaken her now, she would fight me violently to stay in her dream. I cannot picture Solomon. Nor Esther. Nor, can I picture my father's face. It is but that mass of darkness that blended with the walls and eluded the light of the fireplace on that night when he sat beside me while I endured a fever. However, I know that when I see him, he will be smaller than I remembered. Perhaps his anguish will have shriveled him to mere bones, and I shall not recognize him in the light, either.

Or perhaps he will be monstrously large, so large that he makes a mockery of the fear I once had of him, that he becomes a caricature of terror. Perhaps I will look upon him and laugh at the notion that I ever allowed him to haunt my nightmares and waking thoughts. Or maybe not. Perhaps I will look upon him and be reminded of the slave I was and still am. Perhaps I will see him and realize that I shall never be free. Perhaps each step I take at this moment is a step further and further from freedom.

In the slave quarters, I strive not to be seen by any one, not even the slaves. As I creep toward my mother's cabin, I must pass Esther's, and I can hear her familiar humming behind the door. I try my best to pass silently, but much to my dismay, I step on a slick patch of leaves that fail to stay beneath my feet. I stumble, and her humming stops.

"Jasper?" Esther calls into the darkness. "You there? That you, son?"

At first I am silent, hoping that she will figure the sound to be a figment of her imagination and let it alone. However, the hiss of a match sounds and the glow of a flame begins to flicker behind her door and in her window. Her footsteps shuffle toward me, and just as her door opens, I whisper back.

"Ain't no Jasper here,"

"Jasper?" she calls out again.

She raises the lantern before her and steps out into the yard.

"I ain't Jasper," I whisper from the shadows. "But I'm looking for him. Where is he?"

"He's nowhere," she says. "He was here, and now he's gone. I let him get away."

I step forward and into the light of her lantern, clasping my hand tightly over her mouth when I reach her, and grabbing her forcefully by the arm. I am stronger than she remembers, and her eyes widen when she recognizes my face. A shriek threatens to escape past her lips and my hand, and I tighten my clasp on her mouth.

"Which way did he go?" I ask.

She utters what may be an answer in her throat, but the utterance stays there, for I still hold her mouth closed. Realizing my dilemma, I decide to let her speak.

"Shh!" I say to her. "Which way did Jasper go?"

I slowly release my hand, and she whispers harshly to me.

"Where in hell did you come from?" she asks, the stench of whiskey pouring from her mouth. And yet, every semblance of the despair that held her moments ago are gone.

"Nowhere," I reply. "Now, where's Jasper."

"What do you know about Jasper?" she scoffs.

"I know that he's your son."

"Wh-who told you that?"

"Solomon."

Her jaw-stiffens.

"Well, if you heard anything from Solomon," she begins, "he ought to have told you I have no sons."

"But you used to," I reply.

"Yes," she says. "A long time ago."

"And one of them was named Jasper."

"Jasper ran away."

"And Goliath brought him back," I say.

"Boy, how you know that?"

"That doesn't matter. Where is he?"

"Jasper is nowhere. He ain't Jasper no more. His ghost is in them stables, though." She points in the direction of the large pecan tree.

"His ghost?" I ask.

"He don't go by his name no more," Esther says. "And he pretends like I ain't his mama. So, I ain't got no more sons."

"They shot him," I say. "I mean, Goliath shot him before he brought him back here."

"I know," Esther says. "We took the bullet out when he got here. I had to listen to him cry out and go through fever for two days after that. I nursed him back to health just so he could tell me he don't know his own name."

"How do you know he's your son?" I ask.

"You think a mother don't know her own child?" she says, her voice cutting through the darkness. I look around the plantation, expecting lanterns to light up the windows.

"Don't worry," Esther says. "Ain't nobody coming for you. Not tonight."

"Then I'm going to the stables," I say.

"To see a ghost?" Esther remarks. "Have you seen your mother yet?"

I turn away toward the pecan tree.

"Or your father?" she says. I turn back and she continues with misty eyes. "He ain't been well lately. It would do him real good to see you."

"Am I to be his son now and not his slave?" I ask.

"You were always his son," she replies, "just as he is my son." I stare at her dumbfounded, and the tears begin to flow from her eyes.

"Joachim is my son," she says again. "And so is Jasper. And so is Solomon. I gave birth to them. But I am a slave. So I have no sons. And it is a heartache that never goes away."

Her tears fall in torrents, and her body shakes. I feel suddenly that I should console her, but I cannot move.

"So, go and see your father," she says. "And see your mother. Do not runaway to freedom until you do."

She holds out her hand for me to take, and I know that I should not take it. Yet, I step toward her and take it, feeling with its warmth the blood that flows in my veins as well. And too, I feel the cold binds that must be clasped around my wrist if I am to follow her to the Bishop house. And, I follow her anyway. Down the dirt path that cuts across the plantation. Past the tobacco that I once picked with my own hands, that traced my path across the Mississippi, that somehow caused me to back here on the plantation, walking by my own will into the house of my enslaver.

We enter the house through the side entrance that leads to the kitchen, and we traverse the dark halls by Esther's memory until we reach the winding staircase. I have never been up these stairs, and now as I continue upward into further darkness, I feel that I walk toward my doom. And yet, I cannot let go of her hand.

It is only once we get to the top of the staircase that I can see a flicker of light cast upon the wooden floor before the doorway of a chamber at the end of the hall. Esther guides me here, we turn enter the room, and for the first time, I look upon the serene and resting face of my father. In the chair by his side sits Solomon, who does not seem surprised to see me.

"When I was told that Jasper had been brought back to us," Solomon says, "I knew you would soon return as well. Now we are together as a family, aren't we?"

"I will be gone just as soon as I have come," I say.

"You would leave your family?" Solomon asks.

"You are not my family," I say, taking my hand from Esther's grasp.

"Aren't we?" Solomon responds. "Haven't I always treated you as a son? I should have been your father."

"But you aren't," I say. "And I wouldn't be. My mother would have never had you. But you are Esther's son, aren't you?"

Solomon glares at Esther. "So she told you that?" he says.

"Why didn't you?" I ask.

"Because she stopped being my mother the moment this one was born," he gestures to my father who is yet serene in his slumber. "Perhaps I was too young to remember having a brother, but I always suspected it. And when she let him beat her…" Solomon grimaces and stands suddenly from the chair. "Well, let's just say it drove one of her sons away. But not me. I stayed."

"Why?" Esther asks, her shrill voice causing Joachim to stir in his sleep.

"Because I'm the good son, aren't I," Solomon replies.

"But you have shown me nothing but hatred since," Esther says.

"Because that was the only way to show you love!" Solomon cries. "You had two sons as white as snow, one so white that his father allowed him to pass as the heir to the plantation; another so white that he could runaway and survive like I knew he would; and one so black that he must be cursed to be a slave all of his days! Do you know what it was like to be the only son born out of love? To be the only son born to two slaves? To be the only slave that you would not raise to be a man? You loved my father didn't you? And you were sold for it. You hated their fathers and you loved them all the more! So I hated you because it was the only way to show you how much I could have loved you. How much I wanted to…"

"I did not love them more," Esther says quietly. "When Master Bishop took my son—"

"*His* son!" Solomon interrupts and Joachim stirs again. "When he took his son, you knew that you would have a child who could grow into a man. And when Jasper ran away, you knew you had another one. But not me. I am your nigger son. I couldn't do anything more than be a slave. Until today. Today things are different. Today, all of your sons are on this plantation, but I am the only one who is free."

Joachim coughs. Then he coughs again and again, more and more violently until he sits straight up in his bed and opens his eyes. When he sees me, the serene expression returns to his face.

"The prodigal son," he says. His voice is hoarse, and he seems to force the words from his mouth. "You have returned to me."

"I told you he would," Solomon says. "Rest Mister Bishop. Have your tea and rest." Solomon holds the cup to Joachim's lips and he sips, attempts a deep breath, and coughs again. Solomon slowly nudges him back against his pillows.

"It is good to see you, son," Joachim whispers before closing his eyes. Solomon wipes his brow gently. Then he speaks to me.

"Go on and see your uncle. However, you will find that you can't take him far."

Adulthood Rites

Before Joachim was yet a man, he learned how to be a master. And he did so to a woman who ought to have whipped him when he she once caught him being mischievous in the dining room. He accidentally broke a piece of china that day, and Esther fussed about it. He ought to have known better, she scolded him.

Indeed, Esther raised him from babe to master. She bathed him when he came in from a good frolic in the dust outdoors. She fed him with her own milk when he was yet too young to chew. She nursed him back to health when he was ill or injured. But, she was not his mother. She was not allowed to be. And, every time she was caught endearing herself to him— or fussing over him, she drew the ire of his father, Aaron Bishop.

It was due to Aaron Bishop's anger that Esther found herself kneeling with her bare back exposed to the boy in front of her.

"Go on, then," Aaron said to his son who clutched the cowhide tightly in his thin hands so that the blood rushed from them, and the dusky skin between his knuckles turned white.

"Do it!" Aaron commanded, but Esther could sense the boy's hesitation. She looked up and into those dark and somber eyes. She saw in them what she hoped and feared, and so she looked at him pleadingly.

"Do it," she said softly and knelt her head lower to the ground. But, as she felt only the cool breeze upon her bare back, she spoke again, more firmly.

"Now."

The boy raised the whip and brought it down upon her back so that she could feel the potential in it, the capacity in it to tear her flesh.

"Harder," she said again firmly. This time she felt the sting of the blow, and she held back both, the tears that welled in her eyes and the tremor that rose in her throat.

"Harder, still," she said, and this time, she felt the cowhide breach the skin. To stifle the cry that threatened to rise up her throat and out of her mouth, she said again,

"Harder, still!"

The boy raised the whip and lashed it across her back once more, and in this pain, she remembered the birth of her three children. She bore three sons. Jasper was her second.

Her first child did not cry when he entered the world, and he cried seldom thenceforth. He was so quiet, that Esther sometimes reckoned she could runaway with him, and he would never give away her hiding places. He was so quiet, in fact, that Esther sometimes wondered whether he felt anything for her—whether he felt anything at all. He seemed to always know that he was a slave. She sometimes resented his knowing.

"Harder, still!" she cried to Joachim who let rip the cowhide across her back again as she remembered the birth of her second child.

When Esther was sold to Aaron Bishop, she was already with child. She gave birth to her second son, Jasper, not long after arrival. He was much more fair-skinned than her first born. She wished for this child to love her more than her first child seemed to, and so she was more outwardly affectionate toward him. Her affection, it seemed, was not in vain, for this second son adored her. He smiled at her, and she smiled back. She caressed him and sang him songs. In her second son's presence, she often forgot what it was that troubled her about her first son. But, no sooner had she given birth to Jasper than she became pregnant with her third son. This one Aaron Bishop took before she could even give him a name. He took her away so quickly that one night she nearly questioned whether she had ever given birth to him.

"Harder, still!" she finally whispered with the rasp in her exhausted throat until she fainted before the boy and his whip.

"One more," Aaron said to his son.

"But she... "

"It is not up to her. One more."

Only after this last lash was given did he take the whip from Joachim who ran away to the house to hide his tears from his father. When Aaron followed him, it was only Jasper who looked upon the collapsed body of his mother— the blood she once gave to him that now spilled onto the earth beneath her and turned it to clay.

Jasper watched the earth soak up his mother's blood, and for the briefest of moments, wondered what it might be like to mold something from the clay at his feet. He did not venture to find out, however. Instead, he turned toward the crooked ash trees at the back of Aaron Bishop's plantation. Then, he walked toward those trees. When at last he passed those trees, he did not look back. Esther was left with her first born, but even he became increasingly distant. Though he would never leave the plantation, it felt to Esther like she had lost all three of her sons.

Return Of A Native Son

"Where have you been, my son?" my mother asks when I try to awaken her from her slumber. She speaks, but her eyes are still closed, and she smiles dreamily.

"I've been free," I reply. "Where have you been?"

"You know where I have been," she says. "Right here. Where I belong."

"No one belongs here," I reply.

"I do," she replies. "This is my plantation. Solomon told me a long time ago, before you was born. He said, 'this place belongs to you more than anyone else here.' And you know what? He was right."

I shake her out of her sleep and she stares wide-eyed at me. As she realizes who is before her eyes, she begins to cry.

"Oh, Percy!" she sobs. "How have you been, my son?"

"I've been free," I say, holding her in my arms the way she cradled me only so many months ago. "How have you been?" I ask.

"Just fine," she says, placing her hands on my face. "Just fine now that you're here."

"Well, I won't be here long," I say. "We have to go."

"Go?" she asks. "Go where?"

"What do you mean where?" I ask. "Go away from here. Go to freedom." A most satisfied smile lights up her face.

"But don't you know?" she asks. "We're free already. Haven't you heard? Isn't that why you're back?"

"Are you awake?" I ask, shaking her again.

"Perfectly awake," she replies.

"Then why don't we go at once."

"Don't you hear what I'm telling you? We don't have to go nowhere. We are free right here."

"What are you talking about?"

Miriam sits all the way up, and I release her from my arms.

"How did you get here?" she asks.

"What do you mean?"

"Didn't Goliath bring you here?"

"No."

"He was supposed to," she says. "That's why he gone away a few days ago."

"He never had a chance," I reply.

"Well, I guess that doesn't matter. All that matters is that you're here now."

"I won't be for long," I reply. "And neither will you."

"Why won't I?" she scoffs. "I aims to stay right here until Mister Joachim passes away. He should any day now."

"What makes you think that?" I ask.

"Solomon told me."

"How does he know that?" I ask.

"The same way he told me that he knew Master Aaron was gonna die," Miriam says. "He just knows. He has his way, I suppose. He always has had his way."

"And so what if he dies?" I say. "What will that mean for the slaves here?"

"We will all be free!" she whispers, her eyes shining with the moonlight that poured through the window.

"How do you know that?" I ask.

"Solomon. He says that Mister Joachim will free us in his will."

"And how does he know?" I ask.

"Because he helped the master write it. It says that we will be freed and inherit the land."

"If we will be freed, then why should any of us stay here?"

"Because why should any of us leave?" she replies. "We know this place. It has been our home all these years."

"This has never been our home," I say. "Not mine."

"Then we can make it ours," she says, her voice trembling. "Each day, by and by…"

"No," I say. "They won't let us have it. Even if Mister Bishop gives us our freedom, their law won't allow us to take their land."

"They will have to," she says. "What else can they do with it?"

"Who knows?" I say. "But they won't let us have it."

"They don't have to let us!" My mother scowled and rose to her feet. "It is already yours! By birthright it is yours! He is your father. And when a father passes away, his son inherits his wealth. This wealth is already yours!"

"I do not want it," I say, standing and stepping toward the door.

"What do you mean you do not want it? It is your birthright."

"I don't need this place," I say. "I am already free."

My mother steps forward, but I step away again.

"But I need it," she says. "For my own peace, I need it. And I need my son."

"If you need your son," I say, "then go with him to freedom. Because that's where he's going."

"Percy," my mother says. She approaches me, but I cannot step away this time. There is a certain power in a man's name when it is spoken by his mother. I allow her to come close enough to touch my face with both of her calloused palms and all of her slender fingers. "You done seen a bit of the world now, haven't you? A bit of freedom. Maybe you know some things now that you didn't know before. Maybe you know a some things I don't. But you don't know the pain a mother feels when she wakes up every day thinking she lost her son."

"But you haven't lost me," I say, "I'm right here."

"But I still know the pain," she says. "I had it every day I woke up and you weren't here."

I take both her hands in mine.

"Mama," I say. "You don't have to know that pain anymore. Not if you come with me."

"But I already knows it," she says. "I already has it deep down."

"Then let me show you something different," I reply. "Because you are right, and I don't know your feeling. But I did get a glimpse of freedom. I don't yet know what it feels like deep down. But I can and I want to. And I would rather chase that than till this land that I was born to be bound to."

"No, you will till land that is owed to you," my mother interjects.

"Why?" I say, my voice filling the cabin. "Why is it owed to me?"

"Because God put you here for it."

"You sure that was God?"

My mother slowly withdraws her hands from mine.

"No," she says. "It wasn't God. It was me. I put you here for it. And I meant for this place to be yours. I prayed and it came to pass."

"But I don't belong here," I say. "And I won't stay."

"So you will leave me again?" she says.

"Don't be my chains," I reply. "Don't bind me to this place."

"You won't be bound," she says. "You will be its new master."

"That is the same thing," I say. We are silent for a moment before I turn to leave the cabin. It is my mother who breaks the silence.

"What would we do in freedom?" she asks. I turn back to her.

"I don't know," I reply. "Freedom comes first. We can figure the rest out when we get there."

"Okay, son," she says. "I will come."

Chapter 21: Eastward Bound

The Underground Railroad

My mother leads me to the barn inside of which Winthrop is shackled to a large wooden support beam. We swing the heavy door wide, and my mother shines the lantern light upon his emaciated and filthy body. Two horses huff and paw at the dirt in their stables. Winthrop stirs as we enter. His eyes flutter, and when he sees me, his lips, ashen and cracked, part to offer a weak grin.

"Sometimes," I say to him, "you miss the only shot you get."

He forces a chuckle, but it is more of a cough. Then he replies in a hoarse voice, "And sometimes, you get a few more."

"You didn't," I say.

"What do you mean?" he asks. "You're here, aren't you?"

"Me?" I say. "And what if I had run instead?"

"Most of them do," he replies. "I'm glad you didn't."

"How many slaves have you helped escape?" I ask.

"So many more."

"So it is true what everyone in Quincy says about you."

"It's probably true what everyone everywhere says about me."

"Even McAllister and Goliath?" I ask.

"So you heard and saw everything at the saloon," he says. "Did you ever go back to Ms. Maertz's place that night?"

"No."

274

He coughs again. "I suppose I am grateful for that, too." He says.

"You helped my son get to freedom," my mother remarks.

"And now he is here to help us do the same," Winthrop responds.

"Why do we need him to do that?" my mother asks. "We'll be free any day now. As soon as Mister Joachim passes."

"And who told you that?" Winthrop asks. "Solomon? I suppose he would know about Joachim passing. He's the one taking care of him. Just like he took care of his father. But look at me. Do I look like someone who was brought back to be made free?"

"That is only until the master—" my mother begins.

"No," Winthrop interrupts. "Joachim has been sick for as long as I've been here. The only people who have seen me in here are Goliath because he put these chains on me and Esther because she feeds me. And then there is Solomon. He comes in here every once and a while, and I have never seen a more gleeful smirk on a man. If I didn't know any better, I'd say he was gloating."

"That night at the saloon," I say, "Goliath claimed you were a runaway slave named Jasper. Was he right?"

"I don't know any slave named Jasper," Winthrop replies. "My name is Winthrop Goodfellow, and I am a free man." His gray eyes gleam with pride. He glances at my mother beside me and then looks back to me. "But Esther is my mother," he confesses. "And Joachim is my brother. And so is Solomon."

My mother gasps and lowers the lantern so that the light goes out of Winthrop's eyes for a moment before she can raise it again.

"But Mister Joachim don't look like no negro," she says with astonishment.

"Do I?" Winthrop responds. "We were both born to Esther by different masters. Not Solomon, though. He was born before either of us, and when my father died, he used all three of us to settle a debt with Aaron Bishop. That's when Joachim was born. Who knows how Aaron's wife reacted to that. She would later die in childbirth, taking Aaron Bishop's only legitimate heir along with him. That must've been when he decided Joachim would be raised as his son. Of course, Esther would have had no choice but to see it happen."

"How do you know all of this?" my mother asks. "All of this, it happened before you were born and when you were still a child."

"I have spent a lot of time wondering about this place," Winthrop replies. "After all, so much of my kinfolk are on it. It's hard to drop something like that. Maybe I thought I'd some day have an opportunity to take my mother away from here. It must have been hard for her to raise a man who would some day become her master. Maybe even harder than it was for me to watch her do it. She often seemed so proud to watch him grow up."

"So you knew about me all along," I remark.

"Not until you ran away," Winthrop says. "Then I saw the name and knew that I had to find you before the bounty hunters did. It was hard for a slave to escape when I did it. It's even harder now with folks being so afraid of the next Nat Turner or Old John Brown coming along."

"So I am your nephew," I say.

"Yes."

"And Cassandra is your daughter?"

"No," he replies. "Perhaps she ought to have been. I loved her mother. Her name was Phyllis. I helped her get to freedom before she was even showing signs of her master's unborn child. Phyllis gave everything inside of herself to bear Cassandra, and I promised her that I would always watch over her daughter. Phyllis passed away, she in my arms and her child in hers."

The light goes out of his eyes again as my mother lowers the lantern to the ground and begins to weep. Winthrop rises, perhaps to console her, but the rattle of his chains keeps him from stepping forward.

"Hug your mother," he says to me. "Don't let any circumstances spoil the things we ought to hold dearest."

I place my arms around her and her sobs settle into my chest.

"I suppose I did a little of that," Winthrop says. "My mother was beaten before my very eyes, and I wanted to hold her after that. But I couldn't. In that moment, I knew I wouldn't be a slave anymore, and that's about all I knew."

"I know that feeling," I say.

"And yet, here we are," Winthrop says, waving his shackled wrists, the iron ringing staccato into the night.

"Well, I will make sure we make it to freedom for good," I say.

"How?" my mother cries as she pulls away from my embrace. Her eyes are crimson red, and the tears flow freely from them. "Do you not see this man? This runaway you call Winthrop? This slave in chains with a bullet hole in his belly? Is this your freedom?"

"She is not wrong!" a voice calls from outside the barn. We look out to where the moonlight beams to see Solomon approaching on the dirt path. He stops short of entering and says, "You have maybe a day or less to get gone from here, Percy. After that, Goliath will be back, and if Mister Joachim is still alive, Goliath will certainly continue his search for you. Especially once he learns you were here. Better to contend with the slave patrol while they do not have the Wolf's help. Maybe you will make it back to whatever it is you call freedom out there."

"And what do you call freedom here?" Winthrop asks.

"Dear brother," Solomon says with a sly grin, "do not fret over your chains as a sign of your enslavement. See them for what they are: our protection from you."

"Your protection?" Winthrop scoffs.

"Yes," Solomon replies. "We are in the presence of a criminal—a murderous one. You have killed how many people in your crusade against the law?"

"My crusade?" Winthrop says.

"Jasper," Solomon begins, "you must learn that there are civilized ways of functioning in society, and then there is whatever you have been doing."

"Slavery is uncivilized!" Winthrop cries.

"No, stealing is uncivilized," Solomon counters. "And killing, Jasper. Killing is uncivilized. When you are well enough, you will be put on trial for the murder of Chester Albert McAllister, among others. I will see to it."

"You?"

"Yes. Mister Joachim is unwell. So I will see to it, and this great state of Missouri will see that at least some of us negros can act within the law."

"You," Winthrop remarks, "who killed Aaron Bishop and are killing your own brother as we speak!"

Solomon's grin turns downward and he clenches his jaw.

"I," he begins, "have been loyal to my masters. I have been at their bedsides when they have fallen ill, and I have maintained order on their land when they have been unable to do it themselves."

"And you think they will let you run this place when your master is gone," Winthrop scoffs.

"Why shouldn't they?" Solomon asks. I will be a lawfully free man willing to uphold their law."

"But you will be as much a killer as I," Winthrop counters.

"You will have no such proof," Solomon replies. "No one will."

"Oh, I'm sure you have a garden somewhere," Winthrop says. "You've always had a talent for sowing seeds."

Solomon scowls and takes a menacing step toward Winthrop. Before he can take a second step, however, I draw my gun from its holster and point it at his chest.

"I will certainly leave here," I say. "But not without my mother. And not without Winthrop. Undo his chains, or—"

"Or you will shoot me?" Solomon says. "I see you are his kin." He pauses to rub his chin, though his expression was not a pensive one but a smug one. "Well," he seems to conclude, "I cannot argue with that. There is only one problem. I do not have the keys. They are in the house. Will you allow me to go and get them?"

"I will take you to get them," I say.

He turns away, and with my gun pointed to his back, he leads me away from the stables and along the dirt path of the plantation. Pale light falls softly upon the bare, harvested fields, and the silhouette of the Bishop House looms like an immense shadow before us. We are silent as we approach the side entrance, and thus our footsteps seem loud to me. When we enter the hallway, it is longer and darker than I could have ever imagined it to be when the lamps are unlit and the curtains are drawn. The floorboards in the foyer are firm and silent beneath our feet, and I can hardly see the gun in my hands, much less the body to which it is pointed. So, when Esther calls out to us from the top of the stairwell, I am so startled that I point the pepperbox in her direction.

"Solomon?" her voice echoes through the foyer.

"Mama," Solomon replies, no longer standing in front of me. "Your grandson is about to shoot your son."

"Joachim?" she responds.

"No, your other son. The black one. He has his gun pointed at me right now in the dark." I point my gun in the direction of his voice.

"Oh no, child," Esther says, "Why do you wanna go and do that?"

"I don't want to shoot anyone," I say, trying to peer through the dark to find Solomon. "I just want the keys."

"But I can't give them to you," he says, his voice much further left of me than I had thought. "You must understand, Percy. If I have a final lesson to teach you it is this: what belongs to this plantation stays on this plantation. It belongs to us and us to it."

"So you are happy with your enslavement," I say, pointing my gun to the left.

"I am no slave," Solomon replies, this time his voice seeming to come from the parlor, "because I am under no pretense that I am supposed to be happy. You don't understand because you believe in that falsehood, the pursuit of life, freedom, and happiness. But there are no such things. Everyone is a slave to something, so he is never happy. He spends the whole of his life being a slave to their bodies, their hunger, their lust and love, their pleasure and pain. Everyone— black, white, red, or yellow is a slave to material things even though their bible tells them to reject these things. And then the abolitionists will tell you that the Bible is against slavery. But how can it be when it teaches us the most important lessons of this elegant institution? None of us lives for ourselves. All must humble themselves. No one shall be self-righteous. But those are your sins, aren't they? Slavery only errs when it is cruel. That was Mister Joachim's sin. In that way, you truly are your father's son and neither of you belong here. And things will be different when you are both gone."

"Because you will be the new master," I remark.

"Because we will live without slave or master here."

"So all of the slaves will go free?"

"You have not been listening to me," Solomon says. "We need a system here. Perhaps "slavery" is a dirty word, but people do not know what to do with freedom. No one does. All men, even white, suffer with it. They drink too much. They lust. They gamble. They cause great harm. Or they starve to death. No one will do those things here."

"Because you will be their master," I say.

"I will lead them!" he shouts, and I know that he stands outside the parlor door ahead and to my right. I point my gun there. "I will be a leader," he continues. "If you call that being a master, then I regret that I did not teach you to conceive of better words."

"I regret that you cannot conceive of freedom," I say, "because that is not what you will have here."

"Whatever I will have here, I will have," he says. "It will be mine."

"What you speak of is slavery," I remark, "even if you wish to call it something else."

"The word 'slavery' is just fine with me," he replies. "And if slave masters didn't whip their slaves, it would be fine with everyone else, too. There would be no abolitionists. Slaves have existed for all of human history. All of it. We just forgot to abide the Lord's will when we brought it to America. Deep down, no one gives a shit about freedom. They want security without cruelty. That is what we will have here."

"Then I will leave you to it," I say. "But do not lie to yourself or anyone else here. There will be no freedom here." He does not respond. "Solomon?" I call, but he is silent. I can hear neither breath nor footstep. "Esther? Solomon? I will leave y'all to whatever this is. But Winthrop and my mother are coming with me." I hear a click far off to my left.

"I regret that you think so," Solomon says. Then there is a roar of thunder and a flash of light as the wall splinters behind me. In the blink of an eye, I see Solomon's silhouette, and then he is gone. I stumble to my right and fall over the first step of the staircase. As I fall, I aim toward the place in which the silhouette appeared, and I fire. In another blink, I see the scowl on Solomon's face. Then he is gone again. There is a great ringing in my ear, but in spite of it, I hear a groan. Then a shout.

"Damned nigger shot me in the foot!"

I lie at the bottom of the stairs for several moments before I realize that I feel no pain and my legs do move. I scramble to my feet and stumble through the anteroom, down the hallway, and out the door.

When I return to the stables, my mother is frantic.

"Did you kill someone?" she cries.

"I don't think so," I say, "but we must go now."

"I'm guessing you didn't get the key," Winthrop says.

"No," I reply.

"Well," he continues, "by the sound of things in there, you have three more bullets. Let's hope one of them works."

He pulls the chain taut away from the beam, and I take aim at the hinge there. The first shot damages the hinge and splinters the wood. The second shot unhinges the chain from the wall. The horses whinny, and I hurry to calm them while Winthrop readies the saddles. When Winthrop and I have each mounted a steed, I reach down to help my mother up. She stares at my hand for a long while. Then she utters,

"I can't."

"You can," I say.

"You must," Winthrop says. "Regardless of what you hope will happen here, you must know that you will not be free."

"It is not about what I hope will happen here," she says. "It's about what I fear will happen out there."

"You will be with your son," I say. "That's what will happen out there."

She looks into my eyes. Then she takes my hand.

"Okay, son," she says. She climbs aboard, and we make haste to depart Elysium Plantation for good.

The thunderous beating of hooves rumbles beneath us. The earth moves for us. The night wind parts for us like Moses's seas. The moon lights our path. The stars guide us. Eastward, we must head. Godspeed. Into the rising sun. The horses huff and pant and snort as we command them onward. The wolves howl in the distance. The wildcats scream. Their cries are on all sides. But not in front of us. Not before the rising sun.

The black sky yields to twilight blue. Then the color of water. Then dawn. Then day breaks. Then, before the sun has a chance to greet us, we hear steps that are not our own. A man cries in the distance.

"Yee-haw!"

Then shots ring into the air. We three, Winthrop, my mother and me, bury our faces in the horses' hair. Their manes whip back and forth, and we think that bullets whizz by us. But soon the steps, and yelling, and gunshots fade, and we know they were not meant for us. Onward towards the greeting sun.

Before long, we must pause our journey. Our horses need rest, and we must plan for the morning riders who shall soon join our path.

"We are not far enough," my mother says. "Why are we stopping?"

"We must rest here," Winthrop says. "We are too far from any natural resting place, and we needn't ride our horses into the ground, lest we never make it to one."

"But we are not safe here," she says. "They will catch us here."

"You are scared," Winthrop replies. "I know. I've seen it before. But a scared mind never made its way to freedom. Relax. Think clearly. We can build a shelter away from the road. We must bathe. We must sleep. Either Percy or I will keep watch. We'll keep you safe."

Miriam breathes heavily as she tries to be consoled by Winthrop's words.

"You've done this before," she says with only a semblance of her previous panic.

"I've been here before," Winthrop says calmly. "We both have, he continues, pointing to me.

"What is our next move?" I ask.

"We must find food for ourselves and our horses," says Winthrop. It will be a day or two before we can make it to the train. We must avoid it until we are as close to the border as possible. We must go as far as Hannibal and catch the steamboat from there."

"I have a friend on that boat," I say. "He can help us."

"Good. We will rest here. In a few hours, I will see what food and supplies can be found. We will ride farther when the sun has set."

"Okay." I look to my mother reassuringly. She smiles weakly.

"Okay," she echoes me.

We guide our horses a few miles from the pathway. The shrubs and grass is high here, and the ground is difficult to traverse at first. Before long, we are canopied by the woods. My mother falls asleep quickly and Winthrop departs us to find a nearby trading post. I fight sleep in his absence. I take apart my gun and clean it. I watch my mother sleep. She seems more peaceful this way. I count my money and try to calculate the cost of three tickets to New York. I give up after a while. We will be luck to make it back to Illinois. We can figure things out from there. I fight sleep again. I nearly lose before I hear the crackling of footsteps that come closer and closer. I clutch my gun until I hear Winthrop's signal.

His trip was a successful one. We have a bit of kerosine for our lanterns. We have some meat and bread and water. We have fruit. We have oatcakes for the horses. I awaken my mother and we eat quietly. Then it is my turn to sleep. I dream that I am in a sunny room and

Cassandra plays an impromptu fantasy on the piano. I awaken to my mother's gentle beckon. Then it is time for Winthrop to sleep.

As the sun sets, we prepare to ride again.

"What do we do if we are caught?" my mother asks.

"Show him Percy's and my papers and pray," Winthrop replies.

"What if that doesn't work?"

"We pray with bullets," I say. She sighs. We find the road and ride quietly onward. Away from the setting sun.

Between Mother and Son

When at last we arrive at Hannibal, night has fallen upon us for a third time, and the mood is not yet triumphant. "We cannot stay in Illinois," Winthrop says. "It is no longer safe for us there. We must continue eastward."

"Where?" Miriam asks.

"I do not yet know," Solomon replies, "but it will not be safe for us in Illinois. We must take Cassandra and go. McAllister and Goliath will know to look for us there, and by now Isabelle Maertz has outworn her usefulness."

"So our journey is not over, then?" Miriam asks.

"A journey for freedom hardly ever is," Winthrop replies.

"And who is Cassandra?" Miriam asks.

"Cassandra is my daughter. She is safe among friends in Quincy, but this will not last. We must go further."

"Further," Miriam says as she looks off into the distance. "I am already farther from home than I have ever been."

"Home?" Winthrop asks, shooting me a troubled glance."

"I must be making a mistake to do this," Miriam says.

"Freedom is never a mistake," Winthrop answers. But Miriam can no longer see the glimmer in his eyes. It is too dark for her, now. She cannot even see me.

"Things were better back home," she continues. "Solomon was our leader. We worked for each other. We were a family."

"He is your family," Winthrop points to me. But Miriam cannot see me.

"I have not waited. I have not been faithful. I have entered the world where I will have to run forever. I don't want…"

"Stop it!" Winthrop declares with a harsh whisper. I can hear the brush and leaves become unsettled as he grabs Miriam by both of her shoulders and shakes her.

"You must not despair," he says. "Freedom is not an easy path, but it is always worth pursuing. If you turn back now, you go back to death. Even if they don't kill you along the way."

"I will repent. They will forgive me."

"They will take your life!"

"Shh!" I interrupt them, for I hear footsteps. The land only a few yards away is unsettled. Someone approaches. We hold our breaths until we hear a voice, a whisper.

"George?"

I whisper back, "Ain't no George in here."

"I ain't no George, neither," the voice replies.

I move forward, and Winthrop stops me. I touch his hand reassuringly and head into the darkness.

"There he is," Not George says with a smile that outshines the lantern in his hand. "I was afraid y'all ain't make it. There is a y'all, ain't there?"

"Yes. We are all here, the three of us," I reply. I guide him to our hiding place behind the bushes and introduce him.

"Winthrop. And my mother."

"Much obliged," he says, shaking each of their hands vigorously.

"I brought y'all some food," Not George says. "And some clothes. I couldn't get another uniform, but I figure if y'all are traveling with a white man, he should be cover enough. I also got this." He reveals a small piece of paper. "It's the old bill of sale for Elizabeth. I would be powerful grateful if y'all was to get that back to me, somehow. She ain't free without it. But I figure this was a good cause." He hands it to Miriam who takes it reluctantly.

"Well," Not George smiles broadly, "it's best I be getting back before somebody misses me. Good luck, my young friend. I hope you find what you're looking for."

"Thank you, my friend, for everything," I shake his hand firmly and he returns to the darkness.

We sleep together once more in the cover of the woods. I think that I sleep restlessly, for my dreams are uneasy ones, and every sound awakens me. Perhaps if I were sleeping more soundly, Miriam's absence would not have stirred me from my sleep.

"Mama," I whisper into the darkness when I realize that it is just Winthrop and I at our camp. The moonlight illuminates the broken brush leading away from our camp, and I follow it until I can hear her footsteps in the distance. The moonlight illuminates her, then, and I hasten my steps until she turns around in alarm at my presence. We stare at each other for what seems an eternity before she runs to me and hugs me. For both of us, tears fall like rain.

"I'm so sorry, son," she says. "But, I can't do it."

"You can," I implore. "You must."

"I wouldn't even know what to do in freedom," she remarks.

"You'd be free."

"To what end?" She asks.

"That is the end. That is the thing worth working for, worth fighting for."

"But I am tired, son. I am tired of working, tired of fighting. Ain't I suffered enough? Don't I deserve some peace."

"Yes ma'am," I reply before I pull away from her embrace. "We are already so far from there. How will you make it back?"

"I won't," she says. "I will go to the nearest train station. I will turn myself in. They will only return me to my home."

I remove the revolver from my waistcoat. She does not see it yet.

"That is not all they will do," I say.

I raise the revolver until it points to her chest. She does not see it until a glimmer of moonlight shines upon it. Then, her eyes grow as large as the moon itself.

"If you go back, you will alert the bounty hunters. If they don't find us before we can get on the boat, they will find us on the other side. You will jeopardize our escape. We are so close. But I fear that the bounty hunters are closer. Don't go back."

"Would you shoot me, son?" she asks. "Would you shoot your own mother?"

"You cannot go back. It is freedom or nothing."

"And if I choose nothing?" she asks.

"Then I must choose freedom."

"Then choose it." She closes her eyes, and I clutch my weapon, feeling all of the darkness and murkiness that she has held in her soul.

All of these years!

She sighs, and I feel my own breath expelled. The darkness envelopes us both, gathering from within her and from every edge of these forests until I feel that it will swallow us up. She sighs again, and I feel the winds of the forest, the rustling of the grasses, the hush of the trees. She kneels and an entire mountain of darkness rises up behind her. I aim into that darkness and pull the trigger. Lightning flashes and thunder crashes through the whole of the woods as a moan emanates from the shadow. I pull the trigger again, but there is no sound and no flash. Yet, the shadow falls, and with it all of the darkness within and without. The light of the moon shines upon my mother's tear soaked cheeks as the moan behind her grows louder. I walk past my mother to find Goliath writhing in the grass. I look aghast at my mother.

"It was not my father hunting me, was it?" I ask. "Nor was it Solomon. But you! You knew Goliath was here, didn't you?"

Miriam sobs. "I only want you to come home."

"Elysium is no longer my home. But it is clearly yours."

"Then kill me," she says. "Because I cannot go with you. But I will always want you with me."

"I understand," I say. "But I only had one shot."

Holstering my weapon, I turn and leave her behind me. In the darkness.

PART THREE
SPRING OF 1859 (EPILOGUE)

Jeremiah Cobra

My Soul To Keep

Percival Bishop

I was born in the nostalgia of my mother's autumn in a bitter-sweet moment, perhaps before the dawn when she heard a song rendered to her by the meadowlarks, and the wind whispered empty promises through parting blossoms.

I was raised in the foreboding of my mother's winter. She cradled me against her ember soul those cold Decembers, for though her eyes were cool as coal, her heart had burned to cinders. Her sweet-bitter songs were lullabies that I remember.

I was nurtured by the tears that rained in my mother's spring. And, thus I dreamt that willows wept the pigment in my skin. Although I may indeed have been her joy that dwelt within, she never said the words, for love was but a nigger's sin.

I learned to crawl, walk, and run during my mother's summer, amidst the storm torrents, lightning, and menacing thunder. Perhaps she feared that the world would break my bones asunder, but I would rather perish than leave my soul encumbered.

I was born in the reality of my mother's hell. I would surrender heaven if therein I choose to dwell.

And so, as the world passes by outside the window of this train that I ride to Chicago, I try my best to put the memory of our last moment in the Missouri forests behind me. Ahead is the world I shall make my own. And, it is perhaps simply true that she could not go with me into that world anyway. Melancholy, once it has taken root in the heart, grows into every cavity and ossifies therein until the heart can no longer be shaped by joy.

The evil of slavery is not what it does to the body but what it does to the soul. The soul learns to scowl at beauty, to scoff at laughter, to smirk at ambition. When the heart is thusly set, it goes against itself. It rejects all that it ought to desire, for it marks all as unattainable. If slavery is to end in this country, the scars that we will have to heal are not the marks of the whip or even the emptiness of our bellies, for scars are not inherited, and wealth can be earned. Instead, we will have to heal the melancholy, the inexhaustible hopelessness that takes up house in one heart and then is imparted from one generation to the next. My mother passed it on to her, and she sought to pass it on to me. But I will not let it live on.

I reach into my breast pocket and retrieve a sketch of my next sculpture. It is of a man carving himself from an immense tree. He is not concerned with the tree that was there before him. Only what he ought to be. He must create himself. In his own image.

"Abraham," Cassandra whispers, having stirred awake in the seat beside me. I do not respond.

"Abraham, what's wrong?" she asks.

"Nothing. Nothing so big." I say, "Just that I was not born Abraham. That is not my name."

"I know."

"I was born Percival Bishop."

"I do not know that man."

"No, you don't. He did not exist for you to know him. But I think that he does now."

"You have a new name. A better name."

"No. 'Percival Bishop' is my name. My mother and father gave it to me. I was given it the same way that I was given this body. And I would like to keep it."

"Well," Cassandra says with a smile. "Nice to meet you, Mr. Percival Bishop."